Presented by

J. Ellington Ashton Press

www.jellingtonashton.com

&

Hold the Line

APEX PREDATOR: HUNTER'S MOON

APEX PREDATOR:

HUNTER'S MOON

By

D.A. ROBERTS
THE END IS ONLY
THE BEGINNING

HORROR AUTHORS GUILD
MEMBER

APEX PREDATOR: HUNTER'S MOON

Edited by: J. Ellington Ashton Press Staff

Cover Art by: Michael "Fish" Fisher

http://jellingtonashton.com/

Copyright.

D.A. Roberts

©2020, D.A. Roberts

ALL RIGHTS RESERVED. This book contains material protected under International and Federal Copyright Laws and Treaties. Any unauthorized reprint or use of this material is prohibited. No part of this book, including the cover and photos, may be reproduced or transmitted in any form or by any means, electronic or mechanical, including photocopying, recording, or by any information storage and retrieval system without express written permission from the author/publisher. All rights reserved.

Any resemblance to persons, places living, or dead is purely coincidental. This is a work of fiction.

ISBN: 9798681506638

Special Thanks To:
Joshua Dalton,
Steve Monrotus
and
Kerry Davis
For your help and advice

APEX PREDATOR: HUNTER'S MOON

D.A. ROBERTS
Table of Contents

Prelude: Cries in the Night 13

Chapter One: Devil's Due 23

Chapter Two: A Tale of Two Wolves 31

Chapter Three: A Gathering of the Tribes..39

Chapter Four: Council of Wolves...55

Chapter Five: Straight on till Morning 63

Chapter Six: Role Reversal 71

Chapter Seven: Gideon..77

Chapter Eight: Arrival 87

Chapter Nine: On the Hunt..103

Chapter Ten: Owl's Prophecy 123

Chapter Eleven: Blood Oath..131

Chapter Twelve: Exodus 143

Chapter Thirteen: Remembrance..155

Chapter Fourteen: Pathfinder 167

Chapter Fifteen: Battleground 175

Chapter Sixteen: Second Chances 191

Chapter Seventeen: Alphas...199

Chapter Eighteen: Trail's End 213

Chapter Nineteen: Frostbite..223

Chapter Twenty: Voodoo Bayou..235

Chapter Twenty-One: Aftermath...247

APEX PREDATOR: HUNTER'S MOON

Apex Predators: (also known as alpha, super, top, or top-level predators) are predators with no predators of their own, residing at the top of their food chain.

Hunter's Moon - the term "Hunters Moon" is used traditionally to refer to a full moon that appears during October. It is preceded by the appearance of a "Harvest Moon", which is the full moon closest to the autumnal equinox (which falls on the 22nd or 23rd of September). The phenomenon whereby the moon in total eclipse appears reddish as it is illuminated by sunlight filtered and refracted by the earth's atmosphere.

APEX PREDATOR: HUNTER'S MOON

D.A. Roberts

Two Wolves – A Cherokee Parable

"An old Cherokee chief was teaching his grandson about life…
'A fight is going on inside me,' he said to the boy.
'It is a terrible fight and it is between two wolves.
One is evil – he is anger, envy, sorrow, regret, greed,
arrogance, self-pity, guilt, resentment, inferiority, lies,
false pride, superiority, self-doubt, and ego.
The other is good – he is joy, peace, love, hope,
serenity, humility, kindness, benevolence, empathy,
generosity, truth, compassion, and faith.
This same fight is going on inside you
and inside every other person, too.'
The grandson thought about it for a minute
and then asked his grandfather,
'Which wolf will win?'
The old chief simply replied,
'The one you feed.'"

~ Author Unknown

APEX PREDATOR: HUNTER'S MOON

D.A. ROBERTS
PRELUDE:
CRIES IN THE NIGHT

*"It is better to have less thunder in the mouth
and more lightning in the hand."*
Apache

September 24th
4:30 PM
Two Rivers Campground
Eminence, Missouri

It was just beginning to sprinkle when Calvin Martinson decided to call it a day. He'd been standing in the water of the Current River fishing for "brownies", or brown smallmouth bass, most of the day, and his luck had been good. He had six keepers and had thrown back more than a dozen that were almost close enough to keep.

He would have kept fishing if the clouds hadn't rolled in with a few streaks of lighting mixed in. Standing waist-deep in water during an Ozarks thunderstorm wasn't exactly a good idea. Fishermen die every year doing just that sort of thing.

It was getting late in the day anyway and he didn't want to clean his fish in the dark. It would be better to get them gutted and filleted so he could get them on ice, then he would still have enough light left to cook some of his catch. It was hard to beat fresh bass cooked over an open fire. With the weather, he was going to have to settle for pan-fried, but that was almost as good.

Ordinarily, Calvin wouldn't have come to this campground. It had a reputation as being a partier's campground but with the weather cooling down earlier this year, it was almost empty. His normal haunt was more popular with the fishermen, but almost no one fished along this section of the river because of the partiers. As a result, he'd had the river mostly to himself all day. They were calling for an early winter this year, so he figured he'd get in one more fishing trip before it got too cold to camp.

Calvin was still fit for a man in his late forties. A little thicker around the middle than he preferred, but still a strong man. He might have gained weight since back in his Marine Corps days, but he hadn't lost the muscle. Camping and hiking were about as exciting as his life got these days, having left the real excitement behind after the first Gulf War.

He kept his iron-grey hair cut in Marine Corps fashion and people that didn't know him could tell he'd once been a Marine by the way he talked and held himself. As the old saying goes, there's no such thing as an "Ex" Marine. The two eagle, globe, and anchor stickers on the back of his camper and blue Dodge pickup truck didn't help, either. Everything about him screamed "Jarhead." Not that it was a bad thing.

His wife of 25 years, Janice, usually came with him on these camping trips, but she left him for a man from their church last month. This trip, it was just him and he was enjoying the solitude. It wasn't often that he got the chance to get out alone into the woods. Well, except during deer season and that was only while in the deer stand.

He made it back to his cozy little brown and white camper. It was a 2012 Keystone Hideout trailer that he'd bought new and it was still in great shape. When he wasn't taking it camping, it sat out of the weather in a covered garage built for it. He liked to take care of things like this because they were an investment that he could enjoy for many years to come. Besides, it was completely paid for and he didn't need another payment right now.

He made it back to the camper just as the wind was starting to pick up. It wasn't raining yet, but you could smell it in the air. It wasn't going to be long before it started, and it promised to be a good one. He wanted to be finished and comfortably inside the camper when that happened. His mouth was already watering at the thought of the pan-fried fish with cornbread and fried potatoes that he was planning on fixing for his supper. He'd have a few of those ice-cold Budweisers that were waiting in the cooler, as well.

Grabbing the folding table, he unpacked his knives and started cleaning the fish. He was an old hand at it, so it didn't take very long. He tossed the guts, heads, and bones in a bucket as he finished, then put the fillets in a plastic bowl and sealed the lid. Taking them inside, he put them in the small refrigerator and went back outside. Within minutes, he'd cleaned up the table and knives, putting them away before taking the gutbucket out away from camp to dump in the woods. It was just starting to rain when he made it back to the camper.

"Well, shit," he said, softly, "I timed that about perfectly. I guess I'm cooking inside tonight."

Glancing around before he went inside, he was happy to see that one of the two other residents of the campground was leaving ahead of the storm. The other was a small yellow dome tent with a red Chevy SUV parked next to it. Hanging on a makeshift clothesline was a red two-piece bikini and some women's undergarments.

They were whipping around like flags in the wind and he thought that they might fly off when an attractive blonde wearing revealing cut-off jean shorts and a white tank-top emerged from the tent and headed for the line. She rescued them quickly, then turned to head back to the tent when she caught Calvin watching her. Smiling sweetly, she waved at him and started back for the tent. Calvin waved back and shook his head.

"Easy there, big guy," he whispered. "You're still technically married and she's half your age."

Ducking inside the camper, he secured the door and started gathering the cookware he'd need for supper. In minutes, he'd mixed up the cornbread batter and stuck it in the little oven. Then he peeled the potatoes and put them in a cast-iron skillet along with peppers, onions, garlic, and butter. Then he added spices and set them on medium heat to start cooking.

Getting out another bowl with pre-mixed breading for the fish, he smelled it when he opened it. It was his secret recipe, a mixture of cornmeal, garlic powder, sea salt, coarse ground black pepper, and Tony Chachere's Creole seasoning. Dipping the fish fillets in milk before rolling them in the breading, he set them aside while the other cast-iron skillet heated up. Within minutes, the camper was filled with the aroma of cooking food.

"I'm gonna starve before this is ready to eat," he said, smiling.

Putting on some music, he selected a CD from his collection. It was an oldie, but one of his favorites. Chronicle: The 20 Greatest Hits of

Creedence Clearwater Revival. "Susy Q" started blaring through the speakers while he cooked and sang along with the music.

By the time the CD had played halfway through, he was sitting down to eat. "Who'll Stop the Rain" was playing when he took his first bite of the fish.

"Oh man," he said, "this is fucking delicious. Janice, you don't know what you're missing. On second thought, thanks for leaving."

He silently toasted his soon-to-be ex-wife with the beer and dug into the food. Outside the rain was starting to come down heavily. There was lightning flashing through the sky and the wind was picking up. It was enough that it occasionally shook the trailer, but not enough for him to be concerned. The wind was hitting the back of the camper, not hitting her broadside. The odds of it pushing the camper over were practically nil.

He was putting away the leftovers and cleaning up the dishes when he heard the frantic knock on the door. Reaching for the loaded Colt 1911 that he kept on his hip when camping, he started towards the door cautiously.

"Can I help you?" he asked.

"Hey, sir!" shouted a nearly panicked female voice. "Can you help me?"

Taking his hand away from the pistol, he slowly opened the door. The rain was coming down in heavy torrents. Standing just outside the door was the young woman from the campsite down the road. She was soaking wet and he immediately noticed that she wasn't wearing a bra beneath the white tank top.

"This storm is too much for my little tent," she pleaded. "Can I come inside until it blows over?"

She was staring at him with the most intensely blue eyes he'd ever seen.

"Absolutely," he said, stepping aside so she could come in. "Get in here before you catch pneumonia."

Stepping inside, he saw that she was wearing flipflops along with the very short shorts and was completely soaked.

"Let me get you a towel," he said. "You're soaked."

"Thank you," she said, trying to smile with her long blonde hair plastered to her pretty face.

"I'll be right back," he said, ducking into the bathroom to grab a towel.

When he came back, she was completely nude, standing in the middle of the living area. His eyes must have widened when he saw her because she just smiled and shrugged.

"You're letting me get in out of the rain," she said, smiling. "I'm freezing and not all that concerned with modesty, right now."

"I'm sorry for staring," he said, handing her the towel.

He had to force himself to look away. She was very beautiful and had an incredible body.

"Are you…uh…are you camping alone?" he asked, trying to get his mind on something else.

"I am now," she said. "I was supposed to meet some friends down here today, but they never showed. I don't have any cell service, or I'd call them to find out what the hell happened."

"I don't have any either," he said. "I lost mine right after I got into Eminence yesterday and haven't gotten it back since."

She finished drying off and tossed the wet towel onto the floor, standing there naked and unashamed. He noticed that her navel and both nipples were pierced, and she preferred to be clean-shaven. He had to admit, it was affecting him. It had been a long time since he'd been this close to such a beautiful woman. It had been a long time, period. The last few years with Janice had been mostly devoid of any sort of sex-life.

"I…uh…I should try to find you some clothes," he stammered. "I'm not sure I have anything that will fit you."

"If you don't," she said, clearly enjoying his discomfort, "I don't mind being naked. That is if you don't mind it."

"I…uh…I don't mind…uh…at all," he said, stealing another peek at her perfect body.

He wasn't sure, but he suspected that she had pushed her arms together intentionally making her ample breasts stand out even more.

"I'll be right back," he said, turning away and ducking into the back.

He opened a duffel bag and looked for anything that might fit her without covering up too much. He was a gentleman, but he was also a man. No one was going to believe this fishing story when he got home on Tuesday. Selecting a yellow Marines t-shirt with red lettering, he smiled when he realized it was one of his older shirts and was thin enough to mostly see-through.

"Perfect," he thought, heading back with it.

Holding it out to her, he saw that she was smiling at his embarrassment. Taking the t-shirt, she turned around while she put it on, revealing her heart-shaped behind that had no tan lines.

"Fuck," he thought to himself. "Get it together, man."

Turning around, she put her hands on her hips and smiled at him.

"Well, how do I look?" she asked.

He could see the nipples and rings through the shirt, as well as the dark tan of her skin.

"Amazing," he said, his voice a bit husky.

"Good," she said. "Mind if I grab one of those beers?"

"Help yourself," he said, gesturing at the cooler.

She leaned over to open the cooler and the t-shirt slipped up over her buttocks and revealed everything.

"Would you grab me another one, too?" he asked, admiring the view.

"Sure," she said, continuing to fish around in the ice.

Standing up with two long-neck Buds, she twisted the cap off them both and handed him one.

"Thanks," he said, taking a long pull off the beer.

"You don't have to thank me," she said. "It's your beer."

He just smiled and took another long pull.

"Well, since you've already seen me naked," she said, "I should probably ask your name."

"I'm Calvin," he said. "Calvin Martinson. My friends just call me Cal."

"I hope I can call you Cal," she said, smiling mischievously.

"Of course," he said. "What's your name?"

"Alex," she said, smiling. "Well, Alexandra, but I hate going by that. My last name is Venable. Tell me, Cal. Are you married?"

"Technically, yes," he said. "She left me about a month ago for another guy. I filed for the divorce, but it's not final yet."

"Well," she said, making a show of looking him up and down, "it's her loss. You look pretty good to me."

"I'm also old enough to be your daddy," he said, mentally cringing for bringing up his age.

He hadn't wanted to, it just came out. Kind of like her perfect ass when she bent over for the beer.

"I don't care about age," she said, smiling seductively. "It's just a number. What I look for in a man are honesty and good taste. So, I think you're good."

He wasn't sure what to say to that, but she turned and walked over to the CD player.

"I love this band," she said. "CCR is pure Americana Rock."

"They're one of my favorites," he said.

She hit the shuffle and repeat buttons on the player.

"I hope you don't mind," she said, glancing back over her shoulder demurely. "This way, we don't know what's going to play next and it won't shut off until we turn it off."

"I'm good with that," he said, draining the rest of the beer.

"Let me get you another one of those," she said, smiling at him as she turned back to the cooler. "Where are you from, Cal?"

Now he was certain she was doing things like that on purpose, taunting him. She bent over slowly, letting him get a long look at her. It took him a moment to notice that she wasn't digging in the ice to find a beer and she was watching him over her shoulder.

"Uh...Springfield," he managed to say without too much difficulty.

"Like what you see, Cal?" she asked, softly.

"Yes," he replied, not being able to take his eyes off her.

"Good," she said. "Maybe we should forget the beer. Where' the bedroom in this thing?"

"Right behind me," he said, nodding his head. "The bed folds down."

"Then maybe you should fold it down," she said, standing and turning around.

He just nodded emphatically and turned to pull down the Murphy bed. When he turned back around, the yellow Marines t-shirt was laying on the table and she was nude, again. She was smiling at him and he felt drawn into those intensely blue eyes.

She came to him slowly, then started taking off his clothes, tossing them aside like they no longer mattered. She took his pistol and tossed it into the kitchen. Once he was fully naked, she glanced down at him and purred.

"Her loss," she said, smiling broadly.

They fell back onto the bed, a flurry of kisses and caresses. They began making love to CCR's "I Put a Spell on You." Cal's brain was too occupied to catch the irony. They changed positions during "Have You Ever Seen the Rain." Cal was enjoying himself more than he could ever remember.

She was intense, uninhibited, demanding, giving, passionate, and aggressive. Each time he thought he was finished; she'd bring him back to life and they'd start all over again. He felt like he was in his prime, like back in the Marines, all those years ago.

She rolled him onto his back and kept the rhythm going, rocking her hips in a way he'd never known a woman to do before. It was intense and electrifying. The chaos of the storm raging outside only made it more intense with each violent arch of her hips. When she moaned, it was almost a howl. It was strange and somehow intoxicating, as well.

He started to reach for her breasts that were bouncing just above him when she suddenly grabbed his wrists with a strength he wasn't expecting. She pinned his arms to the bed and kept rocking her hips.

"Stay with me, baby," she breathed, never missing a beat.

Concern began to rise in Cal's brain. It suddenly occurred to him that he couldn't move her hands away from his wrists. She was stronger than he thought possible. He was helpless to get away from her and it quickly appeared to him how vulnerable he was.

As the storm reached its peak, the lightning was flashing, and the thunder crashed all around them. She was enjoying herself, even if he was starting to be more afraid than aroused. Something was very wrong here.

The song changed from "Up Around the Bend" to "Bad Moon Rising" and she shifted her rhythm to match the song. He was starting to forget the warning signs and enjoy himself again when she arched her back and leaned her head up and away from him. He couldn't see her face anymore.

When she leaned forward again, her eyes were different. The intense blue eyes were now tinged with a dark yellow where the whites of her eyes should have been. Her mouth was somehow different too.

"What the fuck?" he gasped between breaths.

In the illumination of the lightning, he could see she was changing. There were now sharp teeth in her mouth and fur was sprouting from her body. She was changing into something else, but she never stopped rocking her hips in time with the song.

Her face began to elongate, and her blonde hair darkened to a light brown that matched the hair all over her body. He could hear the popping of bones and the tearing of flesh as she changed. The pain had to be incredible, but she never faltered or showed any signs of discomfort. She was bigger now, too. Stronger and taller, as well as broader.

"Oh my God," he screamed.

"Not quite, lover," she purred back at him, her voice sultry despite the growl.

She howled into the night as she finished her transformation. Seconds later, the screaming began. It went on for a while as she took her time, enjoying every second of the bloodbath she was receiving. She knew she could keep him alive for quite some time. There wasn't anyone here to hear him scream, anyway.

When the screaming finally gurgled to an end, the storm was still raging, and the little camper finally stopped shaking. Blood was dripping from the ceiling, the walls, the windows, and the door. The bed was covered in the dark crimson of blood and the thick viscera that had been slowly stripped away, a small piece at a time. The coppery scent of blood mixed with the musky scent of sex filled the air. Cal hadn't died quickly, nor had he died quietly. She'd made sure of both.

Stepping out into the rain, she let the torrential downpour wash the blood from her fur. Throwing her head back, she howled into the night. From across the river, several others answered her. Their mournful howling mixing with the cacophony of the storm.

Dinner was served.

D.A. ROBERTS
CHAPTER ONE
DEVIL'S DUE

*"He who would do great things
should not attempt them all alone."*
Seneca

September 25th
6:30 PM
Devils Tower, Wyoming

Will sat on the edge, looking down over the greens and browns of the landscape below him. The sun was low on the horizon, bathing the landscape in reds and golds. It was beautiful and awe-inspiring. He felt a sense of loss knowing that, at one time, everything he could see belonged to his people. That was another time, but he had felt an enormous connection to his past ever since he'd taken on the spirit of the Dire Wolf. It remembered running this land, free and unchallenged. The sight of buffalo for as far as the eye could see.

There was another part of him, too. A snarling darkness that wanted nothing more than to devour and destroy. Thus far, Will and the spirit of the Dire Wolf had been stronger, but it was a constant battle. One that he had to win, no matter what, because the cost of losing was unthinkable. The spirit of the Dire Wolf and the spirit of the Old Werewolf battled for supremacy, with Will as the prize.

The First-Born Werewolf inside him was old. Not nearly as old as the Dire Wolf spirit, but its strength reached back through the centuries. Will could feel the power of the beast reaching back to the medieval days of Europe. It longed for the days when it ran unchallenged, hunting the mountains and forests, hunting from the Alps to the Urals with no equal. Will decided that he would think of him as Old Wolf.

"Mind if I join you?" asked Mika, sliding his legs to dangle off the edge, just like Wills.

"Suit yourself," said Will, nodding.

"Fuck," said Mika. "That's a long goddamn way down."

"Yeah," said Will, "but it's not the fall that will kill you."

"I know," said Mika, chuckling. "It's those big fucking rocks at the bottom that'll take care of that. Not exactly how I'd want to go."

"Are they ready?" asked Will, nodding back over his shoulder.

"Almost," said Mika. "You do realize, if we go through with this, we'll go to jail if they catch us?"

"That thought has crossed my mind," said Will.

"But we're going to do it anyway, right?" said Mika, grinning like a schoolboy.

"Well," said Will, "since we've gone to all this trouble. We might as well finish the job. Besides, even if we stopped now, we've already committed a string of felonies just getting up here."

"Goddamn, man," said Mika. "You've turned into a fucking Wildman since I first met you. You're still a cop and we're about to commit a shitload of felonies. Well, a shitload more, I guess."

"What was it you once told me?" asked Will. "It's only a felony if we get caught. So, let's not get caught. Besides, we shouldn't have to ask permission to do something on land that was stolen from us in the first place."

"Fuck yeah," said Mika. "Man, you've changed since you took on the big wolf. I fuckin' approve."

"Somehow," said Will, "I knew you'd say that."

"So, how long do you think it'll take before someone comes after us?" asked Mika.

"Depends," said Will. "They might not risk coming up after us, knowing damned well that we have to come down eventually. But, if they do decide to climb up after us, they'll have to wait until morning. So, in theory, we should have all night to do this."

"Greyeagle," said Mika, in a rare moment of seriousness, "I am behind you on this, even if we end up in prison. This is the perfect place to have a ceremony for the *Hotamétaneo'o* that we've lost."

"We won't go to prison," said Will, confidently. "If we have to, we just change into the wolves and run into the hills. That's why we came up with the meetup point. They can call it in, but who's going to believe that a bunch of werewolves climbed up here just to set a fire?"

"Good point," said Mika. "Let's do it, then."

Mika drew his legs up and slid back from the edge. Will looked out over the land for a long moment before he moved. He felt something deep within him that he hadn't felt since Afghanistan. A calling, almost like a siren call, deep down inside him."

"Are you ok?" asked Sarah, slipping her hands onto his shoulders.

"Yeah," said Will, hesitantly.

"What is it?" she asked, concern in her tone.

"The French call it *l'appel du vide*," he answered. "The call of the void. I've felt it before, back when I was still a soldier. It's stronger now, but I have the distinct feeling that I could step off the edge and live."

"Maybe," she said, "or maybe not."

"Or it might just hurt like a bastard," said Gabrielle. "Everything ok?"

"Will was just being darkly poetic," answered Sarah. "Right?"

"Yeah," said Will, shaking himself out of the moment. "I'm good."

Scooting back from the edge, he stood up and glanced towards where the rest of the group was assembled. After they'd made the climb, they pulled up a dozen large bags that they had attached to ropes. The bags held the equipment they needed to finish what they had come up here for. It had been backbreaking work to haul all the bags up, but it was necessary for what they had planned.

The National Park surrounding Devils Tower was closed for maintenance, so no one had been there to prevent them from climbing it. Friends had brought in three pickup loads of gear, then left once they started climbing. There would be no evidence left behind on how they had gotten up there. If they played their cards right, there would be nothing left for them to be tracked by, either. Just ashes and a cold fire pit.

Will returned to the group as they were constructing the bonfire. The wood was stacked high and would easily burn for hours. It was all dry hardwoods, so it was unlikely to emit a lot of smoke. No one would even know they were up here until after nightfall when they could see the light from the fire. But, by then, it would be too late for the Park Rangers and Law Enforcement to do anything about it. That is if no one had seen them climbing. It would be highly unlikely that they would send a helicopter to chase trespassers. Even if they did, it would take all night to get one here.

Cassie had been listening to her scanner and so far, nothing had come across the radio about anyone on the tower. If their luck held, they would be gone before anyone was in place to prevent their escape. Even if they were waiting for them to come down, they wouldn't be able to stop them.

Once the bonfire was built, they all changed into tribal gear. Even Cassie and Gabrielle had been given ceremonial garb since they were both now claimed as part of the tribe, even if it was just amongst the other *Hotamétaneo'o*. However, that was likely just a formality considering the amount of pull Sarah's father had with the tribal council.

Mika took out a drum that he had brought up with him. It was a nice drum, but it wasn't his normal one he used for ceremonies. This one had been made by him and Will's grandfather, Jay *Matoskah*, just for this ceremony. It was going in the fire when they were done. Their escape depended on being able to move quickly and lightly.

As soon as everyone was dressed, Mika started playing the drum. At first, the beat was slow and soft, but steadily built. While the beat was building, Jason lit the fire. It caught quickly due to the kerosene that they'd soaked it in before lighting. There was a thick layer of wood that would burn for a long time with more they could add, if necessary.

Once the flames were licking into the sky, Will initiated the dance at the northernmost point of the fire. It was a slow shuffle as his moccasin boots scuffed across the stone surface. No one moved while he danced. At each of the cardinal points of the fire, he increased the tempo, slightly. At the southern point, he began softly chanting in Lakota.

When he made it back to the north point, Sarah fell in behind him. Gabrielle followed next with Samuel *Tahmelapachme*, then Cassie, then Jacob *Mingan*. One by one, they all joined in except for Mika. He kept playing the drum. When they reached the northern point again, Sarah started playing her flute. Kayli *Waynoka* and Maria *Dahteste* also began playing flutes as they each passed the northern point. Everyone else joined Will in the chanting.

Will began singing the Lakota Death Song and the others joined in. Apart from the flute players and Will, everyone was now playing handcrafted gourd rattles, made especially for this ceremony. Each was crafted with images and the names of the fallen *Hotamétaneo'o*. The rattles inside were all teeth taken from fallen Dogmen during their first battle together.

The sun was now completely below the horizon and their music continued to grow in both volume and power. Will knew that the spirits of their ancestors would approve of their ceremony here, in this place that was held sacred in the traditions of every tribe that had seen it. This place was sacred, long before the first white settler reached the far eastern shores of the continent.

As they sang the sacred song, they began substituting the names of their fallen brothers and sisters for certain words in the lyrics, thanking their ancestors for each of them, in turn. Jason began adding sage and other herbs to the fire, making it smell sweet and at times, change colors. It ran the gamut from greens and blues to violent reds and oranges.

Dancing in the flames, they all saw the images of their ancestors. They saw the fallen *Hotamétaneo'o* dancing with their ancestors and felt both joy and sadness that they could not dance there with them. They took comfort in knowing that one day, they too would dance with their ancestors. They would be proud to see their ancestors and friends, once more.

The moon came out from behind the clouds, nearly full and bright, casting its orange-hued luminescence onto the ceremony. Somewhere in the darkness, a raven called out its melancholy call only to be answered by another, off in the distance. Wolves could be heard howling in the distance, adding their mournful cry to the death song.

On the eastern horizon, lightning rolled through a bank of dark clouds that were forming there. Above them, the stars stretched out to eternity. They could see the colors of the Milky Way and in the north, the swirling multihued clouds of the Aurora Borealis. The ebb and flow of the Northern Lights seemed to move with their song.

One by one, they began tossing the gourds into the fire. Sacred herbs that had been used in the paints and put inside the gourd began to color the fire in brilliant hues of green and blue. Sparks of those colors began drifting off into the night sky, taking with it the offerings to their ancestors.

Next, the three flutes were added to the fire and the colors changed to reds and orange, adding more sparkles to the night sky. Last to go into the fire was Mika's drum. It, too, was swallowed by the flames, turning the colors to a brilliant purple with sparks that seemed to move of their own accord. They drifted high into the sky and became lost among the stars.

As the drum was devoured by the flames, the chanting stopped. Only the sound of their moccasins on the stone surface and the crackling of the fire broke the silence. The last of the embers drifted upwards and vanished on the cool breeze.

One by one, they stepped away from the fire and stopped dancing until Will was the last one. He continued around, one last time, slowing down at each of the cardinal points. When he reached the northernmost point, he stopped. Now only the sound of the fire and the gentle sighing of the wind could be heard. It was as if the entire world had gone quiet, silently mourning the loss of those who had been memorialized here.

In silence, they removed their ceremonial clothing and added those to the fire. They waited there, staring into the blaze until they were consumed and only ash remained. They all stood there, naked in the moonlight, renewing their pledge to each other and the *Hotamétaneo'o*.

As the fire began to burn low, they opened their packs and began getting dressed. Once everyone had their clothes on, Will opened the final bag. Handing each of them a pack, they began buckling them in place.

"I packed these myself," said Will. "We've gone over how they work, and this isn't your first jump. Doing this at night is a little more challenging, but there should be plenty of moonlight to guide us."

"Once we reach the ground," said Sarah, "if there's no one waiting for us, we'll regroup and head out of the park."

"If there is anyone down there," said Will, "take your wolf-form and get away as fast as you can. We'll meet at the rendezvous point at first light. Any questions?"

"Yeah," said Mika. "Why didn't we just do this naked? I mean, that would have been fucking epic."

"First off, eww," said Gabrielle, "and second, I don't think you'd like how the nylon straps dug into your junk."

"Good point," said Mika. "Never mind."

"One last thing," said Will. "With the direction of the wind, we jump off the southeast side. Then it will blow your chute away from the side of the tower."

"Good to know," said Cassie.

"This is why we practiced this," said Will. "Do this by the numbers and I'll see you all once we're on the ground."

"*Hoka hey*," said Mika.

"Let's hope not," said Cassie, looking nervous.

"I'll jump last," said Will. "That way I'm here if anyone has any issues before they go."

"Alright, folks," said Mika. "Let's fucking do this."

With that, Mika ran over to the edge and dove off without hesitation. He let out a loud, ululating war cry as he jumped.

"He's crazy," said Cassie.

She ran and jumped next. Will watched from the edge as everyone took their turn to leap. He waited until he saw that all the chutes had opened before taking a few steps back, then charging at the edge before leaping over the side.

He felt the wind rushing past his face and a calm detachment that he remembered always having during a jump. It was more than just confidence, this time. There was something more. Something inside of him felt different and he heard the whispered word "*Anunkasan*" in his head. He found that his hand was reaching for the harness release instead of the chute release. Part of him wondered what would happen if he just took off the chute. Part of him wanted him to find out.

"*Anunkasan!*" he shouted into the night.

With the wind roaring in his ears, he hit the release. Right at that moment, even he wasn't sure which one he'd hit.

"*Anunkasan,*" whispered the wind.

D.A. ROBERTS
CHAPTER TWO
A TALE OF TWO WOLVES

"We will be known forever by the tracks we leave."
Dakota

September 26th
6:15 PM
State Highway NN
Southeast of Eminence, Missouri

The sun was low on the horizon and the shadows were growling dark in the trees along both sides of the road. Only an orange sliver of daylight remained and the nearly full moon was already peeking over the opposite horizon, looming large and orange in the eastern sky. The full Hunter's Moon was only days away.

Slowing down as he approached a curve in the road, Miles Jennings was on his way home from a long day at work. He worked at a small mechanic shop in Winona. It was only about a fifteen-minute drive to home, but he'd been running late trying to fix a last-minute repair for a good customer. He was distracted, still thinking about the reason the old Corvette wasn't getting any spark to the sparkplugs. Nothing he'd tried had worked. He was brought out of his thoughts by flashing lights up ahead.

"What the hell?" he muttered to himself.

Through the trees, he could see it was the flashing hazard lights of a stranded vehicle.

"Sucks to be you, dude," he said. "I ain't stopping. I'm already late for supper and I need a goddamned beer."

Slowing down to get a better look as he passed, he saw a blue Dodge pickup with a camper-trailer behind it pulled into the grass at the side of the road. It was facing towards him or he wouldn't have noticed that the hood was up, and he could see a barely clad woman looking under the hood. Her short shorts revealing most of her ass and her tightly pulled yellow t-shirt had been tied in a knot just below her breasts.

"Well, maybe I can stop for a minute," he said, tapping the brakes.

There was hardly ever any traffic on this road once it got too cold to swim at the Rocky Falls Shut-ins. He had one of the only houses along this stretch of road and he loved the solitude here, especially once the tourists stopped coming around in summer. Slowing to a stop beside the front of the truck, he rolled down his window.

"Having trouble?" he asked, smiling.

"Yeah," said the attractive blonde that climbed down off the front bumper.

Now that he could get a better look at her, he thought she could be a model or a stripper. She certainly had the body for it. The yellow t-shirt with red lettering that said Marines on it was thin enough to see she wasn't wearing a bra and had both nipples pierced.

"What seems to be the problem?" he asked, staring at her breasts as she approached his door.

"I have no idea," she said, leaning into the window and pressing her breasts against his arm. "It just quit when I was driving along."

Now that she was close, he was suddenly aware of the intense blue of her eyes.

"Do you have any help on the way?" he asked, relishing the firmness of her breasts.

"No," she said, shaking her head. "I drove out here to go check out the shut-ins and decided to head back to town since there wasn't anyone there."

"Yeah," he said, "that place is usually empty once the weather starts getting cold. How long have you been stranded here?"

"A couple of hours," she said. "I can't get any reception on my cell."

"Let me get out of the road," he said, smiling, "and I'll take a look at it for you. As luck would have it, I'm a mechanic."

"Oh my God," she said, excitedly. "If you could get me going again, that would be amazing!"

She emphasized amazing by touching his cheek with her fingers.

"No problem at all," he said. "Let me back over into the grass so I can use my headlights to see."

"Thank you, so much," she purred, smiling sweetly.

"Don't thank me, yet," he said. "I don't know if I can fix it or not."

She stepped back as he put the truck in reverse and backed off the road with the front of his truck facing the front of hers. Leaving the engine running, he flipped his headlights on bright and got out. She was waiting for him by the bumper of her truck.

"Let's see what we can figure out," he said, smiling.

She turned and leaned over the front of the engine, giving him a view of her long legs and ass. He took just a moment to appreciate them both, then leaned over the front of the truck to look at the engine.

"Why don't you try and start it," he said, taking a small flashlight out of his pocket. "I need to hear what it's doing."

"Ok," she said, heading around towards the front of the truck.

Seconds later, he saw the dome-light come on as she climbed into the cab.

"Here goes," she said, turning the key.

There was a clicking sound but the starter wouldn't engage. She tried it twice before he stopped her.

"Ok," he said, "that's good."

She got out of the truck and came back around to stand beside him.

"It's not turning over," he said. "The starter isn't engaging at all. You've got power, so it's not the battery. You said you were driving when it just died?"

"Yeah," she said. "The dash gauges went crazy and it just died."

"That's got to be something electrical," he said. "I don't think I can fix it on the side of the road. I can call and have it towed to my shop. I'll be able to find out what the problem is and fix it with my tools and diagnostic equipment."

"I don't have the money for all that," she said, pouting. "I just had the gas money to come out here for the day."

"Do you have roadside assistance on your insurance?" he asked.

"I don't think so," she said. "It's an old truck. I just have liability insurance. How much do you think it will cost?"

"Well," he said, "just the tow truck will likely be around a hundred. I can't tell you how much the repair will cost until I figure out what's wrong with it."

"Is there anything I can do to convince you to help me out?" she asked, running her fingers along his arm.

He looked at her and smiled. She was deliberately pushing her breasts together with her upper arms and leaning in so he could look down her shirt.

"Well," he said, looking into her cleavage, "we might be able to think of something."

"How about we go back to my trailer and I give you a down-payment," she suggested, biting her lower lip.

"Sounds good to me," he said.

She took him by the hand and started leading him towards the trailer. They were almost there when she froze in her tracks.

"Is something wrong?" he asked, looking confused.

She was cocking her head to the side and he could see that she was looking around nervously. There was obvious concern in her eyes. The faint breeze was blowing towards them from the trees about twenty yards away and she was looking in that direction, scanning the trees. He smelled the normal odors of the woods, but there was something else there, too. Something faintly musky.

"Hey," he said, "what's the matter."

Turning to face him, she tried to smile but he could tell something had her concerned.

"Why don't you go on inside," she suggested, forcing a smile. "There's beer in the fridge. Help yourself and I'll be right in."

"What's going on?" he asked, glancing around nervously.

"Nothing," she assured him. "I just heard something. You go on inside. I'll be right there."

"If something is going on out here," he said, "I can take care of it. I won't let anything happen to you."

Suddenly, her voice changed. Gone was the demure young woman who had been taking him back to her trailer to give him unimaginable delights. This voice was firm and full of fire.

"Get out of here, you moron," she snarled. "This is your lucky fucking night. I've got bigger problems than you, right now."

"But, what about fixing your truck?" he pleaded, still hoping to get laid.

"I said GO!" she snarled, a guttural grumble to her voice.

He saw the change in her eyes. Something evil replaced the seductive blue eyes he'd seen before. There was a burning yellow where the whites had been.

"What the fuck?" he said, backpedaling away from her.

He stumbled and fell onto his back, then started scooting away from her.

"Run you fool!" she roared, massive canine teeth protruding from her lips.

Getting to his feet, he sprinted to his truck and dove inside. He was vaguely aware of a dark figure standing just inside the trees. His attention was focused on the woman who seemed to be getting bigger as he watched, with hair growing from her skin.

Diving into the truck, he threw it into gear and spun his tires as he slid back onto the pavement. Rubber squealed as he accelerated rapidly away without looking back.

She continued to shift into her full size and strength. She stood just under seven feet tall when transformed and her light brown coat glistened in the headlights.

"I can smell you," she rumbled through her enormous teeth. "You're not one of my pack!"

There was no answer. She knew that the dark figure just inside the trees was another wolf, but it didn't smell familiar. She didn't recognize it as one of her pack and knew that was very dangerous. Her pack was too far away to get here in time to help. She was going to be on her own for this fight. If she called for the rest of her pack, she could be calling them into an ambush because she had no idea how many of them were watching her, despite only smelling the one.

As her eyes grew more accustomed to the darkness, she could see deeper into the shadows. At first, all she saw was the yellow eyes staring intently at her. She felt nothing but malevolence and rage coming from those eyes. Then she saw the shape. It was the form of a werewolf, but there was something strangely different about it. Something that frightened her.

She knew that showing any sign of weakness would only provoke an attack, so she decided to go on the offensive. Snarling and holding her hands out to her sides with the claws extended, she took several steps towards the interloper. It didn't seem to react, at all. Either it wasn't afraid of her or it was unsure how to react.

Before she could figure out which one, he moved impossibly fast. She was too close to the trees to get away from it. In the span of a heartbeat, it shot forward and grabbed her by the neck with a grip like a vice. The massive clawed hand lifted her from the ground without any effort.

She grabbed its wrist and tried to break free, but she wasn't strong enough to even weaken the grip. Her feet dangled above the ground as it brought her up to eye-level with itself. It was easily a foot taller than her. Maybe even over nine feet tall.

The beast's fur was as black as the dead of night without so much as a speck of white in it. The eyes were pure evil with no trace of humanity in them. This wasn't a werewolf. It terrified her to know that this was nothing she'd ever encountered before. She was a woman who transformed into a wolf. This had to be pure wolf without any humanity in it at all. That thought terrified her.

"What the hell are you," she croaked through the powerful hold it had on her throat.

It was squeezing hard enough to prevent her from howling, but it was still allowing her to get enough air to remain conscious. She did not doubt that it could squeeze much harder. It continued to hold her there, all the while seemingly studying her intently.

It didn't seem at all impressed by her, even though overall, their appearances were quite similar. Both were powerfully built bipedal wolves with massive teeth and claws. There the similarities ended, though. Whatever this beast was, it was nothing like her. It seemed curious about her or possibly amused. It was not intimidated in the slightest and she fully understood why. Compared to this beast, she was no better than the humans she'd been preying on.

After several moments of staring at her with an odd expression on its face, it turned and began carrying her back into the woods. No matter how hard she struggled, she couldn't break the beast's grip on her throat. When she began pushing against trees with her feet to try and break away from it, the creature stopped and increased its grip on her throat. Soon, sparks appeared in her vision and she began to blackout.

She fought desperately to remain conscious. She had the horrible feeling that if she reverted to human form, it would simply kill her. Her only hope was for this thing to continue to believe she was like itself. Otherwise, she would just be another piece of meat.

Forcing herself to relax and stop resisting, she felt the creature's grip loosen on her throat. She went limp and pretended she was out cold. It held her up in front of itself for a moment as it watched her. She could feel it's gaze upon her but kept her eyes shut. After what felt like hours, it shifted its grip and threw her over its shoulder.

She briefly considered making a run for it but remembered the creature's speed when it grabbed her. There was no way she could outrun the beast without a significant head start. It would catch her before she made it ten paces. Her only choice was to go along with the beast until it got where it was going. Only then did she have a slim chance to slip away and escape while the beast was either away or asleep. She had to be patient. The question was, where was it taking her and what did it want?

APEX PREDATOR: HUNTER'S MOON

D.A. ROBERTS
CHAPTER THREE
A GATHERING OF THE TRIBES

"I have seen that in any great undertaking it is not enough for a man to depend simply upon himself."
Shooter Teton Sioux

Pine Ridge Reservation
September 27th
4:30 AM
South Dakota

Will stepped out of the camper and headed over to the fire-pit. The coals were still there beneath the ash and he quickly had a fire rekindled and crackling. Once it was going, he sat the coffee pot on the wire rack and started brewing a fresh pot. He was going to need a good cup to get him started for the coming day. There was a lot to be done before the end of it.

"Would you like me to take over the coffee?" asked Jay *Matoskah* as he came out of his camper.

"Yes, Grandfather," said Will, smiling. "You make better coffee than I ever could, anyway."

Grandfather sat next to Will and began taking over the coffee preparations. Will added a few more small sticks to the fire and leaned back in his camp chair.

"You're nervous," said Grandfather.

Will noticed it wasn't a question.

"It is that obvious?" asked Will, smiling. "If we hadn't postponed the ceremony, this would have been done months ago."

"Only to those of us who know you well," said Grandfather. "You should relax. You have nothing to be worried about. When the two of you met Gabrielle, well, that changed the situation. Delaying it was for the best."

"That's easy for you to say," said Will, smiling.

"The three of you are already committed to each other," said Grandfather. "This is only a small ceremony. It changes nothing. After, you will understand that this is not a change. It's a declaration. Nothing more."

"Still," said Will. "How many of our people will be accepting of a union between the three of us? How many will even accept that Gabrielle isn't one of us?"

"It is not for them to approve or accept," said Grandfather. "It merely is. They can acknowledge and celebrate it or not. How they feel changes nothing. This is not their path. This is yours."

"But how will the tribal elders react?" asked Will. "Will they speak out against it?"

"If they say that you are not welcome here," said Grandfather, "then neither am I and I will not return to this place."

Will glanced at his Grandfather, surprised.

"The path you walk is far more important than anyone truly understands," said Grandfather. "The path of the *Hotamétaneo'o* is not just about saving lives from the creatures of this world. It signifies the return of our ancient magic. The old ways are growing stronger and the fact that Gabrielle is part of it is undeniable proof that the spirit of the *Hotamétaneo'o* knows no limits. She might not have been born of our people, but her spirit says otherwise."

"Thank you, Grandfather," said Will, nodding gravely. "I needed to hear that."

"Besides," said Grandfather with a mischievous smile, "Sarah's father is on the council and I don't think many there will openly defy him. He's not a man to be trifled with lightly. Andrew Running Bear is an old friend of mine. He and I already spoke about your marriage and he is in total agreement. He knows that Sarah is happy and understands the importance of the path you are on."

"You might have a point there," said Will, smiling.

"Besides," said Grandfather, "you have other things to consider, as well. After the joining ceremony, another matter needs our attention."

"I thought we were just here for the wedding," said Will.

"Not exactly," said Grandfather. "Months ago, I sent word out to the tribes through contacts I have. I told them about the return of the *Hotamétaneo'o* and the battles you had already fought."

"How did they react?" asked Will.

"You might be surprised to learn that they already knew or at least suspected," said Grandfather. "The people I spoke to are all Medicine Men and Women in their tribes. Respected elders. Some already had visions of the *Hotamétaneo'o*, sensing their return. Others had seen the ancient enemies of our people making their presence known. They knew that if they had returned, then the dog soldiers would not be far behind."

"Well, at least they didn't ignore you," said Will.

"Far from it," said Grandfather. "Many of them offered to send warriors to join the cause. Warriors whose spirit-path was leading them this way, anyway."

"And they're here, now," said Will. "Aren't they?"

"Yes," said Grandfather. "I want you to meet them all and decide who, if any of them, can join you."

"I won't deny," said Will, "we could use the help. We've lost too many people. I mean, we gained back a few, but we're still not strong enough to face what's coming."

"There was a good response from the tribes," said Grandfather. "Originally, twelve were chosen. I sent three back home because I could sense that they would not be a good fit. The remaining nine will be here this afternoon. You can all meet them and decide who you want to join you."

"Nine?" said Will, impressed. "I hope they're all a good fit. We could use the help."

"I am afraid you are probably right," said Grandfather. "I think we are going to be seeing more and more of these creatures and others like them."

"I was afraid you'd say that," said Will.

"This is only the beginning," said Grandfather. "There are worse things out there than the *Oolonga-Doglalla*. Things I hoped would never return."

"Like what?" asked Will, frowning.

"You have enough to worry about," said Grandfather. "There will be time to worry about the other things when the need arises."

"If you say so, Grandfather," said Will, nodding.

"Do not fear," said Grandfather. "I will be preparing and will make certain you are ready when the time comes."

Drums began playing softly in the distance. Will glanced in that direction and all he could see was a distant campfire.

"Someone is up early," said Will, nodding.

"They are preparing for the day's festivities," said Grandfather.

"The wedding?" asked Will.

"No," said Grandfather. "That is a private affair. They prepare themselves to meet you and the others. That is the camp of the warriors who have come to join you if you will have them."

"I'm looking forward to meeting them," said Will.

The drum grew stronger. Will listened and whoever was playing was nearly as good as Mika. Will could already see how they might fit into the existing pack. The only thing would be making sure the order was not challenged. The pack hierarchy was already established. They would find a place in it or leave.

"You're listening to the wolf," said Grandfather, interrupting Will's thoughts.

Will just turned and looked quizzically at his Grandfather.

"No, I did not read your thoughts," said Grandfather, smiling. "I read your expression. You have taken on a heavy burden, dealing with both wolf spirits. One is a protector spirit, the other a ravenous predator. Be careful which one you feed, for that will be the one which grows strongest."

"Thank you, Grandfather," said Will. "I will be careful."

"Now," said Grandfather. "Go get ready. The joining ceremony will begin as the sun breaks the eastern horizon. The others will start arriving soon."

Nodding Will headed inside and got in the shower. Sarah and Gabrielle were already awake and getting ready. Sarah was helping Gabrielle with the ceremonial dress and other gear. When Will emerged from the shower, they were both ready.

"You both look beautiful," Will said, smiling.

"Thank you," said Gabrielle, blushing.

"And you will be severely underdressed for the ceremony if you don't hurry," replied Sarah, grinning wickedly.

"I'll be ready," said Will, dropping his towel and opening the closet.

Sarah slapped him on the butt as they headed out the door.

"Don't be late," she said over her shoulder. "I'd hate to have to drag you out there naked in front of all of our guests."

"You'd do it, too," said Will, chuckling.

"Not alone, she wouldn't," added Gabrielle.

Will scooped up his damp towel and threw it at them as they headed out the door laughing.

Will had just slipped into his loincloth and boots when Mika walked in without knocking.

"Ten seconds earlier and you would have seen me naked," said Will.

"Eh," said Mika. "It's not a thrill. I've seen it before."

"Fair enough," said Will. "Something on your mind?"

"I just wanted to say thank you," said Mika.

"For what?" asked Will.

"For letting me and Cassie be part of your joining ceremony," he said. "We kind of decided to do it at the last minute."

"No problem at all, brother," said Will. "I'm happy to have you out there with me. That way I won't be the only dumbass in a loincloth."

Mika started laughing.

"I almost backed out when I found out about that," said Mika, still chuckling.

"We might want to keep a few of them around," said Will. "I think they might be the only thing we wouldn't shred when we change."

"Now there's a fucking image," said Mika. "A werewolf in a loincloth."

They both started laughing at that thought.

"Go get ready," said Will. "Everyone will be arriving in a few minutes."

Mika headed out of the room, still chuckling as he went. Will turned to finish putting the rest of his wardrobe in place. It didn't take long before he was finished. He had considered braiding his hair but decided against it. He wanted it down for the ceremony.

Heading outside, Will saw that the other *Hotamétaneo'o* were already by the fire, waiting. Sarah's parents were both there along with a few close friends of the family. It was to be a small ceremony. Mika's only living relative was his grandmother and she was too frail to travel. It was customary for the families of those in the joining ceremony to be there. The *Hotamétaneo'o* would serve as a family for them all. Besides, Grandfather had already proclaimed all of them to be his own. No one would question Jay *Matoskah*.

There were others there, as well. Friends had volunteered to play the drums and play other instruments. Will noticed that they were already in place. The fire had been built up and Jason was already adding sacred herbs and incense to the flames. It was nearly time to begin.

The eastern sky was a purplish-red as the light of predawn began to break the night's darkness. As the first rays of the sun crested the horizon, the drums began. Slowly at first, but with growing volume and tempo. Soon, the flutes and gourd rattles. While the others began to dance, Will stood beside Mika, gazing at Sarah, Gabrielle, and Cassie through the flames.

For Will, the rest of the ceremony was a blur of steps and music. He let the rhythm of the moment carry him through the ceremony. It seemed like only a few minutes had passed when he was standing with Gabrielle on his left and Sarah on his right. A large buffalo skin was wrapped over their shoulders. Farther to his left, Mika and Cassie were similarly draped in a buffalo skin. As soon as the skins were placed on their shoulders, the music ceased instantly. The ceremony was completed.

Grandfather began chanting a prayer for a blessing on this joining and soon they all joined in the song. Will felt the power of the song carry through him and he wrapped his arms tighter around Gabrielle and Sarah. He wasn't sure why it happened, but he felt the wolf inside him shift and then the transformation took over.

"Alright!" shouted Mika, joining the change.

Unsurprised, the others joined him as they all shifted. The song ended with the howls of the assembled *Hotamétaneo'o*. Will howled into the morning sky, proclaiming to the heavens the bond that had been formed here today. The bond wasn't just between those in marriage. It was the bond of the pack.

It took a moment before the spirit within him calmed and he looked around. No one seemed scared or tried to run. The word had spread among the tribes that the *Hotamétaneo'o* had regained their ability to take wolf form. Although this was the first time that many of them had seen it, the transformation only served to reaffirm their faith in the legends of their peoples.

Will noticed a slight difference from before. This had been the first time he had allowed himself to shift form since he'd eaten the heart of *Grigore* that night in Arkansas. His form had changed. Before he'd been bigger than the others by nearly a foot. His coat had darkened to almost black on his back and shoulders with it turning to grey on his chest and stomach. He also stood taller than before. He wasn't sure how much taller, but he noticed a difference.

He felt the power of the combined elements that fought within him. So long as he maintained control, the power of both wolves was his. He knew that the spirit of the great werewolf within him fought the restraints, but it fought not only against Will but against the spirit of the Dire Wolf that resided within him. As strong as the werewolf was, it wasn't strong enough to overpower both of them.

As the ceremony came to an end, they all returned to the deeper shadows to resume their human forms, slipping quietly into their campers to change into fresh clothing. While they were getting dressed, Sarah turned to Will.

"What made you decide to change into the wolf?" she asked.

"I don't know," he said. "It just kind of happened."

"Well, they took it better than I expected," said Sarah. "No one panicked and ran away."

"I don't think any of them were expecting that to happen," said Gabrielle, smiling. "But I bet they don't ever forget it, either."

"Can you blame them?" asked Sarah, smiling.

"I hope you're not upset," said Will.

"Not at all," said Sarah. "I think that just emphasized to everyone, my parents included, that we aren't just claiming to be *Hotamétaneo'o*."

"I think the word of this ceremony will spread like wildfire," said Gabrielle. "It might become a legend, told and retold over the years."

"It probably will," said Sarah. "Speaking of legends. What happened to your wolf-form, Will? It changed."

"I noticed that," he said. "I think it has something to do with what happened in the final fight with *Grigore*."

"I knew that would change you," said Gabrielle, "but I didn't expect it to be so dramatic."

"Me either," said Will. "We'd better get back out there before they think we ran off."

Will emerged from the camper wearing moccasin boots with blue jeans and a black t-shirt. Gabrielle and Sarah both wore jeans and boots, but while Gabrielle had a loose-fitting white button-up blouse, Sarah wore a doeskin blouse with intricate colored beads on the back making the pattern of a wolf howling at a full moon. Tassels hung from beneath the arms and shoulders. Both had their hair braided in two long braids. Will kept his down.

Preparations were in progress for a large meal. Several cooking fires had been started for different cooks to prepare dishes of their own. Will could smell delicious aromas drifting around on the gentle breeze. His stomach rumbled in anticipation and he suddenly remembered that they had skipped breakfast for the ceremony.

Mika and Cassie were already sitting together near one of the fires, laughing and talking with some of the guests. Grandfather was sitting near a different fire, motioning for Will to join him. He waved at Gabrielle and Sarah, as well. When they all had taken a seat, he smiled and reached into his pocket.

"I have something for you," said Grandfather. "You asked me to hold onto this for you. It's the present that Claire Parker gave you."

"I had almost forgotten about that," said Sarah, smiling.

Grandfather handed it to her and smiled.

"Open it, my child," he said softly.

Sarah hesitated a moment and glanced at Gabrielle.

"Go ahead," she said. "I'm not upset. You didn't even know me when you got that."

Cassie nodded, then slowly unwrapped the doeskin packet that had been tied shut with a leather strip. When she unfolded the soft skin, she was shocked to see that there were three matching necklaces. They each had an obsidian arrowhead attached to a leather thong by braided metal wire. On the leather thong were beads of turquoise and desert coral.

"How did she know?" asked Sarah, wide-eyed.

"How was she even there?" Grandfather asked by way of an answer. "The necklaces are the least of the questions involved here."

"Fair enough," said Will.

They each slipped one over their head and let them lay on the outside of their clothing.

"They're beautiful," said Gabrielle.

"Yes, they are," agreed Grandfather. "Obsidian is very difficult to work with. It takes a great deal of practice and time to make something like that."

"I'll have to make sure to take it off before I turn," said Will, glancing down at the arrowhead. "I would hate to lose it."

"They're preparing a big meal and festival," said Grandfather, nodding towards the arena to their north. "I can smell the barbeque already."

"Good," said Will. "I'm starving."

"We're also going to have an *Inipi*," said Grandfather. "I want to introduce you to all of the new arrivals before we do. Then we can all join in the sweat and begin the process."

"Then we might as well get started," said Will.

"I'll get the others," said Sarah, heading for the camper.

By the time they had all gathered, the smell of the cooking was making everyone's stomachs rumble in eager anticipation. As they walked over to the arena, they could see that several different trailers had been set up, each containing cooking gear or barbeque grills. It looked as if they were cooking for a small army.

"How many people are coming to the dinner?" asked Jason, glancing around.

"My father invited people he knows on every reservation within two days' drive of here," said Sarah. "I'd expect a large crowd."

Will saw a gathering of people, seated near a set of bleachers just outside of the arena that they used for rodeos and competitions. They were sitting as if they knew each other, but he could tell from the body language that they didn't know each other well. There was still tension among them.

"Is that our group?" asked Will, gesturing towards the bleachers.

"That's them," said Jason. "Grandfather and I have already spoken to them, but it's not up to me. This is a decision that involves all of us."

"Well," said Mika, "let's meet 'em, then."

"I will make the introductions," said Grandfather.

As they approached, all the prospective members stood and waited for them to arrive. Grandfather motioned for everyone to stop and stepped between the two groups.

"Since they are already aware of who you all are," said Grandfather, gesturing at Will and the others, "I will not waste time in introducing you. I will only tell you about them and what they bring to the group."

"That's fine by me," said Will, glancing at the others.

No one voiced a complaint, so Grandfather took that as his cue to continue.

"First," he said, gesturing at the two standing on the left, "this is Richard *Akaash* and his twin brother Robert *Alok*. They're Mohawk from St. Regis Mohawk Reservation in New York. Both were Marine Force Recon and served three tours in Afghanistan."

Will nodded at the two men. They were both fit and stood about six feet two inches each. They both wore their hair long in the back but shaved up the sides in the Mohawk fashion. They were dressed in blue jeans, moccasin boots of the Mohawk style, and red t-shirts. They nodded as they were introduced.

"Next," said Grandfather, "we have Kilani *Nasnane* and Isaac *Kuzih*. They're both Athabaskan from the Tanana Athabaskan Range in Alaska. Kilani was a SWAT team member when she was with the Alaska State Troopers for eight years. Isaac was a big game guide and ran a hunting guide service out of Tanana."

Kilani smiled and waved at them while Isaac only nodded. Kilani wore khaki tactical pants and boots with a blue polo shirt tucked into it. Isaac wore jeans with hiking boots with a green flannel shirt, hanging loose and not tucked in. Kilani had long hair that was pulled back into a single thick braid. Isaac left his long black hair hanging loose. It fell almost to his waist.

"Joseph 'Joe' *Nakai*," said Grandfather, "is a Navajo from the Reservation in New Mexico. He's a former member of the Shadow Wolves, a Native American group of trackers that works for the US Customs and Border Patrol. He quit and returned to the reservation after encountering the *Oolonga-Doglalla* along the US Mexico Border several times."

Joe smiled and shifted his weight from foot to foot. He was wearing tactical boots with desert camo military fatigue pants with a black t-shirt that said Border Patrol in yellow letters. His hair was shoulder-length and moved with the breeze.

"This is Cody *Tapuche*," said Grandfather. "He's *Uintah-Ute* from *Uintah-Ouray* Reservation in Utah. He was an Army Ranger with three tours in Afghanistan. He's been aware of the existence of strange creatures for a very long time. Maybe longer than any of you. He grew up just outside a place that they call Skinwalker Ranch."

Cody shrugged and glanced around. He was wearing black fatigue pants with highly polished jump boots. The black t-shirt had a gold emblem on it that read "Rangers Lead the Way". Cody was one of the few who kept his hair short, cut almost military style. He was also the largest of the group, standing close to six feet eight inches tall and weighing close to 350 pounds. He was built like a tank. He had tribal tattoos down both arms, featuring bears as the totem spirit. The Ute revered the bear above all other animals.

"Nice to meet you all," he said, smiling. "First Sergeant Greyeagle. I was in your old unit. They used to tell stories about you. You're something of a legend. It's a pleasure to meet you, Top."

Will smiled and nodded.

"We should talk later," said Will.

"This is Rain Wind-Singer," said Grandfather, gesturing to a woman off to the right. "She's *Ashalaho*-Crow from the Crow Reservation in Montana. She's an expert tracker and a veterinarian who saw the return of some of these creatures when she discovered a series of animal mutilations on the Rez last year. She's been tracking and documenting them ever since."

Rain nodded. She was wearing a black cowboy hat with a rattlesnake skin band around it. The head of the snake was in the front center with the mouth open, revealing the fangs. The rattle was at the back center of the band. She wore jeans and black cowboy boots with a white t-shirt and a brown deerskin jacket over it with tassels on the sleeves and back.

"Julia *Topsannah*," said Grandfather, pointing to another young woman, "is Commanche. She didn't grow up on a Rez. She's from Lawton, Oklahoma. Her Grandfather was a medicine man and taught her the old ways. After six years in the military, she decided to return to Oklahoma. She married a white cop who was attacked and killed by a Bigfoot. The department called it an animal attack and buried the story. She tracked down the renegade creature and stopped it before it could attack more people."

She nodded solemnly. She wore her hair long and in a single ponytail. She wore running shoes and cut-off jean shorts with a white tank top. There were tribal tattoos on her arms and legs.

"Finally, we come to our final guest," said Grandfather. "This is George Bluesky. He's Arapaho from Wind River Indian Reservation in Wyoming. A former US Army Special Forces sniper and a graduate of the Special Forces Mountaineering School. His team was responsible for tracking insurgents through the mountain ranges in Afghanistan. It was there that he had his first encounter with a Dogman."

George nodded but his face was neutral. He was fit and looked like a weightlifter. He wore combat boots and black military fatigue pants. His t-shirt was black with an Army Strong logo on it. He wore dark Oakley sunglasses and had a tattoo on his right bicep of the Special Forces Mountain Team unit patch.

"Why don't you all take some time to get to know one another," suggested Grandfather, "while Jason and I prepare the *Inipi*. We'll call you when we're ready."

Jason and Grandfather headed off to begin preparations leaving them all to stand in awkward silence for a few moments before Mika spoke up.

"Fuck," he said, glancing around, "don't everyone talk at fucking once."

That drew chuckles from everyone and soon they were all striking up conversations. They didn't realize that over three hours had passed before Jason came for them.

"Hey," he said, glancing around the group that was now chatting and laughing like they'd known each other for years, "are you guys coming?"

"Absolutely," said Will. "We kind of lost track of time."

"Not a problem," said Jason. "As soon as we finish the sweat, it will be time for the big dinner."

"Good," said Mika. "I'm fucking starving. I could eat a dead buffalo right now."

"That's good," said Jason. "There's a lot of buffalo on the grill."

Following Jason, they headed for the building where the *Inipi* was to take place. Since they were on reservation land, a more permanent structure had been made for the sacred sweat. The fires were ready, and the steam was already thick inside the ceremonial chamber. Outside, several elders played drums and chanted, calling for a blessing on the sacred *Inipi*.

One by one, they disrobed and cleansed themselves before entering. After they had all taken their places, more water was added to the heated rocks until the room was thick with steam. Both Jason and Grandfather were inside, directing the ceremony.

Will was proud of Jason's progress as a shaman of his people. He was still very young to have amassed the knowledge that he had, thus far. It would be many years before he would be considered one of the sacred elders of the tribe. In the meantime, he would be one of the *Hotamétaneo'o*. It would be that role which would separate him from others who walked the path of the shaman.

"Before we begin," said Grandfather, "any of you who do not wish to go further in this journey should leave now."

No one made a move, and no one spoke up.

"Good," said Grandfather. "Now, are there any that the *Hotamétaneo'o* who have objections to any of them?"

Again, there was no answer.

"Very well," said Grandfather. "Once this ceremony begins, there will be no turning back from this path. You walk this path for the rest of your lives. You will always be one of the *Hotamétaneo'o*. The hallowed path that you are embarking on ends only in the death of those who walk it."

"The tribal council has met on the *Hotamétaneo'o*," said Jason. "They have decided that this is far bigger than any single tribe. This is something that affects all of us."

Everyone exchanged glances, not sure where this was leading.

"After lengthy discussions," said Grandfather, "they have conferred on Will Greyeagle the title of War Chief of the *Oglala Lakota*. Mika Canowicakte, you have been named a War Band Leader of the *Húŋkpapȟa Lakota*. In this way, we honor the old ways, and all who seek to join the *Hotamétaneo'o* will know the banner they ride under."

There were approving nods from around the group. Will glanced at Mika, who held up his fist for Will to bump. Reluctantly, Will bumped fists with him and nodded.

"We've come a long way, baby," said Mika. "They recognize how important this is."

"This just means that we have to work even harder to be worthy," said Will.

"Don't be so serious all the time, Greyeagle," said Mika. "Relax and be happy. Enjoy the moment, brother."

"I'll try," said Will, smiling. "Thank you for reminding me."

"No problem," said Mika. "I know this is some serious shit, but it doesn't mean we can't enjoy it, too."

"Good point, brother," said Will, smiling broadly. "I'll try to remember that."

"Let us begin," said Grandfather, dipping the gourd in the basin of water and taking a sip before passing it around the circle.

The sun was sinking low in the sky when they emerged from the *Inipi*. Will felt like a different person. He was at peace inside for the first time since he'd eaten the heart of *Grigore*. The werewolf was silent now, but not gone. Will could feel it staring at him from the dark recesses of his mind. It would make its presence known, soon enough. For now, he would enjoy the respite and embrace their new members. It was time to feast.

D.A. ROBERTS

CHAPTER FOUR
COUNCIL OF WOLVES

"Day and night cannot dwell together."
Duwamish

September 27th
3:00 PM
Location Unknown
Near Eminence, Missouri

Alex sat with her back to the wall of the cave. There was just enough light filtering in through the mouth of the cave that she could see fairly well. She wasn't exactly sure where the thing had taken her, but it had carried her for well over an hour. She was hoping that her pack was tracking her, but she was also worried about what would happen if they found her. Her pack was no match for these things. There were eight in her pack. So far, she'd counted at least twenty of these things.

Bones of elk, deer, and even a few humans littered the floor of this cave. There were always at least two of the creatures between her and the exit and she was certain that there was only one way out. For the most part, the creatures had ignored her. A few had been curious about the newcomer but none of them had gotten closer than a few feet. They weren't afraid of her. She was sure of that. They seemed confused by her, more than anything.

She was afraid that if she fell asleep, she would revert to her human form and they would attack her. So far, it hadn't taken much effort to stay awake, but she knew she couldn't stay that way forever. Eventually, she'd doze off and change back to human. It was becoming more of a struggle to stay in her wolf-form than it was to stay awake. That meant it was only a matter of time before she changed, one way or the other.

She could tell that there were more males than females in this pack or whatever they were. They certainly were far more bestial than her pack, in pretty much every sense. She hadn't observed any form of speech other than growls, snarls, and barks. The females seemed to defer to the males and there were an Alpha male and female that ruled over all of them.

The Alpha male was bigger even than the one that had captured her. It was a massive grey male that had to be over ten feet tall. It had a huge scar that ran down the left side of its face, over the eye, and into its muzzle. Whatever had done it had to have been tremendously strong to wound such a powerful creature. The bad part was the scar didn't look like it was very old. Whatever had done it had been recent.

She'd considered trying to talk to some of them, but since she never heard any of them speak, she doubted that they would understand her. From the looks some of them had given her, she didn't think she would find anyone that would be even remotely sympathetic. Her usual tricks of seduction weren't going to work here.

After a few minutes, the Alpha male and female approached her. She stayed crouched against the wall of the cave until the female grabbed her by the arm and yanked her to her feet. She thought about resisting, but the Alpha female was just too strong. She wouldn't have been able to put up much of a fight.

Getting to her feet, the Alpha female pulled her away from the wall and made her stand in the middle of the room. Then the Alpha male walked around her, sniffing and growling low in his throat. When he was finished, the Alpha female got very close to her and started looking her all over, even inspecting her breasts and crotch, sniffing everything.

"What the hell are they doing?" she thought, too scared to speak up.

After a moment, the Alpha female turned and walked away. The Alpha male grabbed her by the back of the neck and pulled her towards the back of the cave. The other pack members seemed to get mildly excited, sensing something was about to happen.

When the Alpha took her to what appeared to be a nest made of pine boughs and remnants of furs, she started to understand what was about to happen. Dragging her into the nest, the Alpha forced her to get down onto her stomach. She tensed in anticipation of what was about to happen, subconsciously holding her breath. After a long moment, nothing happened.

Glancing up, she saw the Alpha standing over her, watching. It wasn't making any move to touch her or attack. It was just watching her as if expecting something to happen. She almost sighed in relief that she wasn't about to be set upon by the massive beast.

"It's waiting for me to change back," she thought, suddenly.

She remembered that the black one had watched her change into her wolf form. Undoubtedly, it had passed that on to the Alpha, despite her not hearing anything she thought was a language. It was watching to see if she would turn back into a human. Waiting for her to change. The question was, would it kill her then?

She thought about it for a long moment before sighing. If they were going to kill her, then they were going to do it regardless. There wasn't any sense trying to fight it any longer. With a nervous glance around the cave, she let herself begin to shift back into her human form.

As soon as she started changing, some of the lesser pack members started growling and getting excited, yapping and snarling as they moved closer. The Alpha male silenced them with one rumbling snarl that sent them all back away in silence.

Seconds later, when the transformation was complete, she lay there nude, staring up at the big Alpha. It just looked at her for a while. She could see that it was mulling something over before it decided what to do. She only hoped that the next thing it did wasn't to rip her head off.

Whatever was about to happen, it seemed to have decided what it was going to do. Reaching down, it pulled her up by her arm. The beast was so tall that her face reached the middle of its stomach. The smell of the creature was almost too much to take. It reeked of dried blood and a thick musk that almost made her gag. Hygiene wasn't one of its priorities.

She was always meticulous about washing blood and gore out of her fur. She had to. Her job was to lure in prey for the rest of the pack. She didn't have to sleep with them, she just enjoyed it. Might as well give them one last night of bliss before she killed them, or at least that's how she felt about it. It was a method that had worked well for her pack for the last few years now. She was able to identify victims who were both easy to lure and not likely to be reported missing quickly. It allowed them time to clear out of an area if they needed to.

Lifting her by the arm with no more effort than a child would lift a stuffed animal, it brought her up to level with its face. Staring into those evil yellow eyes, she felt nothing but malice and darkness there. It stared into her eyes for what felt like forever before it snorted and started carrying her towards the mouth of the cave.

Once they were outside in the fresh air, she finally realized just how rank the air had been inside the cave. It was like she smelled fresh air for the first time in her life. Before she had the chance to do more than take a deep breath, the Alpha brought her up to its face again.

Feeling its hot breath on her face and the sheer fetid stench of it, she thought she was going to throw up, right then and there. It glared at her for a moment before it began growling a deep and menacing rumble from deep in its chest.

"Leave!" it snarled before throwing her almost fifty feet through a mass of bushes and brambles.

She was bleeding from scratches all over her body and she thought she might have cracked a few ribs when she hit the ground, but it wasn't pursuing her. It stared at her like it was starting to reconsider its decision.

Getting slowly to her feet, she held her left arm across her chest cradling the tender ribs. She had the feeling that if she tried to turn back into her wolf form, it would attack her. She didn't want to do anything that could be taken as a challenge.

The rocky ground was cutting into her bare feet and she knew that some of the cuts on her arms, legs, and torso would have normally needed stitches. Glancing behind her, she could see that the big black creature that had captured her in the first place was watching her go. It stood beside the Alpha and seemed to be listening to it, even though she still couldn't hear any kind of language.

As she limped along, she slowly got her bearings and started making her way back towards where she had left the truck and camper. She wasn't about to lead them to her pack. She had little doubt that they would make short work of her and the rest of her pack if they knew where to find them.

Her progress was slowed because the bottoms of her feet were being torn to ribbons.

The command to leave was not just intended for her to leave their cave. She fully understood that it wanted her and the rest of her pack gone. If they encountered those creatures again, it would likely be for the last time. She knew that it was extremely difficult to kill a werewolf, but she didn't think those creatures would have much trouble figuring out how to do it.

She could hear the big black creature following her. It was not attempting to hide the fact that it was right behind her. If she stopped or tried to go back, she had a distinct feeling that it had been instructed to kill her. She already knew that she couldn't outrun or outfight it. It also seemed to be completely immune to any of her usual methods of charming males into doing what she wanted.

She would have to get back to the truck and call the others on her cell phone. She would arrange to meet up with them somewhere miles from here and explain to them that they needed to get as far away from this area as fast as they could go. That they were in grave danger if they didn't leave immediately.

If only she could make her Alpha understand this was a threat they didn't have a chance of beating. If she couldn't convince him, he would refuse to leave this area since the hunting had been so good here. If he decided to stay, she was going to have to do the unthinkable and leave the protection of her pack. There was no way she was going to come back here and challenge those things, whatever the hell they were.

She was limping badly, now. The pain in her feet was excruciating and each step was sheer agony. She couldn't hear the creature behind her anymore, but she did not doubt that it was still there. She could feel it watching every step she took.

Emerging from a thick patch of bushes, she found herself on a rough road that was more rut than the actual road. It consisted of two dirt and gravel paths through the woods with grass and weeds growing up through the center. It was just wide enough for a single vehicle to pass between the bushes on both sides of the road.

To her left went upwards towards the top of the ridge and to her right went downwards into a valley. She could hear distant running water from downhill and knew that had to take her out near some sort of stream. It wasn't loud enough to be the river. Going towards the sound of water was more in the direction that she needed to go than going up the ridge, so she decided to follow the road.

She was leaving bloody footprints in the grass and felt her strength was beginning to fail her. She either had to shift back to her wolf form or stop to rest. If she did either one, she had the distinct feeling the creature that was following her would attack.

Glancing back over her shoulder, she caught a glimpse of the creature watching her from behind a large pine tree. It was about forty yards back, but she knew that it could cover that distance in seconds without any real difficulty. She also knew that on her best day, she didn't stand a chance of outrunning it.

While she was watching the creature, she noticed that it seemed to be looking at something else. It wasn't watching her. It was looking past her and down the hill towards the valley floor. That's when she heard the sound of an engine coming her way. Someone was down here in a vehicle.

Turning quickly around, she saw the familiar dark green of a Missouri Department of Conservation Game Warden's vehicle. It was clear that he'd already seen her because he was stopping and getting out of his vehicle. She could see he was talking frantically into his radio as he reached for the first aid kit behind his seat.

She had no doubt that seeing a naked blonde woman covered in blood was going to get his attention. It was also going to bring a lot of questions she wasn't certain how to answer. Questions that might lead to places she wasn't willing to go. She wasn't sure if anyone had seen her near any of the places where they'd taken men from the campgrounds. If they had, then she was likely going to have to answer even more questions.

"Ma'am, are you ok?" he said, coming towards her.

All his concentration was on her and he was already opening the first aid kit as he approached. She could hear the creature moving rapidly through the trees, towards him. It was staying out of sight until it was close enough to attack.

"Run!" she screamed, trying to warn him away. "Run!"

She was waving frantically and pointing at the trees, but his attention was focused on her. He was looking at her quizzically before he finally turned his head and glanced at the trees. He looked confused until the beast burst from the trees in a flash of teeth and claws. The officer dropped the first aid kit and his hand went for the pistol on his hip. His hand was fast, but the beast was faster. It was on him before he could draw.

She screamed as it bore him to the ground and began savagely ripping him apart. Blood was flying every direction, covering the front of the truck and the windshield in crimson droplets. The officer's scream was cut off quickly as it ripped his throat out, nearly severing the head in the process.

Seconds later, it began shredding off the man's uniform and body armor. Once the clothing had been removed, the beast began tearing the man's limbs off one at a time. The sound was horrifying to hear. The cracking of bones and the splitting of muscle, ligaments, and cartilage seemed ghastly and utterly inhuman.

Despite how she had hunted men before, the sheer brutality of the attack almost caused her to vomit. Compared to this assault, she was practically a surgeon. Despite the violence of the strike, it was over quickly. The beast had the unfortunate officer completely eviscerated in less than a minute.

Picking up the pieces, the beast looked back at her and growled low in its throat. It was a menacing sound, clearly indicating that she was not to come back. Then, it turned and headed back into the trees with the pieces of the officer clutched in its massive hands.

Laying on the ground was only the shredded clothing, blood, and entrails where a living man had stood only moments ago. She stood there in shock, still reeling from the savagery of the attack. It was like nothing she'd ever seen before. These things were nothing like her and her pack. They were pure evil.

The thought suddenly occurred to her that law enforcement was going to be crawling all over this place, now. Killing a cop was a guarantee to end the hunting in an area. At least this would take the attention off the disappearance of the men she'd helped her pack bring down. If anything, they would blame the disappearances on the same animal that had killed the officer. At least that was good news.

Shambling over to the officer's truck, she was careful not to touch anything that would leave a print. Glancing in the vehicle, she found what she was looking for. Most officers carried a go-bag with additional gear in it for emergencies. She opened the bag and found a spare set of clothing and an extra set of boots. Putting them on quickly, she headed down the hill as quickly as she could go. She was going to have to put some distance between her and this place before the search party arrived searching for the officer. The radio call he'd gotten off just before the attack guaranteed they would be looking for him, soon.

She considered shifting into her wolf form and moving away as quickly as she could, but she reconsidered it. Something inside her told her that it was still a bad idea. It was likely that there were more than one of those things following her, anyway.

"This is bad," she whispered, heading down the hill as quickly as she could go.

Despite the boots, she was still limping heavily. Behind her, she could hear something big moving through the trees. They were still following her.

"They're going to kill me, too," she whispered. "They're hoping I'll lead them to my pack."

APEX PREDATOR: HUNTER'S MOON
CHAPTER FIVE
STRAIGHT ON TILL MORNING

"A good chief gives, he does not take."
Mohawk

Pine Ridge Reservation
September 27th
10:30 PM
South Dakota

Will was sitting by the fire with the *Hotamétaneo'o*, both old and new, talking and laughing when he felt his cellphone vibrate in his pocket. At first, he considered ignoring it, but then reconsidered. Almost everyone he knew was here at the Lakota Rez. Even his Grandfather was here somewhere.

Taking the phone out of his pocket, he glanced at the screen. Its caller ID said the call was from Detective Mike Blanchard. That was enough to let him know it was probably serious. Mike never called unless it was something bad. Excusing himself from the group, he thumbed the answer icon and stepped away from the fire.

"Greyeagle," he said, putting the phone to his ear.

"Hey, old buddy," said the familiar voice of Mike Blanchard. "How the hell are you?"

"I'm good," said Will, glancing at the seat where Sarah and Gabrielle waited for him. "I'm doing good, man. How are you?"

"Better than the last time we talked," said Blanchard. "Mostly healed up. I took a job in Sloan County. I needed to get away from Lacland. I'm pretty sure the Sheriff would have fired me because I didn't go along with his animal attack story."

"You didn't tell everyone what happened, did you?" asked Will, frowning.

"No," said Blanchard. "But I wanted to. It pissed me off that everyone believed that the Little Bastard was killed by a fucking pack of wild dogs.

Plus, I couldn't even tell anyone what happened to me. The wife left me over it, too."

"Why?" asked Will, frowning.

"The nightmares, mostly," said Blanchard. "I would wake up screaming a lot and go check the doors. I wanted to tell her, but I don't think she would have believed me, even if I had."

"Shit, I'm sorry, Mike," said Will. "Are you ok?"

"I will be," he replied. "That's why I took the job in Sloan County. It's the Table Rock Lake area. I needed a change of scenery. Little did I know that shit would get weird down here, too."

"What happened?" asked Will, his tone growing dark.

"It's done," said Blanchard. "Next time you're in Kimberling City, buy me a beer and I'll tell you the story. It wasn't me, though. Thank God. It was another kid named Clark. Tough little shit."

"So, nothing going on there now?" asked Will.

"Well, not in my neighborhood," said Blanchard, "but I did hear something a little while ago that just might be up your alley."

"What's up?" asked Will.

"There was a reported animal attack down in Eminence, Missouri," said Blanchard. "Shamrock County. Happened this afternoon. A Missouri Department of Conservation Game Warden is missing. They found a lot of blood at his vehicle and some scraps of his clothing, but the body is missing. They brought in tracking dogs, but they refuse to follow the scent. His last radio call was about a naked woman covered in blood running out of the trees in front of him."

"So, two missing people, possibly?" asked Will.

"Maybe," said Blanchard. "I did a little digging. I called a buddy of mine that works for the Shamrock County Sheriff's Department. He told me that they've had a few odd disappearances lately. Campers that were camping alone in mostly empty campgrounds. There were no bodies or signs of a struggle. They're just gone. Six men, total, if you count the Conservation Agent and one chick."

"I think it's worth checking out," said Will. "Sounds like it might be exactly our kind of thing."

"That's what I was thinking," said Blanchard. "If you need anything, I'll be happy to help with information and shit like that, but I'm not going anywhere near those goddamned things again, man."

"No problem, Mike," said Will. "We've got it. I'll call you if I need you to dig up something for me. Maybe I'll swing by for that beer when we're finished. I'd love to hear what happened."

"My life can't get any fucking weirder, man," said Blanchard. "Maybe I should retire and move to an island where these goddamned things can't get to."

"Good luck, man," said Will. "If you hear anything else, let me know. We're in South Dakota but we can probably be there by tomorrow afternoon."

"I'll text you the locations of the campgrounds and where the Conservation Agent went missing," said Blanchard.

"Thanks, Mike," said Will. "Get me pics of the missing, too. If you can."

"Hey, buddy," said Blanchard, "you be fucking careful. Those goddamned things are dangerous. But please, for the love of God, make sure you get them all. I don't want any of those goddamned things coming up this way. I'll get you as much info as I can find and email it to you."

"We'll do our best," said Will. "Talk to you later. Thanks, man."

"Later, brother," said Blanchard.

Will hung up the phone and put it back into his pocket. Glancing back at the fire, he saw that they were all laughing and telling stories. He hated to interrupt that, but they had a job to do. This would be a trial by fire for the new members. He only hoped that they wouldn't lose anyone, this time.

Heading back to the group, he took his seat between Gabrielle and Sarah. Holding his hands up to get everyone's attention, he waited for them to grow quiet before speaking up.

"I have something I need to tell you all," he began, glancing around at the faces that were illuminated by the firelight.

Everyone settled back and only the sound of the crackling fire could be heard. The warm fall air was laced with wildflowers and a lone coyote could be heard in the distance.

"I think the *Oolonga-Doglalla* may have returned," began Will. "Another group, I'm certain."

"What happened?" asked Mika.

"Several people have disappeared," said Will. "The most recent is a Game Warden."

"Are you certain it's our kind of thing?" asked Jason.

"The Game Warden called in that he spotted a naked woman running out of the trees," said Will. "She was covered in blood and he requested additional units and an ambulance."

"Did he see the creatures?" asked Cassie.

"No," said Will. "By the time they got to his location, he was gone along with the woman. There was a lot of blood and shreds of clothing, but no sign of the officer or the woman."

"What about the others?" asked Mika.

"Just a few missing campers," said Will. "Usually from remote campgrounds with no witnesses. They're just gone."

"Still," said Jason, "this might just be an animal attack."

"Maybe," said Will, "but when they brought in tracking dogs to find the missing Conservation Agent, the dogs refused to track."

"That's odd," said Mika, "but not completely unheard of."

"True," said Will, "but when you add it all up, it's suspicious. I think it's worth checking out."

"Good enough for me," said Mika. "Let's go. Where are we going?"

"Back to Missouri," said Will. "A little town called Eminence. It's in the middle of nowhere."

"What is it with the Ozarks?" asked Mika. "I swear, that place has more creepy shit going on than anywhere I've ever been."

"When do you want to leave?" asked Sarah, glancing at Will.

"I was thinking if we got on the road now," said Will, "we could be there in the early afternoon. We're going to have to drive all night, though."

"We could just wait until morning," said Jason.

"If it is the *Oolonga-Doglalla*," said Will, "then the longer it takes us to find them, the more people will die."

Jason frowned but nodded agreement.

"We can sleep in shifts," said Mika. "I'll take the lead truck with our camper. Will, Sarah, Cassie, Gabrielle, and I will take turns driving it. The rest of you can divvy up the other trucks."

"Let's break camp," said Will. "I want to be on the road in an hour."

"I'll let Grandfather know," said Jason. "He might want to go with us."

"I'll start unhooking the camper," said Mika.

"I'll join you in a minute," said Will. "I'm going to make a phone call and see if I can get more info."

Everyone scattered and headed for different vehicles. Even the new arrivals had already been assigned to different trailers. It was a growing convoy now, with four large trailers being pulled by four dually pick-up trucks. A fifth vehicle, a large Ford Excursion SUV pulled the trailer with the motorcycles on it.

Will stepped away from the fire and took out his phone. Scrolling through the contacts, he stopped when he reached the "G" section and thumbed the contact for Gideon. It rang twice before a gruff voice answered.

"Gideon," was all he said.

"This is Will Greyeagle," said Will. "I hope I'm not catching you at a bad time."

"Not at all," said Gideon. "What can I do for you, detective?"

"I just got off the phone with a friend of mine," said Will. "He told me about a possible issue near Eminence, Missouri. Do you or your people know anything about it?"

"This is the first I've heard about it," said Gideon. "What's going on?"

Will took a few moments to explain everything he had been told. When he was finished, there was a long pause before Gideon spoke.

"Well, it certainly sounds like something we'd be interested in," said Gideon. "However, no official report has been filed with us."

"We're heading that way now," said Will, "but it's going to take us a bit to get there. We're in South Dakota, on the Pine Ridge Rez. We're heading that way as soon as we break camp, but it's a fifteen-hour drive and that's if we don't stop for anything but gas."

"So, you and your people are going to look into it?" asked Gideon.

"That's the plan," said Will. "But who knows what else might happen before we can get there."

"I'm only about an hour from there," said Gideon. "I'll take a couple of people down that way and see what we can dig up. If we find anything, I'll let you know. If it turns out to be nothing, I'll call you off."

"That would be great," said Will. "If I don't hear from you, we'll assume the place is active and get there as fast as we can."

"Most of my team is on a training exercise," said Gideon. "The best I can do is an assessment team. If we run into anything big, you're our only back-up. Well, at least any that could get to us quickly."

"Be careful," said Will. "Just see what kind of information you can dig up. We'll take it from there."

"Sounds good," said Gideon. "We should be there around midnight."

"Be careful," said Will.

"You too," said Gideon.

The line went dead, and Will slipped the phone back into his pocket. Behind him, the others were busily breaking camp. The fire was already out, and they were packing away the camp chairs and tables. Jason was heading towards Will, walking briskly.

"I spoke with Grandfather," said Jason.

"What did he say?" asked Will.

"He told me to tell everyone to be safe and call if we need him," said Jason. "He's going to stay here on the reservation for a few days."

"Alright," said Will. "Let's get the rest of the gear packed and get on the road."

Fifteen minutes later, Mika pulled the lead truck out and headed for the highway. The others followed suit and soon they had a convoy of vehicles making their way southeast. Their path would take them through some very desolate places on their way back to the Ozarks.

Will couldn't help but wonder what was waiting for them at the end of the journey. His instincts were telling him they were heading for something very dangerous. The closer they got, the worse the feeling became.

CHAPTER SIX
ROLE REVERSAL

"Where there are sheep, the wolves are never very far away."
Plautus

September 27th
11:30 PM
Near Eminence, Missouri

There was lightning on the horizon as Alex pulled off the highway and into the campground at Round Springs, north of Eminence, Missouri. She had ditched the blue pickup with the trailer and returned to her red Chevy SUV. She hadn't taken time to shift into her wolf form, so her wounds were still giving her problems. They wouldn't matter soon enough, but for now, she had bigger concerns.

Heading over to the campsite where her pack had set up their camper, she pulled in and shut off the engine. Glancing around as she got out of the vehicle, she noticed that most of the night sounds were gone. Although she couldn't hear or see anything out of place, she had an uneasy feeling and it made her nervous. They were the only camper in the campground.

Bursting through the door, she saw the seven other members of her pack sitting in the living area. It suddenly occurred to her that David only had other women in the pack. She hadn't thought about it before, but it was glaringly obvious now. Only he was allowed to turn new members and he only turned attractive women. It occurred to her that maybe they were more of a harem than a pack, but it was the price they paid for near-immortality. It also occurred to her that he would kill her if she tried to leave.

David, their Alpha, glanced up and smiled at her. There was a feral look in his eyes as if he had been considering the idea of her running from him. The looks that the others exchanged when they saw her confirmed it. They were either planning on tracking her or deciding who would be the next Alpha female in the pack. Possibly both.

"Where have you been?" asked David, trying to sound concerned.

He failed.

"I was captured," said Alex. "I don't know what they were, but they aren't like us. They're wolves, but not anything like us. They were terrifying."

"What are you talking about?" asked Melinda, snidely.

She was a brunette that had been turned after her. Since Alex had been the first one David had transformed, that made her the Alpha female, by default. A position that Melinda had wanted to take from her for some time and had made no attempt to hide the fact.

"They're similar to us," said Alex, ignoring Melinda and concentrating on David, "but they're animals. I don't think they could shift forms. I think they were in wolf form all the time. They were bigger than us, too."

"I've never heard of anything like that," said David.

"Well, they're real," said Alex. "They took me before I could get our next meal. They're stronger than us and faster, too."

"And they just let you go?" asked Melinda.

"I think they were trying to get me to lead them back to you," said Alex, still only talking to David. "We need to get out of here."

"Did they follow you?" asked David.

"I drove for hours and switched vehicles before I came back," said Alex, "but I can't shake the feeling that they're still tracking me. I don't know how I know it. I just do."

"I think she just made up this story to cover for her failure to bring in the prey," said Melinda.

"Do I fucking look like I care what you think, bitch," snapped Alex. "Shut your fucking mouth. I'm talking to David, not you. Besides, I don't remember a single time when you brought in prey."

Melinda stood up but David reacted faster, coming to his feet, and backhanding her onto the couch.

"Mind your place, Melinda," he snarled. "If you weren't so jealous, you'd notice the scent of the other wolves on her. I can smell the fear on her, too. She's not making this up. Whatever they are, they aren't like us."

Melinda didn't move to get up but glared daggers at Alex.

"Go on," said David, turning back to Alex.

"We need to get out of here," she said. "If they were able to follow me, we're in a lot of trouble. There are a lot more of them than there are of us and I couldn't even hurt one of them. The Alpha is massive, too. We need to put some distance between us and them as fast as we can."

"Sounds like you're just a coward, bitch," snarled Melinda.

David turned to Melinda, fire blazing in his eyes. She saw too late that she'd pushed her luck too far, this time. In a flash, David grabbed her by the throat and lifted her off the ground like she didn't weigh an ounce. He was beginning to transform, and his grip was growing tighter as he changed. Melinda was gasping while she gripped his wrist with both of her hands.

"I've had enough of you," snarled David. "Alex has done more for this pack than you ever will. She's kept us fed and never had it tracked back to us. You never even help hunt. All you do is complain about her. I've had enough!"

Alex was sure that David was going to kill her, this time. Melinda had a bad habit of never knowing when to shut up. Her ambition was finally going to get her what she deserved. Alex watched with a small smile on her lips as Melinda's eyes rolled back into her head and her feet began kicking in spasms. Before David could finish her off, there was a loud boom as something heavy slammed into the side of the trailer.

"What the hell was that?" asked David, dropping Melinda back onto the couch.

"They found us!" said Alex, looking at the door with genuine fear in her eyes.

"Let them come!" snarled David. "They might have been stronger than you, but I'm an Alpha for a reason!"

David began shifting fulling into his wolf-form. The transformation took only a few seconds and he was crouched to avoid bursting through the ceiling. At his full height, he was just over seven feet tall and weighed well over three hundred pounds. His reddish-brown coat glistened in the light. It suddenly occurred to Alex that he was overconfident, and he didn't stand a chance against the other creatures.

The others began getting to their feet and shifting form. Melinda started changing but was still glaring daggers at Alex. If they survived this, there was going to be blood between them. The trick would be surviving the attack.

"We fight!" snarled David, reaching for the door.

Before he could grab the door handle, the entire door was ripped from the frame by something outside. The creature outside the door was massive and black, leaning low to look inside the camper. Alex could tell by the yellow eyes and the way it moved that it was the one that had captured her.

Before she could shout a warning, David leaped at the beast and went right for the creature's throat. For a moment, Alex thought that he might succeed. At the last second, the big black monstrosity shifted and caught David without any effort. It yanked him out the door and vanished into the darkness.

With snarls of rage, the others began racing out into the darkness after him. Alex knew that they didn't stand a chance, even if the big black creature had been alone. The might of their entire pack couldn't stop one of those creatures, much less the other pack.

Alex hadn't shifted form like the others. She stepped cautiously to the edge of the door and peered out into the darkness. The big black wolf was throwing David around like a dog with a chew toy. David couldn't even seem to fight back enough to slow it down. The others in the pack were racing to help him but were set upon by three more of the creatures.

For just a moment, Alex felt the urge to race out and help her pack. The feeling passed quickly when she saw the black wolf tear David's head off like it wasn't even an effort. Tossing the head aside, it turned and went after the others in the pack.

Alex took the opportunity to run for her SUV. Since she wasn't in wolf form, the creatures seemed to ignore her. In seconds, she was inside and firing up the engine. When her headlights came on, it illuminated the fight that was going on in front of her vehicle.

David was dead and was already reverting to human form. One by one, the other creatures were knocking the rest of her pack unconscious. It occurred to her that they were going out of their way to avoid killing them.

"They're taking them all captive," she whispered. "What are they doing that for?"

The black wolf turned and glared at her as she put the SUV in reverse. For a moment, she thought it was going to chase her. There were only four of the creatures and all six of her remaining pack-mates were now captured. Instead of chasing after her, the beast began to pick up the remains of David while the others threw her pack-mates over their shoulders.

Mashing the accelerator to the floor, Alex sped off down the road. She briefly wondered what fate awaited the rest of her pack, but she also knew that there was nothing she could do to save them. At least, not on her own. If she tried, she'd only join them in their fate.

Tears stung the corners of her eyes as she sped down the road, heading for the little town of Eminence. From there, she had no idea what she was going to do next. There was no one she could go to for help and nowhere for her to go. She was completely on her own, now.

The ease in which they had killed David told her that the creatures were likely unstoppable. She even wondered if silver would hurt them like it would one of her kind. Somehow, she doubted it. From what she had seen, they didn't have any weaknesses. They were pure evil.

Come hell or high water, she was going to have to find a way to help the rest of her pack. There had to be someone who knew what those creatures were and how to fight them. Even though she didn't care what happened to Melinda, the rest of the pack was still her responsibility as Alpha. Now that David was dead, she was the pack Alpha, not just the Alpha female.

The thought occurred to her that if she didn't find help soon, there probably wouldn't be anyone left to save. Whatever the creatures had planned for the rest of her pack, she doubted that they would wait very long before acting on it.

She briefly thought of calling the police but remembered that the Conservation Agent hadn't even slowed the creature down. The police wouldn't be able to stop these things. There had to be someone out there who could help. The trick was going to be finding them in time.

CHAPTER SEVEN
GIDEON

"The aim of life was meat. Life itself was meat. Life lived on life. There were the eaters and the eaten."
Jack London

September 28th
12:30 AM

Gideon stepped out of the plain blue sedan with government plates. They had stopped at a small gas station in Eminence, Missouri. At this time of night, it looked to be the only thing open in this little town. Despite being the county seat of Shamrock County, the town only had around six hundred residents. To Gideon, it seemed like the only one awake at this time of night was the young man running the gas station.

"What the hell are we doing here, Top?" asked Sergeant Christopher Beale.

"No military ranks while we're here," said Gideon. "Just call me Gideon until we're done. We're not officially supposed to be here."

"Yes, sir," said Beale. "I thought the Major signed off on us coming down here."

"He did," said Gideon. "I mean we weren't invited by the locals. If we encounter local law enforcement, let me do all the talking."

"Got it, Top," said Beale.

"Beale," admonished Gideon with a frown.

"Sorry," said Beale. "Old habits are tough to break."

"Just make sure to remember it when there are people around," said Gideon.

"Speaking of that," said Beale, "why didn't we wait until morning to check this out. I mean, other than the kid at the counter inside, I think we're the only ones in this entire town that are awake."

"Because I promised Greyeagle that we'd check it out," answered Gideon. "I'm hoping we can figure something out before daylight. They won't be here until tomorrow afternoon, so we're here to see what we can do before they arrive."

"In this Podunk town," said Beale, "if there is a deputy or cop on duty, there's probably only one for the entire county."

"What makes you so sure of that?" asked Gideon.

"Because I grew up in a town about this size," said Beale. "Down in Mississippi. After dark, you couldn't find a cop or a deputy unless all hell was breaking loose. And even then, they were likely to be thirty minutes away."

"Alright," said Gideon. "Go inside and ask the kid if there is a hotel around here where we can check in this late. We'll grab a room and hit it bright and early in the morning."

"Copy that, Top," said Beale, heading inside.

"Goddamn it, Beale," growled Gideon, "knock that shit off."

Beale just chuckled as he headed inside. Gideon stayed standing outside the vehicle. The south gate of Fort Leonard Wood was only just over an hour's drive from here, but he much preferred the fresh air. It was cool enough for most people to want at least a light jacket, but Gideon felt refreshed. The air temperature was fantastic. Cold enough where there weren't any mosquitos and warm enough that you didn't need to dress warmly. In other circumstances, this would have been a great place to come to camp.

Gideon glanced at the front of the store and saw Beale talking to the kid. There wasn't any other movement around the area. Even though they were in town, the woods were all around them. Just past the buildings, the woods were still thick. Even the river ran through the middle of the town.

Looking one way, then the other, Gideon noticed a set of headlights heading their way. At first, he thought it might be a local deputy on his regular patrol of the area, but as the vehicle got closer, he could tell that it wasn't an official vehicle. For one, as it passed beneath a streetlight, he could see that it was a red SUV. So, unless the locals used red as their patrol vehicle color, it was probably just another late traveler.

The car slowed down and turned into the convenience store, pulling right up to the gas pumps. Gideon could hear the engine knocking as it came to a stop. Steam was starting to come up out from beneath the hood and he could see that the vehicle was overheating. An attractive blonde was driving and looked shook up. Exiting the vehicle, the blonde saw him and flashed him a nervous smile.

"Having car trouble, ma'am?" asked Gideon.

The woman looked around nervously before turning back to face him.

"Uh, yeah," she said. "I think it overheated. I'm glad this place was open."

"It's just a gas station," said Gideon. "No mechanic on duty. It doesn't even have a garage."

As she stepped more into the light, Gideon could see that she was wearing clothes that didn't fit her and she was covered in scratches and cuts. She wore boots that were too big for her and walked with a pronounced limp.

"Are you ok?" asked Gideon, his voice growing serious.

Before she could answer, a single howl split the night. It sounded like a wolf, only much bigger. It was distant but when it sounded again, it was already considerably closer.

"Shit," hissed the girl, turning in the direction of the howl with a look of terror on her face. "They found me."

"Ma'am," said Gideon, slipping his hand to his Para-Ordnance 14-45 .45 ACP double-stack, "who found you?"

Turning back to face Gideon, she saw his hand on the pistol.

"Look," she said, trying to smile, "I appreciate the offer, but you can't stop these things. The best thing you can do is run. Let's get in your car and get out of here as fast as we can go."

"It won't do any good," said Gideon. "Once they have your scent, they never give up."

"How do you know?" she asked. "I doubt they could follow me across the country. I wasn't planning on stopping until there were at least a thousand miles between me and this place."

"I don't think that's an option," said Gideon, gesturing behind her.

"Son-of-a-bitch," she hissed, turning around.

One of the creatures was standing about thirty yards away, just at the edge of the store. Gideon drew his pistol and cocked the hammer back while flicking the safety off.

"Get behind me ma'am," said Gideon.

"Your pistol won't do you any good against them," she said, backing slowly towards Gideon.

Beale came walking out of the store with a plastic bag in his hand. When he saw that Gideon had his weapon out, he turned and looked in the direction he was pointing it.

"Fuck me!" snapped Beale, drawing his pistol, and backing towards the car. "I go inside for two fucking minutes and you find one of the goddamned things in the parking lot!"

"It's after the woman," said Gideon. "And there's more than one."

"Fuck, fuck, fuck, fuck," hissed Beale as he reached the car. "Run or fight?"

"The long guns are in the trunk," said Gideon.

As the girl got close enough to him, Gideon grabbed her by the arm and pulled her behind him.

"Stay behind me," said Gideon. "We'll hold them off as long as we can."

"That won't be very long," said the woman. "Give me your keys and get ready to jump in."

Another one of the creatures came around the building and stood next to the first.

"How many of those goddamned things are there?" asked Beale.

"Probably just the pair," said Gideon. "An entire pack wouldn't track just one person."

"You guys don't seem too shocked to see that thing," said the woman.

"It's kinda why we're here," said Beale.

The first creature took a couple of steps towards them, growling deep in its throat. Inside the store, the clerk saw the creature through the window and ran over to the door and locked it.

"Thanks!" said Beale. "Asshole."

The creature looked back and forth from Beale to Gideon and then to the girl. There was a feral intelligence in those evil yellow eyes. It was confused that they weren't running in fear at the mere sight of it. It was used to inspiring terror in all who saw it.

"Beale," said Gideon, "get the woman in the car and pop the trunk. I'll keep Fido here distracted."

"Got it, Top," said Beale, motioning for the woman to get into the car.

Beale ducked in on the passenger side and the woman climbed behind the wheel. Beale thought she was going to start the car and drive off, but Gideon had the keys.

"Shit," she said, glancing at the empty ignition.

As the two creatures began fanning out and moving closer, Gideon moved to the back of the vehicle. The closer of the two creatures was now less than twenty yards away. Gideon aimed directly at the creature's chest and glared at the creature. It paused for a moment, looking at the weapon. It was clear that it understood what it was. A growl that sounded almost like mocking laughter escaped the creature as it looked at Gideon.

"Laugh it up, fuzzball," said Gideon, and he squeezed the trigger.

The pistol thundered twice, striking the beast directly in the chest. The look of amusement vanished from the creature's face to be replaced with pained confusion. The bullets had not only hit their mark, but blood erupted from the wounds as the big .45 caliber hollow points did their damage.

Howling in pain and anger, the beast grabbed the wounds with one massive paw and stumbled backward. The other creature looked back and forth from Gideon to its wounded comrade with a clear look of confusion on its face.

"You weren't expecting that to hurt, were you?" asked Gideon.

Wheeling around, the wounded creature ran back around the corner of the building and vanished into the darkness. The other creature growled and then sprinted after its pack-mate, vanishing in seconds. Soon, they couldn't even hear them running away.

Kneeling slowly without taking his eyes off the spot where they vanished, Gideon recovered his two spent shell casings and slipped them into his pocket. He watched for several seconds until he was certain that the beasts weren't coming back. Turning back to the vehicle, Gideon saw the woman climb out and look at him with shock on her face.

"Who the hell are you guys?" she asked. "What did you just shoot them with?"

"Hollow points," said Gideon, "filled with a consecrated mixture of silver nitrate and white ash."

The woman looked wide-eyed at him and let out a soft sigh.

"Who are you?" she asked, her voice barely above a whisper.

"We're the guys that hunt things like that," said Beale, climbing back out and leaning on the roof of the car.

"You called him Top," she said, looking at Beale. "Are you guys in the military?"

Beale looked sheepish and shrugged at Gideon.

"Something like that," said Gideon.

"Let me guess," she said, "you can't tell me?"

"No," said Gideon. "Why was it chasing you?

She stood there in silence for a long moment, clearly confused and afraid. After a moment, she took a deep breath and let it out slowly.

"I think we need to talk," she said, shaking her head. "But not here. I don't want to be anywhere near this place."

"Get in the car," said Gideon. "We should probably get out of here before the local cops show up. I'm sure that kid called 911 as soon as he saw that thing."

"Who'll believe him?" said Beale. "They'll smell the weed on him and assume he was just high. That kid reeks of cheap ditch weed."

"We can send a tow truck for your SUV tomorrow," said Gideon.

"Don't bother," said the woman. "It's not mine. Leave it here. I'm not planning on coming back for it."

They all climbed into the car with the woman in the back seat. Gideon started the car and pulled out of the station, heading through town and across the bridge over the river. Until they were across the river, the woman watched out the back window, searching for any sign of pursuit.

"I don't think they'll be back tonight," said Gideon. "They won't come back until they have reinforcements."

"That's what I was thinking, too," said the woman. "I'm just making sure."

"Ok," said Gideon. "Let's start with your name."

"My name is Alex," said Alex. "Well, Alexandra Venable, but please call me Alex."

"I'm Gideon," said Gideon, "and this is Beale."

"No first names?" asked Alex.

"Gideon will do," he replied. "Now, tell me why that thing was tracking you and how you managed to escape it in the first place."

"I'm Chris," said Beale, winking at her.

"You might not believe this," she began hesitantly, "but I'm a werewolf. I ran when those things attacked and took out my entire pack."

"Holy shit!" said Beale. "You're a werewolf?"

Beale started to reach for his pistol, but Gideon stopped him.

"You won't need that," said Gideon.

"If she's a werewolf," said Beale, "why isn't she trying to kill us?"

"Because she needs us," said Gideon. "Isn't that right?"

"Yes," admitted Alex. "You guys might be my only shot at surviving this. I hope you know, they won't just be coming after me, now."

"I'm aware," said Gideon.

"So, are you going to help me or shoot me?" asked Alex.

"Other than protecting you," said Beale, "what help do you need?"

"Those things attacked my pack," said Alex. "They killed our Alpha and carried off the females in the pack. I want you to help me rescue them. From what I just saw, you might be able to pull it off if you have enough guns and ammo."

"Oh we brought plenty of firepower," said Gideon, "but we're just the advanced team. Now that we confirmed the presence of those things, we call in the rest."

"Will you help me rescue the rest of my pack?" asked Alex.

"It's highly unlikely that they kept them alive for long," said Gideon. "I don't know why they would take them, anyway."

"What exactly are those things?" asked Alex. "They're nothing like us."

"They're called Dogmen," said Gideon. "And they're far more dangerous than your average werewolf. It would take a First Born to go against them directly."

"How do you know so much about my kind?" asked Alex.

"That's a very long story," replied Gideon, "and I'm not sure how much of it I can tell you. For now, we need to find a place to lay low until the others get here. You wouldn't have any idea how many there are in that pack, would you?"

"At least twenty," said Alex. "Maybe more than that."

"Well," said Gideon, "we have to wait until the others get here. We don't have a chance against a pack that large. Not on our own, anyway."

"Do you want me to call the Major?" asked Beale.

"Not yet," said Gideon. "Remember, we have to be invited by local law enforcement and it's not even been officially reported yet. Will and the others will be here before we could even get the team authorized to respond."

"So, what do we do until then?" asked Beale.

"We keep driving," said Gideon. "They can't find us if we keep moving."

"What about her?" asked Beale, glancing nervously at Alex.

"Don't worry about me," said Alex. "I know full-well that my chances of surviving and my best shot at rescuing any of my pack lies with you guys. I won't do anything to you."

"Besides," said Gideon, "the bullets we have work on werewolves, too."

"There is that," agreed Alex. "Do you think we can find a place where I can take a shower and get a change of clothes?"

"I might know a place," said Gideon. "I know a guy who lives a couple of hours from here. I think that will be far enough away to give us a little breathing room."

"How do we know she isn't going to run as soon as she's out of our sight?" asked Beale.

"You can join me in the shower if you're that worried about me running," said Alex, smiling at Beale. "Honestly, after everything I've been through in the last two days, I wouldn't mind the company."

Beale smiled and swallowed hard. He was running the scenarios in his head, wondering if she'd have sex with him, bite him or just kill him. After a moment's thought, he decided that if she did it in that order, it might not be that bad.

While he was driving, Gideon took out his cell and sent a text to Will. It read, "Presence confirmed. Large Pack active. Meet at Two Rivers Camp Ground soonest. Gideon."

D.A. ROBERTS

APEX PREDATOR: HUNTER'S MOON
CHAPTER EIGHT
ARRIVAL

"Sing your death song and die like a hero going home."
Chief Tecumseh, Shawnee

September 28th
3:00 PM

Will and Mika were leveling their camper when the blue sedan pulled into the campground. Other than the campers that belonged to the *Hotamétaneo'o*, there wasn't anyone in the entire campground. Will reached back into his waistband and gripped the handle of his new pistol.

After their last encounter with the creatures, Will decided that he needed a pistol with a little more punch than the 9mm he'd been carrying, despite the advantage the special ammo made by his Grandfather had given them. He wanted something that hit much harder than a 9mm hollow point.

He loved his Hellcat X2 from Guncrafter Industries, so he instantly thought of them when he wanted something new. A phone call to their customer support had put him in touch with the right people. He'd explained that he wanted a pistol capable of bringing down big game. They had exceeded his expectations with what they recommended.

He purchased the Guncrafter Industries M Series Model 5 in .50 GI. It functioned like your standard 1911 pistol, but it was a larger caliber and hit like a jackhammer. It had less magazine capacity than his Hellcat X2, but it made up for that in sheer power. Besides, he still had the Hellcat X2 as his backup.

Will drew the black anodized pistol and held it against his leg, watching the vehicle get closer. When he saw that it was Gideon driving, he put the pistol away and gave a brief nod to Mika. Mika turned and let out a whistle to let the others know to stand down.

The car came to a stop and Gideon climbed out. In the car, Will could see two other occupants, one male, and one female. He didn't recognize either of them.

"Who's with you?" asked Will, nodding at the car.

"Sergeant Beale from the team," said Gideon, "and a civilian woman named Alex Venable. She was running from the creatures when we found her."

"Is she the one that was spotted by the Conservation Agent before he disappeared?" asked Mika.

"Yeah," said Gideon. "That's her."

"Why is she still with you?" asked Mika. "Shouldn't you have gotten her out of the area already?"

"Ordinarily, yes," said Gideon. "There are some *unusual* circumstances involved."

"In what way?" asked Will.

"She claims she's a werewolf," said Gideon, "and that the Dogmen wiped out the rest of her pack."

Will and Mika exchanged glances and both men frowned.

"I've got it under control," said Gideon. "I have the ammo your Grandfather gave me. We drove off two of the Dogmen and made sure she understood that if she tried to turn on us, we'd kill her."

"You shot two of them?" asked Will.

"Well, I shot one," said Gideon. "The other one just ran."

"If you hurt one of them," said Mika, "then they're going to be coming after you, too."

"I was afraid of that," said Gideon. "But not entirely surprised."

"Then I guess you're in this, too," said Will. "You can stay with us. Then we have the best chance to keep each other alive."

"Not to mention you can help me keep an eye on Alex," said Gideon.

"Why don't you introduce us?" suggested Will.

Mika whistled again and the others began emerging from campers and from within the trees.

"Looks like you've added a few new faces since I last saw you," said Gideon, glancing around.

"One or two," said Will. "I'll make the formal introductions in a few minutes. Let's meet your werewolf, first."

Motioning for them to get out of the car, Will noticed that the male was wearing military boots with blue jeans and a Grunt Style t-shirt that didn't hide the bulge of the handgun on his right hip. The haircut, body language, demeanor, and Oakley sunglasses all said military. This guy stood out like a beacon.

The woman got out of the back seat. Will could see that she was very attractive and made certain to show that off. She was wearing a white t-shirt pulled tight and tied off at the midriff. It was clear that she wasn't wearing a bra from the outline of her pierced nipples. She also wore short spandex running shorts and flip-flops. There were scratches on her legs, arms, and face, but they didn't seem to bother her.

As soon as he made eye contact, she involuntarily smiled at him and postured to present herself. Will instantly smelled the wolf on her and knew that the alluring act was part of how she hunted. She pulled in victims with her wiles and took them down. It was an old but simple method of luring in prey. Wild female wolves have lured pet dogs away to their deaths like that for centuries.

Sarah took her place on Will's right with Gabrielle on his left. When Alex saw the two women, she frowned. It suddenly occurred to her that this wasn't going to be quite as easy as she was used to. Will could see the look on her face when her senses told her what they were.

"You're not like me," she said, glancing around nervously. "I can sense something different, but I've never seen it before. What are you?"

"We're *Hotamétaneo'o*," said Mika. "Dog Soldiers."

"And you can all change?" asked Alex, looking around in surprise at the sheer number of them.

"Who turned you?" asked Gabrielle, stepping forward. "Who's your Alpha?"

"His name was David," said Alex. "David Winthrop. Those things killed him last night."

"I know Winthrop," said Gabrielle. "He was part of my old pack before *Grigore* cast him out. I'm surprised that *Grigore* didn't kill him. So, he tried to start a pack of hid own? Not surprised to hear he's dead."

"I remember David talking about a *Grigore*," said Alex. "He said that he was a First Born werewolf. Where is he now?"

"I killed him," said Will, matter-of-factly.

"You killed a First Born?" asked Alex, incredulously.

Will didn't answer. He just glanced at Gideon.

"Why is she here?" asked Will. "Why didn't you put her down?"

"You had good luck getting Gabrielle to help our side," said Gideon. "I thought maybe she might be able to help us, too."

"She never fed on humans," said Will, gesturing at Gabrielle. "I guarantee you, the same can't be said for her."

He nodded at Alex after the second part.

"I won't lie to you," said Alex. "I've fed on humans. It's not difficult. Not to mention, far more satisfying than any deer or elk."

"If you're trying to convince us that we shouldn't put you down," said Mika, "then you're not doing a very good job. You're kinda heading in the wrong direction."

"You're going to tell me that none of you have hunted human?" said Alex, glancing around at the pack.

"Not one of us," said Will. "If we had, the magic that allows us to change would have turned us into the things that took out your pack. The fact that we can still be in human form shows we haven't. We hunt the creatures that prey on man."

"Well, that might be the case for the rest of them," said Alex, nodding at the group. "But you're different. You're not like others. There's something else inside you. I can sense it. There's a darkness there that isn't in the others. Well, she's similar but not the same. You're special."

She was nodding at Gabrielle.

"That's because we're both *Hotamétaneo'o* and werewolf," said Will. "We have both running through our veins."

"It's more than that," said Alex. "How did you kill the First Born? It's not an easy thing to do. For her, yeah. You're different, somehow."

Will didn't answer. He just glared at her.

"He ate that fucker's heart," said Mika, grinning. "Not only did he beat a First Born, but he also took his power. I was there. It was badass."

"That's it," said Alex, seductively. "That's why you're different. You're something else, entirely. There's more wolf in you than you want to admit. What exactly are you?"

Will didn't answer. Sarah glanced at him and saw the struggle behind his eyes. There was a darkness in him since he'd killed *Grigore*. She knew he struggled with it. It wasn't that he'd been distant or cold towards her. He struggled with something that he couldn't explain or share with her, no matter how much she wanted to understand.

"Forget the rest of them," purred Alex, walking slow and seductively towards Will. "They're insignificant compared to you. You and I could start a pack that no one could beat. The two of us could do anything we wanted, hunt whatever we wanted, and go anywhere we wanted, anytime we wanted. We'd be unstoppable."

In a flash of motion, Sarah stepped forward and punched Alex in the mouth. The force of the blow sent her sprawling onto her back and slid about ten feet through the dirt. Gabrielle moved to her left, preparing to go after Alex, as well.

"Stay away from him," said Sarah, her voice low and menacing.

"Well, now we know who the Alpha female is," said Alex, getting slowly to her feet and wiping blood from her lip with the back of her hand. "You can hit hard, but let's see how tough you are."

Getting to her feet, Alex started shifting into her wolf form. Not to be outdone, Sarah started changing as well. As they both changed in a matter of seconds, Alex stood to her full height and was still a head shorter than Sarah. Where Alex's fur was a golden brown, Sarah was dark grey leading to a lighter grey on her chest and stomach. Where Alex as just shy of seven feet tall, Sarah was well over eight.

Looking up at her, Alex realized she'd pushed too far. She might have been an Alpha in her pack, but she wasn't strong enough to challenge the Alpha in this one. Sarah, however, wasn't going to let it go that easily. As she started to step towards Alex, a gunshot broke the tension, and everyone froze.

"Knock it off," said Gideon, his pistol still pointed into the air. "We don't have time for this."

Alex looked back and forth from Gideon to Sarah, grateful for the interruption. Sarah turned and looked at Alex, then backhanded her a full thirty feet, slamming her into a tree and nearly knocking her out. While Alex was trying to clear her head, Sarah snorted, then turned and headed for the camper. She was going to need new clothes.

Alex got slowly to her feet, shaking her head. She had no intention of attacking Sarah while she had her back turned. For one, the rest of the pack would probably have killed her before she got to her. For another, she doubted that it would have done her any good. She couldn't take Sarah and she knew it. Gabrielle was still standing close by, ready to take Sarah's place if she made any kind of move.

"This Alpha is going to be tough to get close to," thought Alex. "Especially with those two in the way."

As she shifted back into her human form, she realized that the clothes she'd borrowed from Beale had been large enough to not shred when she changed. The only problem was that her tail had punched a hole in the spandex shorts, revealing the entirety of the back of her ass.

Having shifted forms, the cuts and scrapes were all gone. She flexed her shoulders and rolled her head, getting the cramps out from the impact with the tree. They could all hear the cracking of bones and popping of joints as she did. Smiling, she shook her head and glanced nervously around the group.

"If you're trying to convince them to help you rescue the rest of your pack," said Gideon, "you're going about it all wrong. I'm beginning to wonder why I even bothered bringing you here in the first place."

"Yeah," said Beale, "I don't think you're exactly making a lot of friends, here."

"That was stupid," said Gabrielle. "What makes you think you would be strong enough to take her on? David wasn't even good enough to be a hunter. He was the pack Omega. He was just a dumbass with a man-bun and skinny jeans that *Grigore* turned because he thought he was funny. He wasn't. He was just a smarmy asshole. He wasn't considered strong, even by the lesser members of the pack. You were turned by the werewolf equivalent of milk-toast. We used to call him the Soy-Wolf. Most of the females in the pack were stronger than he was."

That last comment drew several chuckles from the group.

"Damn!" said Mika. "That's harsh. Props to Gabs."

Mika held up his knuckles to fist bump. Gabrielle smiled and bumped knuckles with him.

"I'm guessing you're the Beta," said Alex, looking at Mika.

"And I'm guessing you don't know when to quit," said Cassie. "What makes you think there would be any chance of us helping you?"

"Because I'm the only one who knows where their lair is," said Alex, smiling wickedly. "If you don't have the point of origin from where I was abducted, you could search this area for weeks before you caught their scent. We never caught the scent of them, and we've been hunting this area for weeks. From the look of their lair, they've been here a while without anyone knowing it. You need me and I need you."

"What makes you think we couldn't find them without your help?" asked Mika.

"I'm sure you could," said Alex, "but it'll take time. I'm sure that this crowd is fully capable of tracking the creatures if they can find their scent. This area is all dense woods and rough terrain. It could take you weeks to find them. How many more people will die before then?"

"And how long do you think your pack will last?" asked Will, his voice low and menacing. "I'm not sure why they bothered to take any of them alive, but they did. So, the question is why and for how long?"

That made Alex stop and think. He was right. If there was any chance of saving any of them, it diminished rapidly as time passed. She also knew that if she wasn't careful, this pack might just kill her and be done with it. She didn't think that Gideon and Beale could stop them, either. Not that they would try. Gideon knew them, and they were working together.

"I'm sorry," she said after a moment. "I get carried away sometimes. I'm used to being the Alpha female in the pack. I guess it's a dominance thing. Sometimes I don't even realize I'm doing it."

That was a lie and everyone there knew it. Whatever else might be true about her, Alex was a manipulator. No one trusted her because she'd tried to challenge Sarah and lost. Her place was now firmly established in order of things. She wouldn't challenge anyone else in the pack. She also understood that no matter how things turned out, she had no shot of joining this pack. Not unless things changed significantly.

"You challenged an Alpha," said Will. "Next time you do something so foolish, I'm going to let Sarah finish it. Not even Gideon will be able to intervene to save you. Make another challenge and I'll let them kill you."

"I won't even try to stop them," said Gideon. "Honestly, I'm already regretting doing it this time."

"If you tell me where you last saw them," said Will, "we can track them from there. The tracks are less than twenty-four hours old. It shouldn't be a problem."

"What about me?" asked Alex. "They're my pack-mates."

"You can't help us," said Will. "You're not strong enough to take on the *Oolonga-Doglalla*. You won't fare any better than they did."

"The what?" asked Alex. "Isn't there an easier, non-Indian, way to say that? Maybe in English, this time."

"Your people call them Dogmen," said Mika. "Our word is cooler."

"That still doesn't change the fact that you can't hurt them," said Will. "You won't win in a fight against them."

"And you will?" said Alex, glaring at him. "What makes your pack so much tougher?"

"We've fought them before," said Mika, "and we won. That was even before any of us could change forms."

"You beat them as normal humans?" said Alex. "Then why can't I fight them the same way?"

"Because the weapons we use will hurt you, too," said Will.

"Then I won't shoot myself," she answered. "I want to help rescue my pack."

Will seemed to think about it for a moment. Before he could answer, they were surprised to see a vehicle pull into the parking lot of the campground. As late in the year as it was and as cool as it was getting at night, very few people were camping now. This vehicle didn't look like it was here for camping. It wasn't loaded down with equipment and tents.

It was a dark green Jeep Liberty SUV with Missouri Plates. Will recognized the stickers on the window and the plastic frame around the license plates. It was a rental vehicle. That meant whoever was driving it wasn't from around here and didn't drive to the area. They'd only driven from the nearest town with a car rental agency and an airport, most-likely Springfield or St. Louis.

A man exited the vehicle and glanced around. He was about average height and a little out of shape. He had dark hair and glasses, with khaki pants on over loafers. He wore a black t-shirt with the phrase "Han fired first" in yellow letters and a grey fleece jacket that was unzipped. On his head was a straw pork pie hat with a black and red band. It was clear that he wasn't here to hike or camp. When he realized that they were all looking at him, he raised his hand and waved at them.

"Who do you suppose that is?" asked Cassie.

"Looks like a fucking tourist," said Mika.

"I don't think so," said Will.

"Are you sure?" asked Mika.

"Why?" asked Will.

"Because he's got his cell phone clipped to his belt," said Mika. "Normal people don't do that shit. That's pure tourist level shit."

"He just doesn't give me the tourist feeling," said Will. "He's not acting like one."

"Besides, this place doesn't get many tourists that aren't here to fish, hunt or camp," said Alex. "It's too far out of the way. That's why we picked it. That and the local law enforcement couldn't catch a cold, let alone find a missing hiker."

Will gave her a dark look but had to admit to himself that would be sound logic from a pack that preyed on people. Although he didn't personally know anyone in Shamrock County law enforcement, it wasn't uncommon for small rural departments to not have the same level of training and experience as the bigger departments. They were usually underequipped, understaffed, and underpaid. That wasn't exactly a recipe for an efficient department.

The man began walking around the area, talking to his cell phone and taking pictures. He was paying particular attention to the entrances and exits to the park and the river access. For a moment, Will thought he was just scouting fishing areas and talking to someone about it on the phone until he remembered that no one got any cell signal in this valley. His phone had died right after they left West Plains, Missouri. Then a thought struck him.

"He's a reporter," said Will. "I bet he's looking into the missing person cases in this area. One of them went missing from this campground."

Will glanced at Alex and she wouldn't meet his gaze. That confirmed it for him. If it had been the *Oolonga-Doglalla*, there would have been blood left behind. The fact that the vehicle had gone missing as well, was the clincher. Dogmen didn't drive. Only werewolves who took what they wanted did that sort of thing. He had read the file that Blanchard had sent him in his email. There was little doubt that Calvin Martinson had been killed by her or her pack.

"Think we should go talk to him?" asked Mika. "Maybe try to warn him off and get him out of the area?"

"No," said Will. "If he doesn't find anything here, he'll leave. He won't find anything, will he Alex?"

"What?" she asked, acting surprised.

"He won't find any trace of him, will he?" Will asked her again.

"Hey, I don't know what happened to Cal," she said, defensively. "He could be anywhere."

"I never said his name," said Will.

"Well, shit," she said, sheepishly.

"You know what happened to him, don't you?" asked Gideon, frowning.

"I'm not admitting to anything," said Alex. "But I can tell you he won't find any trace of him here or anywhere else, for that matter."

"Hey, can't you just show him that Department of Defense ID you have," asked Beale, nodding at Gideon, "and tell him to clear out of the area?"

"I could," said Gideon, "but all that would accomplish is him figuring out he was on to something and the government was covering it up."

"He might think that anyway," said Will.

"Why's that?" asked Gideon.

"I think he just zoomed in on us," said Will. "If he read your plate, he'll see the government tags."

"Well, that's unfortunate," said Gideon, shaking his head. "I need to make a note for scout teams to stop using government vehicles."

"It's better to let him find nothing and leave on his own," said Will. "Let's just hope he leaves the area to write his story before he does find something."

"Or something finds him," said Mika.

"You know he's already suspicious," said Gideon. "That's the nature of reporters. Anything out of the ordinary piques their curiosity."

"Why's that?" asked Mika.

"Because there's more than twenty of us and we're all staring at him," said Gideon. "Plus, no offense, but you all stand out."

"Starting to feel like Custer?" asked Mika, grinning. "Holy crap! Look at all the Indians."

"That's not what I meant," said Gideon, embarrassed.

"I think he's trying to say that you don't look like the usual redneck crowd they see around here," said Alex. "I've been here for almost two weeks and you guys are the first people I've seen that didn't look like extras from the cast of Deliverance. I swear to God I can hear banjo music at night."

Mika started laughing and nearly bent over, then started making squealing pig noises. Soon, they were all chuckling and the mysterious reporter looked at them like they were insane. Then he got back into his SUV and headed out of the parking lot and back towards town.

"Think we scared him off?" asked Cassie.

"I don't think so," said Alex. "He looked Hispanic. He didn't fit the Ned Beatty profile."

Mika lost it, again.

"Fuck," he said, fighting for air. "Werewolf or not, this chick's funny."

"I try," said Alex, curtseying.

"You… uh… you need a new pair of shorts," said Beale, nodding at her.

"Thanks for noticing, pervert," said Alex.

Beale turned red.

"I'm just messing with you, Chris," she said. "It's okay. You can look. I don't mind. I'm not shy."

Sarah came walking back out of the camper, wearing fresh clothes. She tossed Alex a pair of jean shorts.

"Here," said Sarah, "put these on before you try flashing your ass at everyone."

"Too late," said Mika.

Alex just shrugged and took off the spandex shorts. Most of the guys turned their heads. Mika didn't, at first, but received a reminder in the form of a punch in the arm from Cassie.

"Look away, jackass," said Cassie, scowling.

"Oops, sorry babe," said Mika, turning his head.

Beale didn't attempt to look away. Neither did Julia *Topsannah*. Alex saw her looking and locked eyes with her, then smiled broadly. Alex slipped into the shorts and buttoned them up.

"Ok, folks," she said. "Show's over. You can turn around now."

"Now that that's over," said Will, "we need to discuss how we're going to proceed. Do we take her with us or leave her behind?"

"The only way I tell you how to find them is if you take me with you," said Alex. "I think you'd want to go if it was your pack."

"I would," agreed Will, "that's not the issue. The issue is no one trusts you. We have no reason to. You're the kind of creature we hunt."

"And what kind is that?" she demanded.

"The kind that preys on man," said Will.

"Says the guy that ate a fucking heart," said Alex.

"He was a First Born werewolf," said Will. "It was also the only way I could be sure that he'd stay dead."

"Still," said Alex. "You ate it. As far as I'm concerned, we're not that different."

Will was silent, thinking about what she said. Alex smiled softly. She knew that if she kept sowing seeds of doubt in his mind, she could begin to crack his resolve. Once that happened, she could lure him to her side. The rest of this pack was strong, but Will was the one she wanted. He was essentially a First Born, now.

"If you want to leave me behind," said Alex, "you're going to have to kill me."

"I wouldn't push that issue," said Beale. "They just might."

"I'm not an idiot, Chris," she said, glaring at him. "No matter how this turns out, I know I'm not likely to be able to walk away from it. Either by claw, by tooth, or by a bullet, I don't see me surviving this."

"Then what's the difference?" asked Mika.

"I prefer to go out on my terms," said Alex. "And if I can rescue any of my pack-mates, then maybe I can redeem myself. Even if it's only a little. I'm not proud of what I've done but I don't apologize for it, either. In this life, everyone is either a predator or prey. In my own life, I've been both. Now, I choose to be a predator."

"She's not wrong," said Gabrielle, nodding at Will. "Well, not entirely."

"As much as it pains me to admit it," said Sarah, "I agree. If there is any chance for her to get redemption, we should let her try. Who knows, it might break her curse."

"If you're both agreeing," said Will, "then I guess I won't argue. She comes with us, but we keep an eye on her."

Alex smiled and glanced back and forth from Sarah to Will. She had no intention of changing. Every minute she was close to Will was a minute she had to keep working on him. If she turned him, the others would either fall in line or die.

"I'll do it," said Julia. "I'll stay close to her and make sure she doesn't run off."

Alex glanced at Julia. While not ideal, it was better than nothing. Maybe she could use that to her advantage, anyway.

"Fine by me," said Will. "Thank you."

"My pleasure," said Julia, smiling.

"I bet," said Robert *Alok* under his breath.

Julia gave him a dirty look but didn't say anything.

"We've only got a few hours left before sunset," said Will. "We're not going to find them in their lair at night. They'll be out hunting. Let's see if we can get a rough idea of where the lair is on the map and maybe check the area around it for movement. Maybe catch a few of them out hunting and thin the pack a bit."

"You're about evenly matched," said Alex. "Their pack is about the same size as yours."

"What would you like us to do?" asked Gideon. "Since those things are looking for us, I might as well be useful."

"I'll have each of you drive a team," said Will. "Then if we have to change and run, we won't have to go back for a vehicle later."

"Good plan," said Gideon. "When do you want to leave?"

"I want to change into clothes I don't mind shredding," said Will, nodding and turning for the camper. "After that, give us a few minutes for Jason to say the *Blessingway* and for us to prepare for the hunt. It shouldn't take very long."

After Will had left and most of the others were following his lead, Alex turned to Gideon and motioned for him to come closer. Gideon stood next to her and nodded.

"Go ahead," he said, keeping his voice low.

"That one," she said, meaning Will, "scares me. I don't scare easily. You can feel the energy coming from him."

"He's the leader," said Gideon, shrugging. "He's the strongest."

"It's not that," said Alex. "There's strength there, but darkness too. I'm glad he's on our side, for now anyway. You might want to watch him."

"I watch everyone," said Gideon. "I'm glad he's on our side, too."

D.A. ROBERTS

APEX PREDATOR: HUNTER'S MOON
CHAPTER NINE
ON THE HUNT

"Evil can be a teacher if you look at the wisdom if it's negative power."
Tom Brown Jr.

September 28th
5:00 PM

They broke into three teams. Will would take Sarah, Gabrielle, Cody *Tapuche*, Julia *Topsannah,* and Alex with him in the blue truck with Gideon driving. Mika would take Cassie, Jacob *Mingan*, Kayli *Waynoka*, and the Mohawk twins Richard *Akaash* and Robert *Alok* in the big SUV with Beale driving. Jason would be in charge of everyone who stayed behind, ready to back-up whoever needed their help. Alex had shown Will where she'd been taken captive on the map. Will marked it for each team and then made the assignments.

"Jason," said Will, "you monitor the radio and listen for any of us to call for back-up. Also, keep your eyes open in case they show up here. It's not likely, but not impossible. Don't get too comfortable."

"Got it," said Jason.

"Mika," said Will, "you take your team to the Shawnee Creek Horse Camp and RV Park. Start checking around that area. We've had two people go missing out of that park. Vanished without a trace while hiking."

"That wasn't us," said Alex. "We haven't been there. Horses go nuts around werewolves, even in human form. We usually camp close to where we're hunting. We couldn't stay anywhere near that place without freaking out the horses."

"Ok," said Will, "that sounds like a good place to start. I'll take my team and start tracking near where Alex was abducted. Everyone stay sharp and watch your backs. If you run into the entire pack, fall back and call for the rest of us. If you encounter smaller numbers, use your best judgment. Don't risk yourselves unnecessarily. Be smart and be safe."

Everyone exchanged glances and nodded.

"For all of the new folks," said Jason, "pay attention to that. The last time we fought the *Oolonga-Doglalla*, we lost several people. They're not to be taken lightly."

That drew more than a few grim nods. No one would be underestimating the Dogmen, this time.

"I've been thinking about something," said Alex. "If you don't mind me talking."

"Go ahead," said Will.

"When they took me captive," said Alex, "I thought they were going to kill me. Then, I thought they were going to rape me. They didn't do either. What they did do seemed odd at the time."

"What's that?" asked Mika.

"They made me change shapes," said Alex.

"Then what did they do?" asked Julia.

"They let me go," said Alex.

"Just like that?" asked Will.

"Just like that," said Alex. "Well, I later figured out why. They wanted me to lead them back to my pack."

"Which you did," said Gideon.

"I tried to get them to run away," said Alex. "I knew we couldn't take them. David wouldn't hear of it. But, the more I thought about it all, the more it bothered me that they took the others captive. Then something made sense. They can't change shape."

"No," said Jason. "The dark nature of the magic that turned them in the first place prevents that."

"What if they infected themselves with the werewolf curse?" asked Alex.

"It might work," said Jason. "I think it would, anyway. It worked on Will and Gabrielle was able to have both, too. There's no way to know for sure, but it's reasonable to believe it would. We'd be stupid not to take it into account."

"Even if it didn't," said Alex, "they have werewolf females. They could breed a new generation that could. I did notice that their pack was mostly male. They might have wanted my pack as mates for their own."

"Oh fuck," said Mika. "That's not good."

"No, it's not," agreed Will.

"You mean those things might be able to change shape?" asked Gideon, frowning.

"Not immediately," said Jason, "but if they've figured out that the werewolves can change and are smart enough to try it themselves, who knows when it might take effect."

"They're smart enough," said Will.

"Then it could take effect anytime now," said Alex. "It's usually by the next full moon. Sometimes earlier, depending on the strength of the person. But that's for a full transformation. I have no idea for things that are already wolves. This is all new to me."

"When's the full moon?" asked Mika, glancing up at the sky.

"Tomorrow night," said Jason. "It's a Hunter's Moon."

"If they can infect themselves," said Will, "and force a change, then breed with the werewolf females, it'll be permanent in the offspring. We'll be looking at something completely new."

"Fuck me," said Mika, shaking his head. "That's fucked up, man. The biggest advantage that we have is the ability to change and they're easier to find because they can't."

"With that gone," said Jason, "they can hunt with impunity. Anywhere and anytime. They can walk amongst the prey without tipping their hand."

"Then we need to stop them before that happens," said Will. "Once the *Oolonga-Doglalla* regain the ability to change, tracking them will become almost impossible. They'll be able to lose us completely in cities or among people."

"If they can spread it to all of them," said Jason. "As in all *Oolonga-Doglalla* all over the country, then we're going to need a hell of a lot more

Hotamétaneo'o. They'll be hunting without fear. There won't be enough of us to stop them."

"And, if the curse is absorbed," said Alex, "they'll be able to pass it with a bite."

"They already can," said Will. "But I think it has to be through a blood transfer. That's how I was originally turned. I was able to fight the curse through the *Inipi*. I was the first *Hotamétaneo'o* to be able to change in generations."

"He taught the rest of us," said Mika.

"But, if they can change too," said Sarah, "then they can walk amongst us without anyone knowing who they are. If they can change, then tracking them becomes extremely difficult."

"That's terrifying to consider," said Jason. "We've got to stop them cold. If even just one gets away, we might see this spread like a virus."

Once the teams and assignments were in place, Jason built up the fire and started adding sacred herbs to the flames. Softly chanting, he began the *Blessingway* to call the protection of their ancestors during tonight's hunt. They all stood in a circle around the fire, while Jason chanted and danced.

Taking turns, they helped each other into their war-paint. One by one, they approached Jason so he could bless them with sage and call upon the spirit of the *Hotamétaneo'o* to guide them. Each of them took a blessed knife and tomahawk, placing them in their belts.

"So, how long are we going to waste time on the Dances With Wolves cosplay?" asked Alex, whispering to Gideon and Beale.

Beale said nothing but Gideon turned and gave her a dark look.

"Watch your mouth," he hissed. "Just because you don't believe in anything doesn't mean they don't. Keep running your mouth and I'll put a bullet in it. Honestly, I've had about enough of you."

"Sensitive much?" asked Alex, smiling. "I'm kidding. I'm sure this is important, whatever the fuck it is."

Gideon walked away shaking his head.

"I think you pissed him off," whispered Beale.

Leaning in close, Alex slipped her arm around Beale's waist. Kissing him on the neck, she pressed her lips against his ear and whispered directly into it. Her warm breath sent gooseflesh down his entire body.

"All this waiting is making me horny," she said, licking his ear then nibbling on the earlobe. "If they don't hurry up, I might have to tear your clothes off and take you right here in the dirt."

"Well, uh... I... uh," stammered Beale.

He didn't notice her taking his pistol and extra ammo, slipping them into her waistband. His concentration was on her hand roving over the front of his pants.

"Looks like they're all finished," she chided. "Too bad. I guess I'll have to wait until after the hunt. When I get back, I'm going to do things to you that you can't even imagine."

Walking away, she left Beale smiling and watching her go like a lost puppy.

"Jesus, Beale," said Mika, "put it back in your pants already."

"Oh, shit," said Beale. "Sorry."

"No worries," said Mika, slapping him on the shoulder. "You gonna hit that later?"

"I certainly hope so," said Beale.

"Watch out, man," said Mika. "She's a man-eater. Literally."

"Hell of a way to go," said Beale. "Might be worth it."

"That it might," said Mika, watching her walk away. "Anyway, let's get in the SUV. It's time to start hunting."

"Copy that," said Beale.

Alex walked over to Will and stood in front of him. Sarah looked like she was considering knocking her into another tree.

"Relax, sister," said Alex, glaring at Sarah. "I just wanted to ask if I was going to get any weapons to use against those things. Without some kind of weapon, I'm all but useless. I can't hurt them, even in my wolf-form."

"I'm not trusting you with a firearm," said Will, frowning. "I'll give you a knife and a tomahawk. They're blessed so they'll work against the *Oolonga-Doglalla*."

"Well, that's better than nothing, I suppose," she said, frowning.

"Take it or leave it," said Will.

"I'll take it," said Alex.

Will reluctantly handed her a knife and tomahawk but held her gaze.

"Betray us and I will hunt you to the ends of the earth," said Will, darkly.

"Got it," said Alex. "Besides, these enchanted blade things probably only work on the bad magic, right?"

"Something like that," said Will. "They wouldn't be nearly as effective against us."

"See," said Alex, grinning widely. "I'm harmless."

Alex turned and sauntered away towards the truck, climbing in beside Julia.

"We'll see," said Will.

"I still don't trust her," said Sarah.

"Neither do I," said Will.

The groups split into their respective vehicles and headed out. Jason stoked the fire and set guards from those who were staying behind. Joe *Nakai* came over and started helping Jason stoke the fire, then took out his knife and started carving on a piece of wood.

"I hate the waiting part," said Joe.

"Me too," agreed Jason.

The hoot of an owl caused them both to turn and look in that direction. Perched on a tree branch just at the edge of the firelight was a large grey great horned owl. It was watching them with those large luminous eyes.

"That's not good," said Joe.

"No, it's not," said Jason.

Both men knew that the owl was a messenger of death. Jason started adding more wood and herbs to the fire.

"What are you doing?" asked Joe.

"Praying," said Jason. "I'm going to sing songs of protection until they all come back."

Fifteen minutes later, Gideon brought the truck to a stop right where Alex had been parked when she'd been captured. They all climbed out and started grabbing their gear.

"This is the place," said Alex. "When I first saw the thing, it was standing over behind that big oak tree."

"Did you try to run?" asked Julia.

"No," said Alex. "Like an idiot, I tried to scare it off. I didn't realize until it was too late that it was much bigger than me. I thought it was after my dinner, not me. It beat me without much effort."

"It carried you off into the woods," said Will, glancing at her.

"Yeah," she said. "We went pretty far, too. A few miles, at least."

"Which way?" asked Sarah.

"It didn't take a direct route," said Alex, "like it was making sure it wasn't followed. Ultimately, it took me north of here. If we're going to follow the trail we used, it's going to be less direct than the path I took getting back here."

"Maybe we should just backtrack the way she escaped," said Gabrielle. "It would be the freshest tracks."

"That way will also take you by where the Conservation Agent was killed," said Alex. "It's not far from here."

"Alright," said Will. "We go that way."

"Are we changing?" asked Alex.

"No," said Will. "Not until we have to. We'll be able to follow the trail like this. Staying in human form gives us a bit of an advantage. They won't know our scents. If we change into the wolves, they'll know that scent instantly."

"Good point," said Alex. "But at the same time, we'll smell like food."

"Which will bring them to us," said Sarah. "Which is exactly what we want. We'd much prefer to deal with them in smaller groups than with the entire pack at one time."

"Let's go," said Will, heading into the trees.

"Won't we have to shift for him to be able to follow the trail?" asked Alex. "That's what I have to do."

"Did you ever climb up into the trees?" asked Sarah.

"No," said Alex. "Why would I?"

"When the *Oolonga-Doglalla* wants to make it difficult to track them," said Sarah, "they climb into the treetops and move tree to tree. If you stayed on the ground, Will can track you. He's the best tracker I know."

"Even in the dark?" asked Alex.

"That's the advantage we have over your typical werewolf," said Sarah. "The *Hotamétaneo'o* possess the improved senses all the time."

"I bet that comes in handy," said Alex, shaking her head.

Sarah only smiled, then headed into the woods after Will. Gabrielle motioned for Alex to get moving. Alex headed into the woods and gave Gabrielle a cold and calculating look.

"What's your problem?" asked Gabrielle.

"Why is it that they'll accept you into the pack?" said Alex. "You're just werewolf trash like me."

"Just get moving," said Gabrielle. "We don't have time for debates. Will's already tracking."

Alex started walking into the trees and mumbled to herself loud enough so that Gabrielle could still hear her.

"Stupid bitch," muttered Alex. "What makes you so fucking special?"

Gabrielle didn't bother to answer. Julia walked past Gabrielle and shrugged but kept going into the trees. Cody walked up and Gabrielle headed into the trees beside him.

"I do not trust that one," whispered Cody. "She's deceiving us. Don't turn your back on her."

"That's the plan," whispered Gabrielle, smiling.

"Once she gets the rest of her pack," whispered Cody, "she's going to betray us and try to escape."

"Then we're just going to have to be careful," replied Gabrielle. "Good thing these weapons work on werewolves, too."

Moving beneath the canopy of the trees, everything seemed surreal. It was just getting to be fully dark, but the woods were alive with sounds. Animals were scurrying through the underbrush and the treetops. The cicadas were singing a symphony that seemed to echo back to them from every direction at the same time. If it wasn't for the fact that they were hunting the *Oolonga-Doglalla*, it would have been relaxing.

The rich aroma of the woods was intoxicating to Will. This was how it was supposed to be. Stalking prey through the wild, relying on his skills and strength. Oddly, both the Dire Wolf and the Old Wolf inside him agreed and were relishing the hunt. It suddenly occurred to Will that if he appeased Old Wolf by hunting, then it wouldn't fight against him so much. He made a mental note to remember to stalk a deer or an elk with Sarah and Gabrielle often enough to keep Old Wolf satisfied.

Following the trail was easy for him. Will could follow the scent of Alex easily. The fact that she'd been followed by at least two of the creatures made it even easier. For one, it was pungent and oily, clinging to the area like an invisible fog. For another, they weren't trying to hide their tracks. It was as if the creatures had no fear of pursuit. Then the thought occurred to him that they were eager to find the rest of her pack. They wanted to find them out in the open. Only, it didn't work. That's why they let Alex go.

It wasn't long before Will found where a herd of elk had crossed the path. The scent was older than the track he was following, so the herd had crossed a few hours before Alex and the *Oolonga-Doglalla*. Since they loved acorns and buckeyes, it was likely that the herd wasn't that far away. Old Wolf howled, wanting to follow it and taste the fresh blood of the kill. Will had to remind it that they had bigger prey tonight.

They moved through the woods for almost half an hour before Will motioned for everyone to get down. They ducked into a thick section of wild blackberry bushes. They were thick enough that you could be standing on top of someone and not see them. Will put his finger to his lips to instruct everyone to be silent.

At first, they didn't see anything. Then, faintly, they heard soft movements in the underbrush. They were trying to be quiet, but the enhanced senses of the *Hotamétaneo'o* made it far easier to hear even the slightest noise. After a moment, they began to see movement heading in their direction. Finally, the first creature emerged from the underbrush. It stopped with just its head out of the brush, sniffing the air and looking around.

It was about fifty yards away, on the far side of a clearing. Will smiled when he realized they were downwind of the creatures. The creatures couldn't smell them, but he could smell the creatures. It was pungent and musky; an easy scent to recognize as a large predator. A dangerous scent.

"They're hunting," mouthed Will. "They don't know we're here."

Everyone nodded their understanding. When Alex saw the head, she began to visibly shake. It was the same creature that had abducted her. Julia put her hand on her shoulder and Alex smiled at her. They were both wearing shorts and Alex put her hand on Julia's thigh. At first, Julia tensed but then relaxed and smiled. Sarah made eye contact with Julia and frowned at her but didn't say anything.

Once the creature was satisfied that no threats were close, he stepped out of the bushes and went up on two legs. Will heard the distinctive popping sound as the creature's paws straightened out into hands. It was strange, but the *Oolonga-Doglalla* morphed their hands into paws when they ran on four legs. Will decided it must have been a defense mechanism, making them indistinguishable from other animals when they ran on all fours.

He'd seen their tracks while they were running on four legs. Although they were larger than normal for a wolf, they were otherwise identical. In an area with a large wolf population, it was a good survival trait. The *Hotamétaneo'o* didn't do that because they hadn't spent generations hiding from society.

Will readied his weapons and nodded at the others. They began taking out their weapons. Alex pulled out her knife but thought better of letting them know she had the gun unless it meant saving her own life. She'd been pondering when to use the gun since she'd first gotten it. She doubted that she would be able to kill more than one or two of them, once they were in wolf-form. But while they were still in human form, she was confident that one to the head would do the job.

"Be patient," she thought to herself. "Bide your time."

The creature stood to its full height. It was just over nine feet tall. Alex had thought it was bigger, but she was a little preoccupied at the time. Then a second creature emerged. Will got ready to give the signal to attack when two more emerged and stood up. Will motioned for everyone to hold. When four more emerged from the bushes, Will knew they were in trouble. They were outnumbered, but Will knew they could still beat them. They just had to be smarter.

Will motioned for everyone to wait. If the odds had been even, he would have considered it. But his group had two new people that he'd never taken into battle before. They also had Alex, who was too weak to effectively fight the Dogmen. Even with the blessed weapons, Will knew she wasn't a real fighter. That's why she lured men into her bed before she killed them. That meant she was a schemer and a planner. Will had little doubt that she was already looking for a way to turn the tables on them and escape. The more he was around her, the more he had the feeling that bringing her along had been a mistake.

The creatures glanced around for a moment before the big black one, the Beta, motioned for them to follow. He then headed off roughly southeast. Undoubtedly, they were looking for the elk herd that moved through this area. Will had already seen signs of their passing. Tracks and scat were easy to find, especially when an elk herd goes through an area.

Once they had moved away, Will leaned close to the others.

"The direction they're going will intersect with our trail in about four hundred yards," Will whispered. "When they cross it, they'll pick up our scent. My guess is they prefer long-pig to elk venison. They'll follow us instead of the herd."

"So, they'll be coming for us," said Sarah, shaking her head.

"It is the fresher scent," said Will. "If you were them, which would you follow?"

"Well, shit," whispered Alex. "Think we can take them?"

"Only if we do this right and lull them into a situation where we have the upper hand," said Will.

"Well, what do we do next, oh fearless leader?" said Alex sarcastically.

Will didn't answer. He just glanced around the area. He was looking at all the angles of approach and possible directions. Then he saw something that caught his eye. About thirty yards away, he saw a deer stand about thirty feet up on the side of a large walnut tree. Beneath it was a well-worn trail leading northwest. It was away from the road, so either there was another road or a camp.

"This way," said Will, heading off quickly but careful to not make too much noise.

The others followed as Will moved in a crouch until they were clear of the area. Following the trail proved to be the right thing to do. About a quarter of a mile from the deer stand, Will found a crude hunting cabin. It wasn't anything spectacular, but it was cover and it was defensible.

"Come on," said Will, heading directly for the cabin.

When they reached the edge of the clearing where the cabin stood, they could tell there was no electricity or running water. A small "outhouse" had been constructed behind the cabin by nailing boards in between two trees, cutting a round hole in the board and digging a hole beneath it. They could all smell the outhouse indicating that it had been used recently.

There was no sign of light inside the cabin and Will didn't detect any sound coming from it. It was made log cabin style, using logs that had been cut and roughly fit together. They had at least planed down the sides of the logs so that they fit closely together instead of having large gaps that had to be filled with tacking. Despite the crude construction materials, it was solidly built.

"Let's get inside," said Will.

"Great plan," said Alex. "Let's just hide from the big bad wolf. How long until they huff and puff and blow our house down?"

"Shut up," snarled Gabrielle. "You have no idea about tactics. No wonder your entire pack was taken so easily. This is called a choke point. We force them to come at us in smaller numbers. They can't rush us all at once. We pick them off as they come through the door or the windows."

"The windows are too small," said Will. "They'll have to come through the door."

Alex just shrugged but said nothing.

Once on the porch, Will noticed that it was closed with a combination lock and a hasp. Taking out his tomahawk, he began digging at the edge of the hasp. In a few seconds, he had a small opening. In the distance, they hear the *Oolonga-Doglalla* begin howling. They'd just found their scent.

"Well, they know we're here," said Sarah. "You might want to get that door open, my love."

"I'm working on it," said Will, not taking his eyes off the hasp.

Finally, he had enough to get the edge of the blade beneath the hasp. Using the tomahawk for leverage, he pried slowly and the hasp reluctantly broke free. Once the lock was removed, Will opened the door and looked inside.

The cabin was roughly twenty feet by twenty feet, with one large room inside. There were bunks along the back wall for ten people. Made bunk bed style, they were constructed from 2x4 boards nailed to the wall and together. There were three racks along the back wall and one in each corner. To the left was a crude kitchen and to the right was a few chairs and two couches. All in all, it wasn't that bad.

"It's empty," said Will, motioning for them to all get inside.

Will watched the woods while the others went inside. In the distance, he heard the Dogmen howl again. They were getting closer but they were still several minutes away. Part of him wanted to shift form and go directly after them, but that would be a mistake. Despite the confidence expressed by Old Wolf, Will doubted that he could take that many of them, even with the help of the others.

Ducking inside, Will shut the door. There was a large wooden crossbar that could be fit over the door, effectively preventing anything from getting in without a battering ram. Dropping the bar in place, Will glanced around. Julia and Alex were on the couch, Alex leaning against Julia. Will was starting to grow concerned about how close they were getting. Alex's hand was on the inside of Julia's right thigh, very close to her crotch.

Cody found a lantern and got it going with a book of matches, then looked at Will and grinned. With the light, they could see that there were large door-flaps that were screwed into the wall above the windows with a pull cord. They could close off the windows with thick boards. Sarah and Gabrielle started shutting the boards, blocking off the windows completely.

"That'll slow them down," said Gabrielle.

"For a while," said Will. "They'll rip the walls down if they have to."

"The trick is to hold them out long enough to make them think they broke the door," said Gabrielle. "If we can get them coming through the door one at a time, we can control the fight."

"Rack 'em and stack 'em," said Cody, smiling. "Let's do it!"

"I'm ready," said Gabrielle.

Sarah just nodded. Will glanced over and saw Alex look over quickly, moving her hand away from Julia like a teenager who had been caught making out by a parent. Although Will didn't see anything going on, he was sure that they had been kissing, possibly more by the sudden movement of her hand and the guilty look on her face. Considering where the hand had been before, he had a good idea of where it had been. Julia looked a bit flushed but recovered quickly. She smiled and got up, tugging her shorts down a bit as she stood.

"I'm ready," said Julia.

Will glowered at her for a moment. He was going to ask her what was going on and put them both on the spot when the silence was shattered by a howl. It was close.

"They found us," said Gabrielle. "Here they come."

Will listened as the sounds of movement spread out around the cabin. They were looking for ways in and if their prey had an escape route. They were also looking for a scent to verify that they hadn't left. Once they were certain their prey was inside, the movement stopped. It was as silent as the proverbial tomb outside. Not even the wind broke the stillness.

"What are they doing?" mouthed Julia.

"Intimidation," mouthed Gabrielle. "Scare tactics."

BOOM!

Something heavy slammed against the door. There was an immediate grunt of pain and surprise when the door didn't splinter apart and explode inward. Will smiled softly, knowing that the beast was now off-balance, not sure what to expect. That would be to their advantage.

BOOM!

Another blast against the door, followed by a snarl of rage when the door still held.

"Act scared," Will mouthed at the women.

Alex immediately started acting scared, whimpering but smiling and giving them the thumbs up while she did it. Julia started mimicking the sounds that Alex was making. It didn't sound sincere, but Will doubted that the creatures could tell the difference. Sounds were sounds and if they seemed even remotely in distress, it was likely good enough.

BOOM!

Another massive hit on the door was followed by the cracking of wood. There was a grunt of pain, but the door still held. It wasn't going to hold much longer. Will had planned on removing the wooden crossbar to let it break inside but realized that they were going to break through anyway.

"Get ready," Will said softly.

Everyone began readying their weapons.

"When do we turn?" asked Alex, softly.

"You're better off staying human," advised Will. "You can use weapons. They'd be like toys in your wolf-form. We'll turn if the fight's not going our way. I want us to remain in this form as long as possible. Once we transform, we can't turn back without being naked and without weapons."

BOOM!

This time, visible cracks began forming in the crossbar and door. It wasn't going to take many more hits before they came through the door. Motioning for everyone to get into place, Will slowly removed the crossbar. With it out of the way, the next time they hit the door it was going to crash through easily, likely sending it sprawling to the floor.

Will lined up Sarah and Gabrielle to jump it once it was down. Alex and Julia moved to the side. Will couldn't tell if they were moving to be ready to help or to avoid the fight. Warning bells were starting to sound in his head about those two. Something wasn't right and Will was fairly certain that Alex was attempting to turn Julia against them. Will doubted that Julia realized she couldn't go with Alex and remain a *Hotamétaneo'o*. The magic would turn into a curse if she left the path.

BOOM!

The door exploded inwards in a shower of splintering wood. The creature, a grey male that stood close to eight feet tall, came sailing through the door and slid onto its stomach. Before it could try to stand, Sarah and Gabrielle began slashing and hacking into the beast's head and neck. As expected, Alex and Julia made no move to help.

The next one through the door was more prepared. It was a reddish-brown female with a set of jagged scars that ran down the right side of her face. It looked like bear claws had made the wound. She saw Will and snarled but failed to see Cody. He stepped out from behind what was left of the door and slammed a tomahawk into the side of her head. The wound began to steam and crackle as the creature screeched and fell to the floor, writhing in pain. A second shot from the tomahawk ended the spasms.

Will stepped over the dead female and threw his tomahawk in one fluid motion. It sank to the shaft in the face of a grey male about thirty feet away. With the knife in his right hand, facing backward with the blade along his forearm, Will moved to engage another creature. Cody stepped out, right behind him.

"I'm right behind you, Top," said Cody.

With three down, there were still five of the creatures remaining, although they could only see three now. Cody stepped off the porch to engage another creature when a grey and white beast leaped from the roof of the porch onto his back, knocking him to the ground. The creature expected Cody to be an easy meal once on the ground but didn't count on his massive strength. Cody was built like a tank. With a grunt of rage and pain, Cody did a push up with the beast on his back, then dipped his shoulder sending the creature sprawling into the dirt.

With a roar of anger, Cody stood up. The knife and tomahawk lay in the dirt where he fell. Cody was changing. Since this was his first transformation, they weren't fully certain of what he would look like. Bets had been made among the group that he would be as big as Will, possibly bigger. If Will hadn't been watching the transformation, he might not have believed it, himself.

Everything seemed to freeze when Cody began to shift forms. Will noticed that the fur growing from his back and arms was dark brown and course. It didn't look like typical wolf fur. Something else looked different, as well. The structure of the head was different, too. He wasn't turning into a wolf.

In the span of just a few heartbeats, Cody transformed. From the shape of the snout and length, Will knew he wasn't looking at a normal bear. This was something as old as the Dire Wolf within him. He was looking at the giant short-faced bear that went extinct during the Pleistocene Era. Cody just kept getting bigger and bigger.

The wolves looked shocked as Cody grew into his form. It was well over 12 feet tall and had to weigh more than a thousand pounds. Standing on two legs, he towered over the wolf creatures. The creatures stood dumbfounded, unsure of what they were looking at or what to do about it.

With a roar of fury, Cody stepped forward and with a swipe of one massive hand, tore the head completely off a reddish-brown female. With a snarl, the grey and white beast that had knocked him down jumped onto his back and began biting and clawing at his neck and shoulders.

Will ran forward and snatched up the weapons that Cody had dropped. Whirling around, he threw the tomahawk and struck another creature in the side of the head. It never saw the blade coming because it was too busy watching the fight between its pack-mate and Cody.

The remaining creatures were fixated on Cody. Another grey male dove onto Cody's back while the big black male wolf started glancing around for the best escape route. Will knew it was considering running to tell the rest of the pack that something new had entered the fight. Something they never encountered before.

While it stood indecisive, Will threw his knife and it buried to the hilt in the black creature's shoulder. With a snarl of pain, it yanked the knife free and threw it away into the trees. It looked at Will and started advancing. That was the moment that Will chose to release the wolves inside him.

With a roar that split the night, Will began to shift forms. It happened quickly and in seconds he stood revealed before the creature. As it turned to flee into the woods, Will dove onto its back and took it to the ground. It quickly turned into a mass melee of teeth and claws.

Cody twisted and was able to get a grip on one of the creature's legs. He turned to his left and threw the creature like it didn't weigh an ounce, slamming it into the front of the cabin and buckling the wall inward. The creature slowly got to its feet and was watching Cody continue to struggle with the beast on his back. It was shaking its head, trying to snap out of the trauma that it had just experienced.

Before it could move, Alex ran out the front door and dove onto its back, stabbing with her knife and screaming, "Die you bastard, die!"

She was stabbing it in the neck and shoulders. As it turned to snap at her, she grabbed its lower jaw and held onto it. It bit deeply into her fingers but let go almost instantly as she jammed the knife into its eye. With bloody fingers torn open, she shoved the wounded hand into the beast's neck and grabbed the big artery. With a scream of triumph, she pulled the artery out and snapped it. Blood sprayed into the air.

The beast fell to its knees and Alex knew the end was near. Yanking the tomahawk out of her belt, she slammed it into the side of the creature's head, ending its life. It crumpled lifelessly to the ground. Alex stood and looked down at her mangled hand and watched it heal almost instantly. Smiling, she shook the blood from her hand and closed her eyes.

She could feel the power of the *Oolonga-Doglalla* bonding with her werewolf blood, making her more powerful than she'd ever felt. The trick was going to be keeping it from the others until she was ready. After all, she was an Alpha of her pack and she could control her changes. She was a new breed of animal now. One that wouldn't be controlled or killed so easily.

As Julia emerged from the cabin, Alex swooned and fell to the ground, moaning loudly. Instead of helping the others, Julia ran to Alex. Feigning injury, Alex grabbed Julia around the neck and pulled her close.

"I got one," she said, whimpering as she spoke. "I'm hurt. Help me."

Julia lifted Alex and carried her towards the house as Sarah and Gabrielle were coming out.

"What happened?" asked Sarah.

"Alex is hurt," said Julia. "She killed one."

Both Sarah and Gabrielle looked surprised.

"Get her inside," said Sarah, turning back to the fight.

Cody threw himself backward and crushed the wolf on his back against a large oak tree. The creature released its grip on him and fell to the ground. They weren't sure if the cracking sound they heard on impact had been the wolf or the tree. Before it could get up, Cody grabbed it and threw it at a large walnut tree about the diameter of a hubcap.

The beast slammed into the tree with the force of a runaway locomotive. Branches fell out of the tree and the beast bent backward around the trunk. This time, it was clear that the wet cracking sound had been the creature's spine. It might not have been a mortal blow, but it took the beast out of the fight.

It began trying to crawl away, using only its hands. The legs wouldn't move, and you could see the spot just beneath the shoulders where the spine had been snapped in multiple places. Cody walked over, his footsteps booming like a mythical giant, and placed one foot in the middle of the beast's back. Reaching down, he grabbed the creature by its upper jaw.

Straightening up, there was a wet tearing sound as the beast's head came away from its shoulders. Blood fountained from the ragged stump of its neck, staining the ground a dark crimson. The mouth spasmed open a few times before the eyes went completely glassy.

Will continued to fight the large black Beta. The benefit of being *Hotamétaneo'o* and werewolf was not just in strength. It was the fact that Will still had all his mental faculties. He hadn't surrendered to the power of the wolf. Using training he received in the military, he transitioned from brawling to ground fighting techniques.

In seconds, he'd gotten a grip on one arm then wrapped his legs around the torso and shoulder of the beast, then lay back in an armbar. Will wasn't going for a submission. Using the shoulder as a fulcrum, he wrenched back and tore the arm from the socket, then ripped it from the beast's body.

Rolling away, Will got to his feet quickly. The Beta tried to stand but was still in shock from having its arm torn off. Will rushed in and drove the beast back to the ground. This time, he got his arms around the creature's head, locking in what was called an LVNR, or Lateral Vascular and Neck Restraint. Instead of going for the chokehold to put the beast out, Will wrenched and twisted, breaking the creature's neck.

Still holding the beast, Will nodded at Sarah. She ran over and drove the blade of her knife into the beast's neck, heart, and forehead. The light dimmed in the creature's eyes and faded out. The Beta was dead.

Getting to his feet, Will glanced around. All the creatures in the hunting party were dead. Unlike werewolves, these creatures did not revert to human form after they died. They were wolves and nothing would change them back. Their curse was not broken by death.

"They're all dead," Will said, his voice a deep rumble.

Cody stretched and roared into the night; the deep bellow of a bear that had not been seen in this world for millennia.

CHAPTER TEN
OWL'S PROPHECY

"There is no death, only a change of worlds."
Duwamish

September 28th
9:30 PM

Will stood next to Cody. Neither had shifted back into human form. Cody stood more than a foot taller than Will.

"How did he turn into a bear?" asked Gabrielle.

"The Ute are spiritually connected to the bear," said Cody in a deep resonating voice. "It does not surprise me."

"Let's get these bodies inside the cabin," said Will. "Then we'll burn it to the ground."

"I'm on it, Top," said Cody, heading for the nearest body.

"Is everyone ok?" asked Will, looking at Sarah.

"For the most part," said Sarah. "Even Alex got into the fight at some point. She dove on a creature's back and stabbed it to death. She's beaten up a bit but getting better. Her werewolf blood will heal her, just slower as long as she remains in human form."

"Tell her not to change, just yet," said Will. "I want you all to remain in human form until you have to change. Cody and I will stay this way."

"I think we could all ride Cody," said Gabrielle, walking over to them. "He's massive. If we can turn into bears, then what's next? Someone going to turn into a mountain lion or something."

"At this point, who knows," said Sarah.

Cody grabbed the leg of a creature in each hand and dragged them to the house as if they didn't weigh anything, throwing them unceremoniously through the door. By the time he'd dragged all of the creatures to the house, Julia and Alex came out the door. Alex was leaning heavily on Julia and limping on her left leg.

"Are you ok?" asked Gabrielle.

"I think so," said Alex, her voice pained. "I've been worse. Give me a few minutes and I'll be ready to go. I might have to have Julia help me from time to time."

"No problem," said Julia, smiling.

Will considered confronting the two of them but thought better of it. He'd do it when the others weren't around, just in case it was nothing. He didn't want to poison the group against Julia. However, thus far, Alex had killed more of the *Oolonga-Doglalla* than Julia. Before he could say anything at all, Cody walked up.

"All done, Top," he said. "They're all inside the cabin. Now what?"

"We burn it down," said Will. "We can't leave the bodies of wolf creatures for just anyone to find. If they do find bones, they'll assume it was from large wolves. The DNA won't come back as a human."

"Good call," said Sarah.

"I'll take care of it," said Gabrielle, heading inside.

She went inside and they could hear her smashing the lanterns. Then she doused the oil all over the floor and came outside with a book of matches.

"Who wants to do the honors?" she said, smiling.

"I'd do it, but it would be like trying to strike a grain of rice against a postage stamp," muttered Cody.

That drew a few chuckles from the group.

"I'll take care of it, then," said Gabrielle, lighting one match then igniting the entire book. Tossing it in through the door, they heard the whoosh as the kerosene caught fire. Instantly, flames were licking their way around the interior of the cabin. Gabrielle got back away from the porch and they watched as the cabin was engulfed in flames within minutes.

"That ought to do the trick," said Sarah. "That cabin's built from hardwoods. It'll burn hot enough to get rid of most of the bones."

"Let's get moving," said Will, turning to head into the trees.

"Don't walk too fast," admonished Sarah. "The rest of us aren't over ten feet tall."

"Speak for yourself," said Cody.

"Cody-AK," said Gabrielle. "That's your new nickname."

That drew a few groans and a few chuckles.

"I like it," said Cody. "The Kodiak is a big bear."

"Good," said Gabrielle, smiling. "It's settled. Cody-AK, it is."

Will kept the pace slow enough that they could all follow. He kept an eye on Alex and Julia. There would be times that Alex would lean heavily on Julia, but when no one was looking she seemed to walk perfectly fine.

"What game are you playing?" Will wondered.

The moon emerged from the clouds. It was nearly full and brightly orange in the night sky. The Hunter's Moon loomed close, giving them plenty of light to see by. Will glanced at Alex but she didn't seem to notice the full moon.

"That's odd," muttered Will, softly.

"What's odd?" asked Sarah.

"The full moon does not affect Alex," Will said, nodding her way.

"That is odd," said Sarah. "I wonder why?"

The moon shed enough light on the area enough that they could see in great detail. Tracking was much easier now that he was in wolf-form. His senses were good while still in human form, but much sharper once he transformed.

They emerged on a rough road. Will knew this had to be where the Conservation Agent was killed. Within minutes, he found the exact spot. The massive area of dried blood only confirmed it.

"This is where the Agent died," said Will. "They tore him apart and carried him away through the trees, over there."

"Poor guy," said Sarah. "A bad case of wrong place at the wrong time."

"Exactly," said Will. "He didn't even have time to draw his gun."

"Not that it would have done him any good," said Gabrielle. "Not against those things."

"True," said Will. "Let's go."

He continued, now following Alex's bare footprints. There was blood in the prints, making it much easier to follow. Will had read the file. No one had made any attempt to track them. Although he did read that when they brought in tracking dogs, they refused to follow the scent. That probably saved their lives, too. If they had found the den, none of them would have made it back.

It took the better part of an hour, but Will followed the tracks to where they were heading for the large rock outcropping. He stopped the group because the scent was strong. They were approaching from downwind so they wouldn't smell them coming.

"This is it," whispered Alex. "The cave is behind that big boulder on the right."

"Got it," said Will. "How many did you say are in the pack?"

"I only saw about twenty," she replied. "You've already almost cut that in half."

Will didn't say anything. He was watching the area where the cave was located, looking for any signs of movement.

"I don't see anything moving," he said, after a moment. "I'm going to risk getting a bit closer."

"We're all going," said Sarah, adamantly.

"Fine," he said, "just stay quiet."

They began creeping closer to the mouth of the cave. Just as they were almost in a position to peer around the boulder, they heard growling coming from just to the right of their position. From the sound of it, they couldn't be more than fifty yards away.

Whirling that direction, Will saw four of the creatures emerge from the trees.

"Cody and I will deal with them," said Will. "Scout the cave and see what you find. If the rest of the pack is in there, change forms and regroup."

"You don't think they're in there, do you?" asked Gabrielle.

"I think most of them have to be out hunting," said Will. "If anyone is in there, it's only a few. Just enough to guard the captives."

"Is there another way out?" Sarah asked Alex.

"I don't know," she replied. "I only ever saw the one."

Will and Cody began advancing towards the four creatures.

"Go," he said. "Be careful."

As Sarah and the others headed around the boulder, they could hear the battle that had just exploded behind them. Sarah said a quick prayer for their safety and success.

Once they reached the mouth of the cave, they could smell the overwhelming scent of the creatures but saw no sign of movement. Heading into the cave, they slowly scanned the darkness. There was no sign of movement or anything living in the cave. There were numerous nests on the ground, made from boughs of trees and moss but they were all empty. Bones from animals of all sorts littered the ground, including humans.

"They were here recently," said Sarah.

"But, where did they go?" asked Alex.

Just then, they heard a soft moan come from the back of the cave. As they cautiously approached, they saw a human woman laying naked in a large nest.

"That's the Alpha's nest," said Alex. "That's where they took me to watch me change."

Moving closer, Alex recognized who was in the nest. It was Melinda.

"That's one of my pack," said Alex, excitedly.

"Check on her," said Sarah. "We'll cover you."

Sarah watched the entrance while Gabrielle covered a side tunnel that led deeper into the bluff. Julia stood close to Alex and watched her but kept glancing around the cave.

"Melinda?" said Alex. "It's me. It's Alex."

"Alex?" moaned Melinda, weakly. "Get out of here. Don't let them find you."

"I think they're all gone," said Alex. "What happened?"

Alex rolled Melinda over onto her back and leaned close to talk to her. She was covered in cuts, scratches, and bruises and had a haunted look in her eyes.

"They brought us to the Alpha," said Melinda. "We couldn't even fight back. They're too strong."

"I know," said Alex. "What happened to the others?"

"The Alpha forced us to change into our wolf-forms," said Melinda. "When we changed, they got excited. Then it gets really weird."

"Weird?" asked Alex. "How?"

"They made us bite them all," said Melinda. "Why would they do that? They're already wolves."

"I don't know," said Alex.

She already knew why. The same reason she made the one she fought bite her. To get the powers of both werewolf and Dogman.

"The Alpha and the Beta," said Melinda, struggling to talk.

"The Beta is dead," said Alex.

"Good," said Melinda. "They brought us back here and tried to force us to join their pack. Force us to bow and present ourselves to the Alpha. The others did it, but I refused. I fought back."

"Shit," said Alex. "Go on."

"I already have a pack," said Melinda. "They tried to make me. Oh my God, they hurt many times, trying to make me. But I think they finally figured it out I wasn't going to do it. When they did, they hurt me, really bad. I don't even think I could force myself to change. It hurts so bad. Why wouldn't they just kill me?"

"Because they wanted you to suffer," said Alex. "Where did they take the others?"

"I think they were all starting to turn into those things," said Melinda. "They were changing and didn't smell like werewolves anymore. They would smell them all over until they were sure the change was working."

Alex waited for her to continue.

"Seriously," thought Alex, "this is like dragging information out of a stump. She's a moron, even now."

"They can talk," said Melinda. "Not much, but some. They said something about finding a new lair. I think they're trying to hide until the changes are complete."

Alex wondered if it would take until the next full moon or if it was different for the Dogmen.

"They left hours ago," said Melinda. "Please, you've got to help me."

"Well," said Alex, "there's only one problem with that."

"What?" asked Melinda, with tears in her eyes.

"You challenged me, bitch," whispered Alex. "I won't forgive or forget that. I can't trust you, so I've got no use for you."

"Please!" pleaded Melinda.

Alex put her hand over her mouth and shoved the knife into her heart. Holding her there for several seconds until she was sure she wasn't going to make any noise. Once she was certain she was dead, she took her hand away and pulled out the knife, wiping it on the bedding. Slipping the knife back into the scabbard, she rolled Melinda back over facing the wall.

"She's dead," said Alex, drawing the pistol from her waistband. "Now that I've dealt with one rival, I'll deal with the others."

"What?" asked Gabrielle, turning around to face Alex.

Standing up as she turned around, Alex fired once and shot her in the forehead, killing her instantly. Gabrielle dropped to the ground with only a short moan. Sarah turned at the sound of the gunfire and Alex shot her three times in the chest. Sarah crumpled to the floor trying to fight for air. The bullets had completely obliterated her heart and one lung.

"Looks like I've just dealt with two more rivals," said Alex, smiling.

Before Julia could react, Alex spun and aimed directly at her head.

"Think hard about this," said Alex. "You can join me, or you can join them. Decide now because I don't have time to waste."

Julia looked at Gabrielle lying dead and saw the light fading from Sarah's eyes. She was gone.

"Are you going to kill me?" asked Julia.

"Not if you join me," said Alex.

"If I do," said Julia, "I'll turn into one of those things. I won't be able to turn human anymore."

"Then I bite you and you become like me," said Sarah. "We'll start a pack of our own. Forget those other bitches. They got what they deserved. Fucking traitors."

Julia frowned, debating the prospects.

"Hurry up," snapped Alex. "Decide right now!"

"Will we be together?" asked Julia.

"You'll be my mate," explained Alex. "We'll rule the pack together."

Julia paused for just a moment, doubt on her face.

"I'm in," she said, smiling.

"Then let's go," said Alex, slipping the pistol into her waistband. "You made the right choice."

Together, they headed down the second tunnel and vanished into the darkness. As the last light faded from Sarah's eyes, she was reaching towards the mouth of the cave. She was reaching for Will.

CHAPTER ELEVEN
BLOOD OATH

"May the stars carry your sadness away,
May the flowers fill your heart with beauty,
May hope forever wipe away your tears,
And, above all, may silence make you strong."
Chief Dan George, Tsleil-Waututh Nation

September 28th
11:00 PM

"You take the two on the right," said Will. "I'll get the other two."

Instead of a reply, Cody roared and changed the two on his side. Will headed in more cautiously, gauging their response. The two creatures he approached fanned out and tried to flank him. Will feinted to the left, then dove into the creature on his right. They immediately tangled up in a mass of teeth and claws, then went rolling down the side of a ravine. The other creature bounded after them, eager to help its pack-mate kill the interloper.

Bouncing over rocks, downed trees and through brambles, Will and the dark grey creature rolled out into the middle of a small creek. It wasn't deep enough for them to drown it, but it did make it more difficult to regain their footing. Will shoved the creature back with all his strength, trying to gain some distance when the second creature dove right on top of him, bearing him back to the ground.

Above him, he could hear the smashing of trees and howls of pain and rage. Will knew that Cody was wasting no time in engaging his targets. He didn't have time to ponder it because he had his own hands full with the two creatures who were now trying to shove his head beneath the shallow water.

Driving his left elbow back with a sudden violent jerk of his arm, he felt it impact the side of one of the creature's heads. Immediately, one of them let out a yelp and was knocked clear of him. Reaching down, he grabbed the ankle of the other beast and yanked its feet out from under it. It flailed as it fell and Will rolled over on top of the beast, punching it several times in the face. Each blow sounded like a sledgehammer striking the ground.

Before he could press the attack, the other creature drove into his side like a linebacker, knocking him off the dazed beast. The two of them grabbed for each other, looking for the upper hand. As they rolled, they fell farther down the creek and off a small embankment. They splashed into a pool that was well over six feet deep and about as wide as a large SUV.

They rolled over and over in the water, grappling for position. Will drove a series of short punches into the beast's face, then pushed away from it. Getting to his feet, he gulped in a huge breath of air. Before he could take a second, the other creature dove from the top of the embankment and took him back into the water.

Behind him, Will felt the second creature sink its teeth into his right shoulder. The warm sensation of blood oozing from the wound seemed in stark contrast to the coolness of the water. Will resisted the urge to roar in pain, knowing it would cost him his breath. Instead, he reached over his shoulder and jammed a claw into the creature's eye. It instantly released its hold and he could hear as it tried to howl and only ended up sucking in water.

Shoving away, he knocked the feet out from under the second creature. Grabbing hold, he held the beast's head just beneath the surface of the water and drove fist after punishing fist into the beast's face and head. The creature's eyes were beginning to roll back into its head when a sudden crash of breaking wood caused Will to look up.

Above him, Cody must have thrown one of the two creatures he was fighting because one came crashing through the canopy of trees and hit the water right next to Will. Giving the creature he was holding one more shot to the face, Will released him and turned as the one with the bloody eye stood up and snarled at him.

"Well, shit," thought Will.

One-eye dove onto him, but Will was ready this time. He caught the creature and twisted around, shoving it face-first into the boulders at the edge of the embankment. Will could hear the crunching of bone and felt the creature go slack in his hands. It wasn't dead, but it might be out of the fight long enough for him to get the drop on the other two that were now getting up out of the water.

One drove its shoulder into Will's stomach, and he kept his footing, driving blow after blow into the beast's back. While it had him distracted, the other creature stabbed him in the chest with a broken tree branch about the diameter of a bottle of soda. He felt the jagged wood dig deeply into his flesh and he roared in pain.

The creature drew back to stab him again, but Will hooked his arms beneath the arms of the creature he'd been pummeling and lifted it out of the water. With a twist, he threw the beast into the one with the sharpened piece of wood. They both slammed into the wall of the ravine, landing on jagged rocks.

One-eye was just getting back up and Will grabbed him by the neck. One-eye slashed him across the chest with both sets of claws, cutting him almost to the bone. Blood was flowing freely down his chest, but he knew that it would heal. It was just going to take it a while.

Above them, there was more crashing and breaking of wood. Will glanced up to see Cody and the other wolf rolling down the ravine, breaking trees as they fell. The wolf was missing several patches of fur and was covered in its blood. Cody, while still looking angry, didn't appear to be hurt.

Picking One-eye up off the ground, Will kept his grip on its throat and grabbed one of its legs. Once he had a grip on an ankle and the throat, he lifted One-eye above his head and threw him through the air. One-eye slammed into a tree with a broken branch, impaling him on the stump. One-eye wasn't dead, but he couldn't force himself off the jagged branch that was sticking out of the center of his chest. He was stuck there, at least for now.

Behind him, one of the remaining creatures brought a large rock down on Will's left shoulder with tremendous force. Will felt the shoulder break under the blow, leaving his left arm to fall useless at his side. The pain was excruciating but he couldn't let it take him out of the fight.

As the creature brought the rock up to strike him again, Will kicked it in the stomach. The force of the kick propelled the creature back into the embankment and it dropped the rock to fall onto its chest. Will heard the telltale sound of several ribs breaking.

Cody emerged from the water, holding the beast he had been fighting by the throat. It was limp in his hands and Will could see it was almost unconscious. Grabbing it by one thigh, Cody raised it high into the air, then brought its back down onto his left knee. Will heard the beast's back snap like thunder. Tossing the creature aside, Cody began looking for another target. Above them, in the direction of the cave, they heard what sounded like gunshots.

"That sounded like a gun," said Will.

"No one was carrying one," said Cody.

Before they could ponder it further, the other two creatures attacked, forcing Will to defend with only one arm. Cody allowed the creature to leap at him, then drove his fist into the beast's chest while still in mid-air. The sudden application of force severely altered the creature's trajectory, sending it to slam into a walnut tree about the diameter of a bowling ball. The tree snapped off from the force of the blow and the creature did not rise. From the way it was laying, it was clear that it had multiple broken bones.

"Go," said Cody, grabbing the beast that was attacking Will by the scruff of the neck. "I've got this, Top. Go see what's going on up there."

Will just nodded and headed out of the water. He was badly hurt, but it was healing. It was just going to take time. The side of the ravine was steep, and it was slow going. Several times, Will slid back down in the leaves and mud, forcing him to start all over again. It would have been a much easier climb if he had the use of both arms.

By the time he clawed his way back to the top, he was exhausted. The bleeding from the wound in his chest had stopped but the wound was still raw and ragged. He could feel the bones in his shoulder trying to reset themselves. Getting to his feet, he stretched both arms and felt the bones go back into place.

With a roar of pain, Will stretched and straightened to his full height. He looked around for any signs of a shooter but saw nothing going on outside the cave. He was starting to get a bad feeling, deep inside him.

Heading for the mouth of the cave, he ducked beneath the opening and waited a moment for his eyes to adjust. Once they had, he moved deeper into the cave. Ahead, he could see someone laying on the ground. The sick feeling in his stomach increased. He moved closer and the feeling turned to sickness when he realized what he was seeing.

On his right, he could see Gabrielle. She'd been shot in the forehead and the back of her skull was open. Her eyes were open wide, and it was clear that she was dead. Will felt like he was going to scream, then his eyes fell on the other body. She was lying to his left, almost hidden in the deep darkness of the cave.

He saw Sarah laying on her back with her face looking towards the mouth of the cave. Her left hand had been reaching for the cave entrance. There were multiple bullet holes in her chest and her eyes stared blankly into Will's. She was dead. What's worse, Will knew she'd been reaching for the mouth of the cave. She'd been reaching for him.

He screamed and fell to his knees. He cried into the darkness, howling mournfully from deep within him. Both Old Wolf and Dire Wolf howled with him. They felt the loss as deeply as he did. They were part of Will and those were his mates. They both roared their pain and fury. In the darkness, Old Wolf made him a promise. Their unity of purpose would bring those responsible to the justice of the pack. Dire Wolf agreed. The shared pain made the impossible, possible. They were now one in their pain and their fury. They were one, now.

He wasn't sure when he gathered up both of them, but he found himself screaming and crying, holding both of them in his lap. He'd reverted to human form and was stroking their hair. He screamed until his voice was cracking and ragged. His body was wracked with sobs and the tears were stinging in the corners of his eyes. He was far beyond consolation.

When he felt the hand on his shoulder, he barely registered it. Cody leaned down beside him, but Will couldn't hear his words. He was beyond hearing anything. Grief had taken him to a place away from words. A place outside reason. A place almost beyond sanity. Only his rage kept him from going into the darkness of insanity. Only his rage kept him alive.

He wasn't sure who started singing the death-song first, him or Cody. They were both singing it. Will cradled Sarah and Gabrielle while Cody held him. Their tears both fell like rivers for the fallen. Although Cody had only known them both for a short time, they were his family. He felt their loss as much as he would have his mother. There was going to be vengeance. This could only end in the blood of those responsible.

Will was still singing when Mika and the others arrived. Will didn't see them come in nor did he answer when they spoke to him. His voice was almost gone, yet he continued to sing the death-song. No one could reach him. His pain had taken him to a place beyond reason.

"Let him be," whispered Mika. "We need to know what happened here."

"I'm already on it," said Cassie. "From what I can tell, they were alone in the cave when it happened. From the casings and the tracks, I think Alex shot them both. I found a knife wound in the chest of the naked girl at the back of the cave. Alex probably killed her, too."

Mika growled but didn't say anything.

"I think the gun came from either Gideon or Beale," said Cassie. "It's those big .50 caliber rounds like Will uses."

"Beale," said Mika. "Gideon carries a double stack .45. What about Julia. Where did she go?"

"I'm not the tracker," said Cassie, "but the Mohawk brothers are. They said that it looks like Julia left with Alex."

"Goddamn it!" snapped Mika. "That fucking bitch!"

"I suppose she could have been taken against her will," said Cassie.

"You saw the way those two looked at each other," said Mika. "If you ask me, she's as responsible for what happened here as Alex is."

"Besides," said Robert, "the tracks don't bear that out. They were side by side, not one in front like a captive."

"You're probably right," said Cassie. "I don't know."

"Who's the dead girl at the back of the cave?" asked Mika.

"I have no idea," said Cassie, "but I think it's safe to say she was one of Alex's pack. From her scent, she was a werewolf."

"So, what happened to the rest of the pack?" asked Cody.

"The Dogmen took them with them," said Cassie. "I have no idea why they left this one behind."

"I think it was because she wasn't changing," said Cassie. "I only smelled werewolf on her, not Dogman. I'm going out on a limb and guessing that they left her behind because she wouldn't join them. The others must have joined their pack. There should be five more, according to what Alex told us."

"Then we've got to find them," said Mika. "We have to prevent the *Oolonga-Doglalla* from being able to shift forms again."

"We killed twelve of them," said Cody. "Eight back at a cabin we found in the woods and four just down in a ravine about a quarter of a mile from here. If there were around twenty in their pack, then there can't be many of them left."

"We have to find them first," said Mika. "I hate myself for saying it, but we have to. We can't go after Alex and Julia until we stop the *Oolonga-Doglalla*."

"I don't think Will is going to be in any shape to do anything," said Cassie. "He's completely unresponsive."

"Can you blame him?" asked Mika.

"Not at all," said Cassie. "I just meant he's not going to be doing anything for a while."

"He'll come back to us," said Mika. "He won't quit until Alex and Julia face justice."

"I know," said Cassie. "Let's get them all out of here."

"I've already taken care of it," said Mika. "We're going to meet Jason on the road. We're all going back to camp."

With that, they began gathering up Sarah and Gabrielle. Cody and the Mohawk brothers built a fire and threw the bodies of the dead Dogmen along with the dead werewolf onto the pyre. Under the circumstances, it was better than any of them deserved but they couldn't leave the bodies to be found by anyone. Once the pyre was burning, they got ready to carry their fallen with solemn reverence.

"I'll carry them," wheezed Will, picking up Sarah.

Before he could pick up Gabrielle, Mika stepped in.

"Let me, brother," said Mika. "Let me help you. I know how bad you're hurting but let me carry part of it."

They locked eyes and Will nodded.

Reverently, Mika picked up Gabrielle's body as gently as he could. Side by side, they headed through the woods, returning to the road. Will didn't speak until they were laying them both in the back of the truck.

"Walk in beauty," said Will, closing both of their eyes.

Jason placed a blanket over them as Gideon got out of the truck and stood watching. No one said a word as Will got into the truck and lay down next to them.

"Drive slowly," said Jason, nodding at Gideon.

Without a word, Gideon got back into the truck and they headed to the campground. It was a long, quiet ride. By the time that they made it, Jason had already made several phone calls in the other vehicle. He'd reached Grandfather and he was already on his way.

Once they made it back, Jason began preparing them for the funeral. There would be no official investigation nor a trip to any funeral home. They would handle this within the tribe, within the pack. There was no need for an investigation because none of them had any intention of seeing those responsible go to jail. This would be a more permanent solution. One that only blood could provide with the finality of death. Blood demanded blood, after all.

Will never left their side the entire night. He sat beside them, never moving to do anything other than to get dressed. Jason sat with him, singing and saying prayers for them both. Will's silence only added to the pain felt by the others. They not only mourned the loss of Sarah and Gabrielle, they mourned for Will. They feared that he would never be the same again. Time would prove them right.

Hours later, Will was sitting with Jason, staring into the fire. Sarah and Gabrielle were inside the camper. They were already prepared for the funeral. Will hadn't said a word since he'd been back to camp. Jason did the only thing he could do for him and that was to just be there. No words needed to be said.

Will barely registered when the old red Toyota pickup pulled into the campsite. Grandfather climbed out of the truck slowly, glancing around at the looks of loss on the faces of everyone there. With a grim nod, he headed to where Will and Jason sat by the fire.

"I am here, my grandsons," said Grandfather, sliding into a camp chair.

"How did you get here so quickly?" asked Jason.

"I flew back to Lebanon and drove down," explained Grandfather. "I have several friends who are pilots."

"Thank you for coming," said Jason. "I've done all I can, but I don't think anything can reach him."

"He is listening," said Grandfather. "He will speak when he is ready. Do we know what happened?"

"We had a female werewolf with us named Alex," said Jason. "She stole a gun from Beale, one of Gideon's men, and shot them. It was loaded with the bullets we made for them to fight the *Oolonga-Doglalla*."

"And where is Gideon?" asked Grandfather.

"He said he was returning to Fort Leonard Wood," said Jason. "He went back to deal with Beale, but he said to call him if we needed him."

Grandfather said nothing. He seemed to be lost in thought.

"And we've not found any sign of the *Oolonga-Doglalla* since last night," said Jason. "I told you on the phone about what we suspected was happening. It may already be too late to stop them."

"I see some of the others are missing," said Grandfather, glancing around.

"Mika took several people with him to try and track them down," said Jason.

"The *Oolonga-Doglalla* or this Alex person?" asked Grandfather.

"The *Oolonga-Doglalla*," said Jason. "As bad as it sounds, we need to prevent them from regaining the ability the change shapes. Besides, I'm sure that Will would want to be there when we find Alex and Julia."

"This Alex," said Grandfather. "If she is as smart as I think, then she is long gone. I would not remain in the area if I were in her position. I would be putting as much distance as possible between me and Will as possible."

"That's what we thought, as well," said Jason. "The *Oolonga-Doglalla* can't just drive or take a flight. They're moving out of the area on foot and we can track them."

"Mika will track them if anyone can," said Grandfather. "He is an excellent tracker. If they do learn to change shapes, they will not be as difficult to find as you suspect."

"Why is that, Grandfather?" asked Jason.

"It is far easier for a man to act like a beast than for a beast to act like a man," said Grandfather. "They might be able to blend from a distance, but they cannot walk among humans and not be noticed. They have forgotten how to act like men. That is if they ever were before. They could have been born *Oolonga-Doglalla*."

"That might be true," said Jason, "but for how long? They're smart enough to learn."

"Perhaps," said Grandfather

"So, what do we do now?" asked Jason.

"We take them back home for burial," said Grandfather. "Sarah's family will be there tomorrow."

"What about the hunt?" asked Jason.

"I will take Will back home with me," said Grandfather. "I will make the preparations for the funeral. You can continue the hunt and come when you can."

Will stood up and glanced at them both. Jason looked at Will, curious about what he was doing.

"I will go with Grandfather," said Will. "When this is done, I will hunt down Alex and Julia, personally."

"What will you do then?" asked Jason.

Taking a knife from his belt, Will cut a slit into his palm, then presented it before him.

"I swear before the sacred moon," said Will, "I will have their blood and take their heads. I will not rest until I have done so."

Will walked away and went inside the camper. Jason and Grandfather exchanged glances. The words Will had just spoken had chilled them both to the marrow. Not for just what he said, but the cold way he said it. They had little doubt that he would carry through on his threat. A blood oath could only end in blood.

APEX PREDATOR: HUNTER'S MOON

CHAPTER TWELVE
EXODUS

"Live your life that the fear of death can never enter your heart."
Chief Tecumseh

September 29th
9:00 AM

Mika, Cassie, the Mohawk twins, Cody, Joe *Nakai*, and Isaac *Kuzih* were moving through the undergrowth. This hunt was different now. They all wore the war paint and buckskins traditional to the *Hotamétaneo'o*. They all carried traditional weapons that had been consecrated for the hunt. Mika's face had black circles around the eyes with parallel stripes running down both cheeks. It made him look like his face was a skull, which fit the mood he was in. This hunt wasn't just about finding their quarry. It was about vengeance.

Jason had mixed the pigments that they used in their warpaint. Using a special blend of herbs, he had built upon the original recipe created by their Grandfather, Jay *Matoskah*. Using the herbs against prey animals like deer and buffalo was one thing. Using them on another predator required a whole new level of scent elimination. If the *Oolonga-Doglalla* smelled anything at all, it would be the faint aroma of sage and pine. Things that would already exist in the woods around them.

They had been tracking the *Oolonga-Doglalla* all night. From what they could tell, there were only seven survivors of the entire pack, plus the five surviving members of the werewolf pack. It seemed like the werewolf females were willingly staying with the *Oolonga-Doglalla*. Mika had little doubt that they would be looking to find others of their kind. After all, there was safety in numbers.

Robert *Alok*, one of the Mohawk twins, had been monitoring the tracks. From what they could tell, the *Oolonga-Doglalla* had split up. Four groups had headed in different directions. They were trying to ensure that at least some of the hybrids survived to spread it to other packs. Mika had decided to hunt them down one group at a time instead of splitting up the group. Time was on their side, for the moment.

"So, when we find them," said Richard *Akaash*, "are we rescuing the werewolf females?"

"No," said Mika. "If what we're afraid is true, they've already been turned. We can't let that get loose in the world. Besides, Cassie believes they joined the pack willingly."

"Fair enough," said Richard. "I don't have a problem with it. Besides, they were hunting people here before the *Oolonga-Doglalla* showed up. If it weren't for that, we'd have been hunting the werewolves anyway. It's not like they were innocent before any of this started."

"I don't have a problem either," said Robert. "Look what happened the last time we tried to help a fucking werewolf."

"They had better pray I don't find them before Will does," said Cody. "I'll rip their goddamned heads off with my bare hands."

No one argued the point. Cody had been there when Will found the bodies of Sarah and Gabrielle. Cody had wept and sang the death-song with him. His rage was terrible to see and when they found out that his other form was of a massive bear, they were even more worried. None of them thought they could stop him, even if they wanted to.

"These tracks are fresh," whispered Robert, crouching low beside the trail.

The others fell silent, listening for any sound that their quarry had detected their presence. The sun was high enough in the sky that the *Oolonga-Doglalla* couldn't risk traveling. They only traveled by night. It was extremely difficult to kill one of them with normal weapons, but it was completely possible. A large enough shot to the brain would incapacitate them long enough to finish the job before they could recover. They still feared man, as long as they had numbers. One on one, there was no fear at all.

Mika motioned for everyone to stay silent. All eyes were on him as he assessed the avenues of approach. They were near a ravine that likely had caves hidden inside it. That was the place where they were most-likely hiding for the day. To their left, the ground rose sharply, forming the northern edge of the ravine. Directly ahead, the small stream went deeper into it. In the soft earth beside the stream, they'd found a fresh track.

"They're either hiding in this ravine until sundown," whispered Mika.

"Or this is a trap," whispered Robert. "As smart as these damned things are, I can't believe it would step right into the soft earth and leave such a perfect track for us to find."

"They might if they don't know they're being followed," whispered Richard.

"They know," whispered Mika. "They're well aware that we're tracking them."

"Then it's a trap," said Cody. "So what? There's only two of the Dogmen and one she-wolf, and she's not likely to fight for them. We can easily take them."

"Something's not right, Mika," whispered Robert. "All night, I've been tracking partial prints and mashed down grass. Now, out of the blue, I get an almost perfect print. They don't make this big of a mistake."

"He's not wrong," said Richard. "I've been double-checking the tracks. This is the clearest print we've seen in hours."

"I think they doubled around and met up with another group," whispered Robert. "Or they all met at a designated place. Either way, we're walking into a bigger fight than we expected."

"By the time we could get the others here," whispered Mika, "they'll be long gone. If we don't act now, we might not get another shot for days, if at all."

"Even if they did meet up with the entire group," whispered Cody, "then we're pretty much evenly matched. I don't see the she-wolves fighting all that well, even if they joined the pack."

"Unless they turned them," whispered Cassie. "Then they're just like the rest."

"Can they do that?" asked Cody, keeping his voice low.

"I think so," whispered Mika. "I mean, that's how Will got turned originally. He fought the darkness and won. If he hadn't, he would have become one of those things."

"Then so could the she-wolves," whispered Cassie. "Only, they're already cursed, so they wouldn't be able to fight it like Will did."

"Fuck," whispered Joe *Nakai*. "That's five more of them, then."

"Worse than that," whispered Mika. "Five that are both werewolf and Dogman."

"That could easily mean they're stronger than us, now," whispered Cassie. "Will had both and look how strong it made him. If they turned the she-wolves and then they turned the rest of the pack…"

"Then we're looking at twice our number of enemies that are far stronger than we expected them to be," whispered Robert.

"I think we'd be stupid to think it hasn't happened already," whispered Cassie. "If we go in expecting it, then they won't have surprise on their side."

"Alright," whispered Mika. "I'm going up on top of that ridge to get a look into that ravine. Cassie and Joe will come with me. The rest of you, sneak into the ravine and we'll guide you in. I'll use the owl call. One hoot for every creature I see."

They all moved off, their moccasins making almost no noise on the soft grass and soil. As they climbed higher above the ravine, they could see the others making their way slowly along the edge of the creek. Mika carefully studied the ravine below them and the path they were taking, looking for sentries or any signs of movement.

As they climbed higher above the floor of the ravine, Mika was beginning to see the sides of the ravine growing rockier and steeper as they went. The others on the ground were moving slower to give them a chance to get into place before they reached the area where they suspected the cave might be.

Mika could feel the air below him change. It was cooler and smelled like damp earth. They were fifty feet above the floor of the ravine and almost directly above what he suspected was a large cave opening. There was another scent in the air, as well. The musky scent of the *Oolonga-Doglalla*.

"They're right below us," mouthed Mika, careful to not make any unnecessary sound.

Cassie and Joe both nodded, crouching down behind a large honeysuckle bush. The last thing they wanted now was for their shadows to give away their position. The sun was still low enough in the sky that it was casting long shadows and could easily throw enough of one into the ravine to alert the creatures.

Mika crawled on his stomach to the edge of the ravine and peered down into the deep shadows below. Below them, there was a rocky outcropping that angled back into the side of the bluff. Mika considered leaning down below the edge to try and get a look into the darkness when movement caught his eye. He instantly froze.

Directly across the ravine was an area with several boulders that were about the size of a draft horse. He hadn't considered that there might be a cave behind those boulders until he saw one of the creatures stick its head up above one and begin sniffing the air. It was a large male with dark grey fur. It also had a recent scar down the side of its face.

Pressing his face down into the grass, Mika peered through it with just one eye. The last thing he wanted to do was to have the beast sense his presence. Animals had the uncanny ability to feel when a predator was watching them, even when they couldn't see it. That primitive instinct had served them well, down through the ages.

As if to prove him right, the creature turned and looked almost directly at Mika. Narrowing his eyes to bare slits, Mika held his breath and waited for the creature to either sound the alarm or look away. After what felt like an hour, the creature looked away and started glancing around the area. Cautiously, it stood up from behind the boulders and walked out away from the entrance to the cave.

Glancing around for a moment, it seemed to study its surroundings before it moved over to a tree and started relieving its bladder. Mika could hear the urine stream splattering against the tree and onto the rocks at the base of it. The acrid smell of the urine was easily detected, even from their vantage point.

Down the ravine, Mika could see Robert and Richard were creeping through the bushes, just around a slight bend in the creek. They were close to exposing themselves without ever knowing that the creature was there. Mika raised a few inches and let out a single hoot.

The creature's ears came up instantly and it began looking around. Mika knew that the beast had heard the owl and suspected it wasn't an owl. Fortunately, Robert and Richard both immediately went to the ground, hiding behind the thick bushes. Behind them, Mika could see the others doing the same.

When the creature finished urinating, it turned and stepped out into the center of the ravine, nearly standing in the creek. It was staring directly towards where Robert and the others now hid. Mika knew it hadn't smelled them, since there would be no wind down in that ravine. The slight breeze was coming almost directly into his face, which meant that it was passing over the valley. No, it had to be something else.

It occurred to Mika that any sound in that narrow ravine would likely be magnified. That meant it had probably heard them approaching, despite how slowly they had been moving. When it took a few more steps in that direction, it was confirmed. It had heard enough to make it curious, but not enough for it to sound the alarm. They had to either get it to look away or prevent it from sounding the alarm. Neither was going to be easy.

The creature had moved far enough away from the boulders that it was unlikely any of the others could see it. The only way it was going to sound the alarm was by either howling or making a lot of noise. If they were going to take the beast out, then they had to do it quickly. If it saw the others, then the element of surprise was going to be completely gone.

Leaning close to Cassie's ear, Mika pressed his lips against her and whispered very low, "I've got to take that thing out."

Cassie looked at him quizzically but didn't say anything. She had no idea what Mika was planning but wasn't sure she liked the sound of it. Mika winked at her, then slid back away from the edge. Getting to his knees, he made sure he was back far enough where the creature couldn't see him. Staying in a crouch, he got to his feet and crept far enough forward where he could get a glimpse of the beast.

"What the hell is he about to do?" thought Cassie.

Mika took several steps back and drew his knife. It hit Cassie exactly what he was about to do, but it was too late to stop him. All she could do was hope it worked and that he didn't kill himself in the attempt. She locked eyes with him for a moment. Mika just winked at her and gave her the wry smile that made her fall for him in the first place.

"I love you," she mouthed, "but you're an idiot."

"I know," he mouthed back.

He didn't elaborate which he meant, but it was likely both. Joe nodded his approval and drew his knife just in case he had to follow in his footsteps. Cassie winced because she knew that falling from that distance was going to hurt even if he struck his target. Fifty feet was a long way down.

Mika took a running start and leaped into the air, arms and legs pumping to give him more momentum. Cassie watched as he arced high into the air and seemed to be falling right on target. Raising the knife above his head with both hands, Mika covered the distance without making a sound. Although, she'd half expected him to let forth a war cry that would have shaken the entire ravine. She wouldn't have put it past him.

Mika dropped without so much as a whisper of sound betraying his fall. Just before he struck, the creature seemed to sense his approach. It could have been his shadow giving him away, but the creature wasn't expecting a flying Indian. The look of surprise on its face registered clearly and it brought its hands up to try and block him.

Mika struck the beast full-force and it caught him as if he didn't weigh anything. However, catching him was a mistake. Instead of blocking the attack, it had merely prevented him from striking the rocky ground of the ravine. Mika buried the knife deep into the beast's skull right between the eyes, snapping the blade off from the impact.

The creature held him in a bear-hug, but there wasn't any force to it. The blade had done its damage. Smoke was coming from the wound and the beast opened and closed its mouth soundlessly, a shocked look still on its face. It was already dead; the body just hadn't gotten the memo yet.

It crumpled to the ground and Mika kicked free of the beast, landing on his feet several feet away. Mika flashed Cassie a broad smile and gave her a slight bow. She just shook her head at him.

"That was fucking badass," whispered Joe.

"Yeah," agreed Cassie, "but if you tell him I said so, I'll deny it."

Mika rolled the dead creature over and concealed it behind a large bush. He had just ducked down when another creature stuck its head out over the boulder, looking around for the other one. This creature was smaller and lighter colored. When it came out around the boulder, they could see it was a female. Something metallic glinted on its breasts. The nipples were pierced.

"That's one of the she-wolves," whispered Joe, leaning close to Cassie.

"She doesn't look like a captive to me," whispered Cassie.

The creature stepped into the creek and leaned down, drinking deeply. For a moment, Cassie considered repeating Mika's leap but thought better of it. Mika had been lucky. There was no way to know if they would be that lucky, twice.

Cassie saw movement from below. The Mohawk twins were sneaking into position, preparing for a strike. Just as they were approaching the flank of the she-wolf, it suddenly stood up and snarled at them.

"Damn it," hissed Cassie, getting to her feet and taking several steps back.

The creature crouched low and let out a roar, alerting any of the creatures still inside the cave. The Mohawk twins drew their weapons and fanned out, but their stealth was for nothing. They could already hear movement from deeper in the cave.

Cassie took several running steps and leaped into the air. Joe watched in amazement as she reached her apogee and began hurtling towards the she-wolf. Unlike Mika, she didn't have a weapon in her hand as she fell. Joe was astounded to see her shift into her wolf-form in mid-air.

"Now that's badass!" he hissed, getting to his feet, and getting ready to leap after her.

He started shifting into his wolf form as he ran. By the time he launched himself into the air, Cassie had impacted with the she-wolf and slammed her to the ground. Joe shifted forms and landed beside the creek, snarling as he threw the remnants of his clothing away from him.

Out of the cave, four more creatures emerged. This group had met up with at least one other group, looking for safety in numbers. As the creatures moved to surround the two interlopers that were in their midst, the Mohawk twins shifted form and strode out into the water, snarling a challenge.

They were both silver-grey and the ruff on their necks both looked like the Mohawk style haircuts that they both wore. It was clear who they were, even in wolf-form. Mika shifted form as he ran, moving to protect Cassie as she fought the she-wolf.

When Mika shifted, he was larger by half-a-head than even the *Oolonga-Doglalla*. Mika was terrifying to behold since the skull-like face paint was still coloring the fur on his face. He was the largest creature by far until Cody blasted out of the bushes, fully enraged and in his bear-form. With a bellow of raw fury, he charged directly at the creatures emerging from the cave.

Mika ran and leaped up on top of a boulder, then slammed into one of the largest males as it left the cave. They hit the ground in a mass of claws, teeth, and fury. The thought suddenly occurred to Mika, if all these creatures were now infected with the werewolf curse, then likely so would all of them by the end of the fight. He'd already been bitten at least three times.

Cody slammed into a large male Dogman and bore it to the ground with very little resistance. The Dogman simply wasn't strong enough to outmatch an enraged bear, especially since Cody was close to six feet taller than it was. It bit and scratched him, but the outcome was never in any doubt. Cody got a grip on both the upper and lower jaws of the *Oolonga-Doglalla* and started forcing them apart.

The creature slashed at Cody with its claws, but he was beyond feeling any pain. He continued to force the jaws open wider and wider. The sound of ripping flesh and breaking bone began sounding loud as the snarls of the beast turned into whimpering cries of pain. Cody continued relentlessly until he tore the beast's head apart and threw the pieces in opposite directions, the lower jaw landing in the water and the top of the jaw and head landing on top of a boulder with the eyes still flicking from left to right.

Slowly, the light faded from the eyes and the beast was dead. No amount of healing was going to fix that wound. There would be no recovery from that. Cody picked the body up by the ankles and slammed it several times down backward on top of a large boulder, shattering every bone in the body.

Cassie had knocked the she-wolf into the water and held her beneath the surface. The she-wolf fought back, sinking its teeth into Cassie's leg. Cassie drove her fist into the side of the she-wolf's head like a piston, over and over again. The beast released the bite on her calf and fought to get to her feet.

Exploding up from the water, the she-wolf knocked Cassie over onto her back. Diving on top of her, the she-wolf forced Cassie's head below the water and wrapped her fingers around her throat. Cassie struggled to get air and felt like she might be losing the fight when Joe drove his shoulder into the side of the she-wolf, knocking her off Cassie.

Bearing her to the ground, Joe sunk his teeth into the she-wolf's throat, pinning her to the ground. Cassie got to her feet and dove onto the she-wolf's legs, preventing her from kicking Joe off her. Once she was that close, Cassie's senses told her that the she-wolf was indeed changing into a mixture of Dogman and werewolf.

With a tearing sound, Joe got to his feet. The throat of the she-wolf was still gripped in his teeth, but the bitch was still on the ground. Blood erupted from the massive wound and Cassie could hear her gurgling on her blood. Snatching up a tomahawk that lay on the ground, Cassie drove the blade into the she-wolf's temple, ending her suffering and her life.

Another she-wolf sprinted away from the group, heading down the ravine trying to escape. The Mohawk twins were right on her heels and she didn't make it more than twenty yards before they took her to the ground.

Mika was still battling the large male but was holding his own. The beast circled Mika, feinting to the right then lunging to the left. It almost made it past Mika in an attempt to reach the water when Cody's massive hands wrapped around the beast's head, totally engulfing it in his enormous grip. Crushing the skull like an eggshell, Cody twisted and ripped the beast's head from its shoulders without much effort.

Blood fountained into the air as the body crumpled lifelessly to the ground. Isaac and Joe took another male to the ground and began ripping into the beast as it savagely bit at both, trying to free itself but to no avail.

When Mika glanced around the fighting was over and they all stood looking at one another. They were all bloody and wounded, but they had won the fight without losing any of their own. However, the thought played through Mika's mind, they had all been bitten multiple times. They were going to have to fight the werewolf spirit, the same as Will.

"Well, that changes things," thought Mika.

APEX PREDATOR: HUNTER'S MOON

CHAPTER THIRTEEN
REMEMBRANCE

"Hold on to what is good, Even if it's a handful of earth.
Hold on to what you believe, Even if it's a tree that stands by itself.
Hold on to what you must do, Even if it's a long way from here.
Hold on to your life, Even if it's easier to let go.
Hold on to my hand, Even if someday I'll be gone away from you."
Crowfoot

September 29th
2:30 PM

Their wounds were mostly healed by the time they all made it back to the campground. Mika waded out into the deeper part of the river and washed the gore and war paint from his fur before he reverted to his human form. Cassie joined him, as did the others. There was a lot of blood to wash off and none of them wanted to wear it any longer.

Jason met them at the edge of the water with towels and fresh clothing. None of the men were embarrassed in the slightest, but Cassie slipped behind some bushes before she got dressed. Mika waited until she came out before slipping his arms around her and hugging her tightly.

"Are you ok?" he asked, smiling gently at her.

"Yeah," she said, "but I'll be doing better once we've located all of them."

"There was six there," said Mika. "That means there are only six more out there somewhere."

"Somewhere," echoed Cassie. "That's the real trick. They're not going to be easy to find. The Alpha is one of the ones still unaccounted for."

"I'm not worried about the Alpha," said Mika. "For one, he's kind of a bitch for leaving his pack to be picked apart. For another, if I can't take him, Cody will fuck him up. Holy shit, he's strong."

"I saw that," said Cassie. "He's also taking the loss of Sarah and Gabrielle personally."

"Just because they're new," said Mika, "doesn't mean that they don't take the bond very seriously. We all went into the sacred *Inipi* together. That means something strong to our people. Well, to everyone except that fucking bitch Julia."

"She'll get hers," said Cassie. "If Will doesn't get her, all of us would love to take a shot. She betrayed all of us."

"Will swore a blood oath," said Mika. "He'll follow them until he dies if it takes that long. I honestly don't see it taking that much time. Will's relentless. He's also the best-damned tracker I've ever seen."

As they headed back into the campground, Mika could smell food cooking. He'd forgotten how hungry he was. He couldn't remember the last meal he'd eaten, and he wanted to make certain everyone got a good meal and some rest before they went back out after the other creatures.

"What did you find?" asked Jason, taking a seat by the fire.

"We found six of them," said Mika. "It looks like not only have the she-wolves been taken into the pack, they've infected each other. The *Oolonga-Doglalla* can take human form again. I know they infected the werewolves, so they're now all part of the pack."

"Damn it," said Jason. "That's not good."

"We should have three of the werewolf chicks and three of the *Oolonga-Doglalla* remaining," said Cassie, "if our counts are accurate. Certainly not much more than that, if any. But they're all changing, and I don't know how long until they've got all the abilities of both."

"Well, that's not good," said Jason. "The last thing we need is a small army of those things running around."

"That's exactly what we'll have if we don't stop them before they hook up with another pack," said Mika.

"Well, that's not going to happen today," said Jason. "It's not like those things have a Facebook page or use Google Hangouts. The Alpha and the others will have to find another pack to link up to. I seriously doubt they stay in contact with each other."

"That's possibly the best news we have in all of this," said Cassie. "If they have to hunt for the other packs, we have time to track them down."

"So, what are you going to do next?" asked Jason.

"We're going to eat and get some rest," said Mika. "After nightfall, I'm taking more of the group out and trying to pick up the trail of the other groups. We need to finish this before the trail goes cold."

"Well, we've got the food part taken care of," said Jason. "I made a big batch of frybread and we've set up a big taco bar in the camper. We'll use the frybread as taco shells."

"God, that sounds delicious," said Cassie. "I'm starving."

"I bet," said Jason. "It's been damned near twenty-four hours since you all have eaten."

"How's Will?" asked Mika.

"Still not talking, last I knew," said Jason. "He went with Grandfather back to his place to make the funeral preparations."

"I feel so bad for him," said Cassie. "I can't imagine how he must feel. It's got to be pure hell."

"That's pretty much how I'd feel if it was me," said Mika, squeezing Cassie's hand.

"As soon as the funeral is finished," said Jason, "I think Will is coming right back. He'll want to go after Alex and Julia as soon as he can. The only reason he agreed to stop hunting now is that Grandfather asked him to."

"He needs to grieve," said Cassie. "If he doesn't take time to mourn, I think he might give in to the werewolf side. If he does that, we're going to have to stop him ourselves."

"Do you think we can?" asked Mika. "Will might be unstoppable with what he has inside him. I mean, most of us have some werewolf in us now, but he's Dire Wolf on top of First Born Werewolf. He's stronger than any of us."

"All the more reason he should take some time and mourn," said Cassie. "If he goes dark-side, we're in a lot of trouble."

"Not just us," said Jason. "Everyone who crosses his path. I seriously wonder if Gideon's team could take Will down."

"Maybe they could," said Mika. "The trick would be finding him. If Will didn't want to be found, they wouldn't be able to track him. He'd vanish like smoke in the wind. I'll put my skills up against almost anyone, but I don't think I could track Will if he didn't want to be tracked."

"Between his abilities in wolf-form and the skills he's picked up as a Ranger and cop," said Jason, "he'd be one difficult man to find. Even harder to stop."

"Let's just be glad he's on our side," said Cassie. "I think we could stop him, but it would take us all to get it done."

"And we'd lose half the group," said Mika. "Maybe more."

"I think the only one of us that could go toe to toe with him would be Cody," said Jason. "And even then, it might be a tough fight."

"Honestly," said Cassie, "if Will goes over the edge, I think Cody would go with him. He wants to get Alex and Julia as bad as Will does."

"Will would never surrender to the darkness," said Cody, taking a seat near them. "He values helping people and saving lives as much as I do. Besides, he won't have to go into the darkness. He won't be hunting them alone. We just have to make sure he knows that."

"He's right," said Jason. "Will wouldn't want to hurt anyone but them. I don't think even the werewolf spirit could tempt him to hurt innocent people. It's not in his blood."

"Cody-AK," said Cody, sounding sad.

"What?" asked Cassie, putting her hand on his arm.

"That's what Gabrielle nicknamed me," said Cody. "I liked her. She was so awesome. That's such a badass nickname, but it only makes me sad now."

Cassie didn't know what to say. Cody looked like he could cry but held it together by sheer determination. He also looked deeply tired.

"Hey," said Cassie, "why don't we all go in and eat some of those tacos. After we eat, we can all get a few hours' sleep before we go back after those things."

"I could eat," said Cody.

"And you're right," said Cassie. "Cody-AK is a fantastic nickname."

"Thanks," said Cody, smiling. "I like it."

"Let's go, then," said Cassie, taking Cody by the hand and leading him towards the big camper.

Mika and Jason followed behind them, heading inside and joining the others. There was a table filled with large bowls of taco ingredients, with more than enough to fill them all. Soon, they were all seated around the camper eating in silence.

Mika ate two tacos and ducked into his bedroom. Emerging with his drum, he sat down beside Cassie. Robert went to his camper and returned with his drum. Without saying anything, they both began playing softly. Soon they began singing with the rhythm of the drums. One by one, they all joined in the singing. It was an uplifting song about peace and tranquility. It helped to soothe the wound that they all felt inside.

Once the song was complete, Jason performed a *Blessingway* for them all. The mood seemed lighter in the group. Their sorrow had been shared and in doing so, diminished. They all knew that neither Sarah nor Gabrielle would want them to be sad but to remember them with joy for all the things they shared. That was exactly what they intended to do.

"Let's all get some rest," said Mika. "We're going back out hunting once it's dark."

People began heading for their beds. Mika continued to sit and watch them all go without moving. Cassie stayed next to him, holding his hand until they were alone.

"What's on your mind?" she asked, softly.

"I keep thinking what if it had been us that had gone there instead of Will's group," said Mika. "I don't think I could lose you and keep my sanity."

"Yes, you could," she said, putting her hand on his face. "You can and you would. They all look to you for strength and leadership. Especially now, with everything that's going on."

"I can't lose you," he said, quietly. "I don't know what I'd do."

"Well, I hope we never have to find out," she said, "but just remember that works both ways. I don't want to lose you, either."

Mika just shrugged and smiled softly.

"Now, let's go get some rest," she said, taking him by the hand. "We've got a long night ahead of us."

It was well after dark when everyone got up and started getting ready for the hunt. They all dressed in clothing that they didn't mind shredding, since it was likely that they'd be changing into wolf-form when it came time to make the takedown.

When they headed outside, they found that the fire was already built up and burning brightly. They were surprised to see that Will and his Grandfather were seated next to the fire, already dressed and ready to go.

"I am glad that you all decided to join us," said Grandfather, smiling.

"Glad to see you're back," said Jason.

"We had the funeral earlier today," explained Grandfather. "Will was eager to get back here and hunt the creatures down."

"How are you feeling, Will?" asked Cassie.

Will stood up and walked over to her and Mika. There was a deep sadness in his eyes, but they saw strength there, too. Their fears seemed to be completely unfounded. Will was going to remain himself. There was no darkness in his eyes. Hugging them both, Will held them for a long moment before slowly releasing them.

"I would be lying if I said that I was fine," said Will. "I may never be fine, but I'm back in this fight."

"We were worried," said Cassie.

"That I might surrender to the darkness?" said Will. "For once, the Old Wolf and the Dire Wolf are in complete agreement. There is no temptation. They both want revenge. Besides, if I gave in to the darkness, it would go against everything that Sarah and Gabrielle stood for. I won't dishonor them by giving in."

"You know that Alex and Julia are probably hundreds of miles away by now, right?" asked Mika.

"I know," said Will. "They'll have to wait. We can't let the *Oolonga-Doglalla* escape. If they could all change shapes, it might be impossible to stop them."

"It would damned sure make finding them a lot harder," said Mika.

"And much stronger," said Grandfather.

"They have to be stopped first," said Will. "I'll find Alex and Julia afterward."

"We'll find them," said Cassie. "You won't have to do it alone."

"We'll see," said Will. "I feel like finding them is something I have to do alone."

"We can worry about that later," said Grandfather. "For now, let's concentrate on finding the *Oolonga-Doglalla*."

"So, how do we run this hunt?" asked Mika, glancing at Will.

"There are seventeen of us, now," said Will.

"Eighteen," corrected Grandfather. "I will be joining you tonight."

"No offense, Grandfather," said Will, "but if we have to change, you won't be able to keep up."

Grandfather started laughing. The smile that split his face seemed to ease the tired lines of age and they caught a glimpse of the fierce warrior that still lived within him.

"Listen to me, my grandchildren," said Grandfather. "There is something that I must tell you all. For so long, I have watched you all. You have struggled to learn the lessons that you had to learn as *Hotamétaneo'o*."

Will glanced around and saw that they had all gathered close to hear what Grandfather had to say. Even though he spoke softly, his voice carried a power that captivated them all.

"I was unable to do the things I wanted to do," said Grandfather. "Some of these lessons, you simply had to learn on your own."

"What do you mean, Grandfather?" asked Will, confused.

"When I told you that the *Hotamétaneo'o* were not all gone," said Grandfather, "I did not mean just you. There were others, long before any of you took up the cause. There were others, long before any of you were born."

"I thought the last of the *Hotamétaneo'o* died out long ago," said Will. "Before the knowledge was rediscovered."

"That is what you were meant to think," said Grandfather. "For the true power of the *Hotamétaneo'o* lies in how they gain their knowledge, not just in the knowledge itself. Lessons learned without struggle are knowledge that is easily taken for granted. Knowledge can easily be underestimated. Only when it is learned through adversity and triumph can it truly be appreciated. Only then, do you have the discipline to appreciate the power and not be overwhelmed by it."

"You've been able to change the entire time," said Jason, looking wide-eyed at his Grandfather. "Haven't you?"

"Yes," said Grandfather. "I learned long ago. However, there is more than what you realize. After seeing Cody's transformation, I thought you might begin to suspect."

"The wolf is only one form," said Will.

"Yes," said Grandfather. "As you master the ability, you can choose any shape in nature. Some are more difficult than others."

"How long does it take to master other forms?" asked Jason.

"It takes as long as it takes," said Grandfather. "Some of you may never learn to change to anything but your first form. Others may find it comes as naturally as breathing. It is different for each person. You must first embrace the spirit within you, not just the spirit of the wolf."

"When did you first learn to change?" asked Jason.

"I changed for the first time on the battlefield," said Grandfather. "I grew angry when my best friend fell to the enemy's guns."

"Was this in Korea?" asked Will, frowning. "At the Chosin Reservoir."

"No," said Grandfather. "It was during the Battle of the Greasy Grass against General Custer and his Seventh Cavalry. What the white men called the Battle of Little Bighorn."

"That's impossible," said Mika. "You'd be over a hundred and fifty years old."

"Something like that," said Grandfather. "I could only call the wolf spirit for many years until I met a great man who taught me to embrace the spirit within myself. To not see it as a single spirit within me, but an opening of the self to the spirit world."

"If you're that old," said Mika, "then how old is Gideon?"

"I am afraid that's not my story to tell," said Grandfather. "He told me in confidence, and I will not betray that."

"Who taught you?" asked Jason.

"That is a story for another time," said Grandfather. "I feel that this revelation is enough for one night. I will tell you all more when the time is right. For now, we must hunt. The spirits are calling, and we must answer them."

"At least tell me his name?" asked Jason. "This is going to drive me crazy. You can tell me the story later; I just want to know who taught you."

"His name was Wovoka," said Grandfather. "I accepted the spirits when I joined the Great Ghost Dance."

"Holy shit," whispered Mika, his voice full of awe. "I've got to hear that story."

"In time," said Grandfather.

They decided who would be going where. Jason would stay at the camp as a back-up and defend the campsite. Staying with him would be Jacob, Samuel, Rain Wind-Song, George Bluesky, and Maria. They would be armed and keeping vehicles ready to come to assist whoever needed them.

The rest would all go as one group but once a trail had been established, they would split into two groups. One would be led by Will and the other by Mika. It was likely that the Alpha had further split his pack to better their chances of someone getting away. They would be ready for just that event.

Will's group was Grandfather, the Mohawk Twins, Cody, and Kayli. Mika would take Cassie, Kilani, and her brother Isaac, along with Joe and Melissa. Both teams had expert trackers in them, to improve their chances of following the trail. The chances of fooling them all were very slim.

"We'll change here," said Will. "No sense waiting until later. We can move faster if we change and they already know we're following them. Speed is of the essence."

"I agree," said Mika. "We might as well go quickly."

Will grabbed a large black range bag and tossed in several handguns, tomahawks, knives, and extra magazines for the pistols.

"I can sling this over my shoulder when we run," said Will. "Then, if we have to change back for some reason, we won't be unarmed."

"I'll do the same," said Mika. "I'll carry a bag for my team. We might want to throw in some shorts and t-shirts, too. Then, if we do have to turn back, we're not naked."

"Good call," said Cody. "I get embarrassed easily."

"From what I've seen," said Maria, "you've got nothing to be embarrassed about."

That drew a round of chuckles from the group.

"Just a friendly reminder, folks," said Will. "The Alpha is going to be strong. The Beta was a hell of a fight and he wasn't tough enough to take the Alpha. Remember, if you run into the Alpha male and female, expect them to be much stronger than the rest of the pack."

"If we don't get them stopped," said Mika, "then we can expect every time we face the *Oolonga-Doglalla* from now on, they're going to be a lot stronger. If we don't stop them, they'll all be able to shift back to human form. That's going to make them damned hard to find."

Once the bags were prepped, they all started shifting forms. They were all surprised when Grandfather turned into a pure white wolf, nearly nine feet tall. It wasn't an albino form, just the coat was pure white. The nose and eyes stood out like points of darkness against the radiant coat.

Shouldering the bags, Mika and Will headed for the river. They would ford it here where it was relatively shallow and move through the forest. Glancing back at Jason, Will nodded at him once. Jason returned the nod grimly. Then, Will vanished into the darkness. His dark coat hiding him completely.

Grandfather's white coat stood out like a beacon in the moonlight, until he hit the trees. Then, somehow, he too vanished like smoke. In seconds, Jason could no longer hear them moving through the trees. He stared after them until the sounds of the crickets and other insects returned.

"Good luck," he whispered.

Turning back to the fire, he started chanting softly.

APEX PREDATOR: HUNTER'S MOON

Chapter Fourteen
Pathfinder

"If you talk to the animals they will talk with you and you will know each other. If you do not talk to them you will not know them and what you do not know, you will fear. What one fears, one destroys."
Chief Dan George, Tsleil-Waututh Nation

September 29th
9:45 PM

Will set a fast pace. There would be no need to attempt to track until they reached the abandoned lair. From there, it would be a matter of sorting out their trail. They had successfully removed two groups and their trails would have to be eliminated before they moved after the others. That would take time. The more time it took, the colder the trail grew.

With their enhanced senses, running through the trees required no effort. They could all see in the darkness as well as they could in the light. Especially with the bright light of the moon shining down on them. It was just past full, but still bright enough in the sky for them to read by.

They had been fortunate in the fact that it had rained in the last week. The ground was soft and took prints well. It hadn't rained since they encountered the *Oolonga-Doglalla*, but that meant the rain hadn't washed out any of the tracks. If there had been a hard rain, then the chances of finding the creatures would be reduced to almost nothing. They would have to rely on sightings and watching the police blotters for missing persons. If the creatures were careful, then they could go unreported for months.

They ran for almost an hour before Will stopped to get his bearings. They were on a ridge overlooking a campground. The place was mostly abandoned except for one old camper with a campfire going beside it. Will could see two figures talking in low tones. One was an older man with a red ball cap on. He was sipping from a large coffee mug.

The other person seemed to be holding out something as they spoke, most-likely some type of recording device. Although they were too far away to make out facial features, Will recognized the straw porkpie hat. It was the reporter that they'd seen at their campground on the day they arrived. He was still working on the story. Will wondered who the man was that he was interviewing. He didn't have time to dwell on it, though. They had bigger fish to fry. Besides that, if they were successful, they would be leaving this area by tomorrow. Let him keep digging for a story that left nothing behind.

With a curt nod at the others, Will slipped off into the trees. Seconds later, he was moving at high-speed through the trees. He'd gotten his bearings and adjusted his course, now he had to make up for the lost time. Part of his mind kept nagging him about the reporter. Something more was going on than he realized. Since when did reporters take creatures like this seriously? This reporter seemed to be tenacious like he knew it was more than just a story.

Will wasn't sure why the reporter intrigued him so much, but he just couldn't shake it. Maybe when this was all over, he'd find the reporter and strike up a conversation just to find out what he knows. But that was a thought for another time. He had work to do and couldn't waste time on such thoughts, despite how hard they were to shake.

Then it hit him. In the files that Blanchard had sent him on the local disappearances, he'd also sent all files about the incident that happened at Table Rock Lake. It had been a reporter named Noriega who had broken that story wide open and forced an investigation into the incident, along with an investigation into the sheriff's department. Although that investigation was still ongoing, it had to be the same reporter who had broken that story. Now, Will was more intrigued than ever.

Emerging from a thick patch of brush, Will found himself on the edge of the ravine where the creature's lair had been. He was standing right where he and Cody had fought the four *Oolonga-Doglalla* when Sarah and Gabrielle had been killed. Pain stabbed through him like a hot knife when he thought of that moment.

Slowly, he moved towards the mouth of the cave. He couldn't force himself to move any faster. The closer he got to the mouth of the cave, the heavier his feet felt and the tighter the pain in his chest became. His knees were growing weak when he felt a strong hand on his shoulder. He glanced to the side to see his Grandfather standing there. Another hand on his other shoulder was Mika. Grandfather just shook his head slowly.

"I'll go," said Mika. "You stay here."

Will felt tears stinging the corners of his eyes, burning hot on his cheeks. From somewhere deep in his chest, a mournful howl rose and he leaned back to release it. It was a long, sorrowful cry, full of deep sadness and loss. It was echoed by everyone there and the notes seemed to roll off into the night and reverberate around the deep ravines and hills.

Mika headed inside the cave with Cassie and the Mohawk twins behind him. No one was going anywhere alone. If they encountered anything at all, they were not going to be taken unprepared. Grandfather kept his hand on Will's shoulder and Cody stood beside him without saying anything. Cody was the only one in the group that Will had to look up to see his face.

"I'm sorry, Top," said Cody.

"For what?" asked Will.

"If I had fought harder," he said, "we might have made it inside the cave before they were shot."

"You do not know that," said Grandfather. "There are a great many factors at work. We all blame ourselves in different ways. The truth is that what has happened cannot be undone. We can only go forward and be certain that it never happens again."

Cody nodded, but Will continued to stare into the darkness of the cave. After a few moments, Mika and the others came out of the cave and headed back to the group.

"There's another exit," said Mika. "It looks like all of the tracks go that way. It leads off in that direction."

Mika was pointing over his left shoulder.

"You take your group through the cave," said Grandfather. "Will and the rest of us will follow the bluff around in that direction. We can meet on the other side."

"It would be faster if we all went through," said Will.

"Possibly," said Grandfather, "but if there is more than one exit, then they could have gone in more than one direction. If we do not locate any tracks, we will meet at the other exit."

"And if we do find tracks?" asked Cody.

"We will alert the others and decide who goes which direction," said Grandfather.

"Okay," said Mika. "Let's get moving."

Nodding at the group, Mika headed back into the cave. His group followed along with him while Will and the others started around the edge of the bluff. Will was grateful for the excuse not to go into the cave, but he doubted they would find another exit. It was a kind gesture from his Grandfather to allow him to save face. The truth was, Will didn't think he could force himself to go back inside. The pain was too much for him to bear.

Moving quickly through the underbrush, Will edged his way around the bluff. After about fifteen minutes, they came to an opening in the side of the bluff. It was big enough for them to go inside, but they would have to walk in a crouch. Fresh tracks were coming out but none going back in. From inside, they could hear the others making their way out of the darkness.

"We're here," said Will, letting Mika know they weren't walking into an ambush.

Will and the Mohawk twins began studying the ground outside the cave. There were three distinct sets of tracks. One set was wearing shoes, so they knew that had to be Alex and Julia. The other two sets were all massive paw prints. They seemed to pause briefly outside the cave, then headed in different directions, three each way. One set seemed to be quite a bit larger than the others. That had to be the Alpha.

"You take these tracks," Will said, gesturing to Mika. "I've got the Alpha."

"I put a cellphone in each of our bags," said Mika. "Call when you're done or if you need help."

"You too," said Will.

With that, both groups headed out following their quarry. Will could tell from the depth of the impressions that the creatures had been running. They were not attempting to hide their tracks. Instead, they were counting on covering as much territory as quickly as they could. Will figured that they would likely do that for hours before either doubling back on their trail or attempting to hide their tracks. Possibly both.

Will set a quick pace, moving just slow enough to avoid losing the trail. It was easy enough to follow with the bright moonlight and the fact that they weren't trying to hide them. He knew that they would have a real advantage when the sun came up. The *Oolonga-Doglalla* preferred to hide during the day. They would hide in a cave or an abandoned building. It wasn't the light. It was the fact that they avoided being seen whenever possible.

The thought occurred to Will that they might prefer to keep moving during the day to avoid being caught by the *Hotamétaneo'o*. If that was the case, then it was going to take everything they had to catch them. It was also far more likely that the creatures would be seen. Will wasn't certain if the general public being aware of the existence of these creatures was a good idea or not. Even with visual sightings, some people would never believe it.

Will was distracted enough that he missed a change in the tracks and had to be called back by Grandfather. It was just a short snarl, not a verbal call. Will heard it and immediately stopped to look back. He saw Grandfather kneeling beside the tracks, closely examining them. Will quickly returned to the group and crouched down beside Grandfather.

Once he got closer, he could see the change in the tracks. The two smaller sets had gone off to the right while the Alpha had gone to the left, alone.

"Why did they split?" asked Will.

"I'm not sure," said Grandfather. "Possibly to split us up, as well."

"I wouldn't put it past this Alpha to try and save his skin," said Cody. "He hasn't had any problem sending them out to fight without him leading the way."

"There's six of us," said Will. "Grandfather, you take three of the others with you and I'll take one with me. We'll finish them both."

"If you find and stop the Alpha," said Grandfather, "then you can follow our tracks and catch up with us."

"If you all find the others first," said Will, "head back to camp. I'll handle the Alpha."

"Who's going with you?" asked Grandfather.

"That would be me," said Cody.

"I think it's settled, then," said Grandfather, smiling. "Will, it seems Cody and you are inexorably linked."

"I'm with you until the end," said Cody. "Where you go, I go, Top."

"Fair enough," said Will. "Let's move."

Will handed Grandfather the duffel bag containing the weapons before heading off after the Alpha. Cody nodded at the others and turned to follow Will. They headed off down the trail at a quick pace. Will could see that the tracks were old enough that they still had a considerable distance to make up.

"How far behind are we, Top?" asked Cody.

"A day," said Will. "Maybe more."

"We need to make up some time," said Cody. "Got any ideas?"

"He can't run at this pace forever," said Will. "He'll have to stop, eventually."

"So will we," said Cody.

"Remember Ranger School?" asked Will, chuckling. "We had to go days without sleeping. We're going to push through with no rest. We'll catch him."

"Hooah," said Cody.

Three hours into the run, they slowed to take a break near a fresh spring that bubbled out of the side of a bluff. While they were both catching their breath and drinking, Will glanced to the side and found a nest. Tapping Cody on the shoulder, Will pointed at it.

He could smell the scent of the beast and found the bones of several small animals. They looked like rabbit bones. It had camped here long enough to hunt and rest. From the scent and tracks, Will estimated that he had been here until it got dark tonight. That meant they were much closer than they had thought.

"He camped here and hid during the day," said Will, moving towards the nest. "The sun will be up soon, so he'll be looking to go to ground."

"How close is he?" asked Cody.

"He's only a few hours ahead of us," said Will, chuckling. "His tracks show he isn't running. He thinks he's shaken us."

"He probably thought we'd go after a group instead of him," said Cody. "As I said before, he's willing to sacrifice the rest of the pack to save himself. Fucking coward."

"I think you're right," said Will. "He counted on us following a group over an individual. He's probably planning on starting a new pack once he can change into a human."

"If he's moving slower, we can catch him," said Cody.

"I'll bet we'll overtake him by dawn," said Will. "If we hurry."

"I'm right behind you, Top," said Cody.

"Rangers Lead the Way," said Will.

"Fucking Hooah," said Cody.

Turning, they rushed off into the night following the trail. The fatigue they had been feeling melted away in anticipation of catching the Alpha. Will kept his pace slow enough to let Cody keep up. Being the wolf, he was faster. However, pound for pound, he knew he was no match for the raw strength of the big bear.

Two hours later, Will motioned for them to come to a stop. Pausing beside a small stream in the woods, they both took the chance to get a drink before speaking. Will, drank deeply then sat back and just listened to the sounds around them. After a moment, Cody sat back and joined him.

"We're close," said Will, softly.

"Do you think he knows we're behind him?" asked Cody, keeping his voice low.

"From the tracks," said Will, nodding, "he's not far away. I don't think we were close enough for him to hear us coming, but we're going to have to be quiet from here on out."

Cody just nodded and looked around the area.

"If he hears us coming," whispered Will, "it'll be another footrace. I want to catch him sleeping. It'll be daylight in about an hour. If we're careful, we should find him bedded down for the day."

"I hope the others are as lucky as we are," said Cody quietly.

"Me too," whispered Will.

CHAPTER FIFTEEN
BATTLEGROUND

"Upon this earth, on which we live, Unseen has power.
This power is mine, for locating the enemy.
I search for that enemy, which only
Unseen the Great can show to me."
Lozen - Chihenne Chiricahua Apache

September 30th
5:45 AM

Mika knelt at the edge of the river. The tracks had brought them right to the water's edge. The three creature's that they'd been tracking had been moving slowly and it didn't take them long to catch up. They would have already caught them had it not been for them going into the water. That was going to make tracking them much more difficult.

"Which way?" asked Cassie, keeping her voice down.

"If they didn't go straight across," said Mika, frowning, "then tracking them is going to be tough. We'll have to send out people in both directions on both sides of the river."

"That's not good," said Cassie. "There's only six of us."

"I'm not excited about that, either," said Mika, "but if we don't, we'll never find their tracks. There's no way to know where they left the water."

"Mika," whispered Joe. "I think I found something."

Mika nodded at Cassie and they headed back into the trees where Joe was crouched down.

"What've you got, man?" asked Mika.

"Look at these impressions in the grass and dirt," said Joe, pointing.

"Those aren't footprints," said Cassie. "What is that?"

"There was a tree laying here," said Mika. "Probably a fallen log."

"Yep," said Joe. "Looks like they pulled it out of the dirt and took it to the water. It's not laying around here anywhere."

"They're floating downriver," said Mika, smiling. "That's fucking brilliant. We would've missed that impression if you hadn't spotted it. Nice job, Joe."

"I just happened to glance over while we were catching our breath," said Joe, shrugging.

"What do you think the odds are that they tossed the log in the water to throw us off?" asked Isaac.

"I'd say the odds are low," said Joe. "For one thing, it's off the trail and I just happened to see it. Also, they took care to avoid leaving tracks leading to and from where they took the log. They weren't counting on me spotting the impression. Hell, I almost didn't."

"If you hadn't seen it," said Mika, "we would've split up and chased our tails. Meanwhile, they'd be floating downriver quickly without really exerting any energy."

"The water's cold," said Cassie. "How long do you think they could stand it?"

"The cold doesn't bother us," replied Mika. "I don't see why it would bother them, either."

"I was afraid of that," said Cassie.

"How deep's the water?" asked Isaac, nodding at the river.

"Right here," said Mika, "from the looks of the current, I'd say pretty deep. Deep enough to float a log."

"How deep does this river stay?" asked Joe.

"I have no idea," said Mika. "If Will was here, he might know. He's from this area. I'm from Standing Rock."

"If I remember what the map said," said Cassie, "this is either the Current or the Jack's Fork River. I'm not sure which. From what I remember, they're both pretty deep. People canoe both rivers all summer."

"Then I'd say it's a safe bet that they could float for a long way," said Mika.

"What's the plan, boss?" asked Joe.

"Who here's a good swimmer?" asked Mika.

"What do you have in mind?" asked Isaac.

"I'm a strong swimmer," said Melissa.

"Me too," added Kilani.

"Alright," said Mika. "I can swim, but I ain't exactly good at it. You two cross the river right here and see if you can find tracks. Check about a hundred yards in both directions. If you don't find any tracks, let me know and we go downriver."

"I'm guessing it's time-critical," said Kilani.

"Faster would be better," said Mika, nodding.

"Alright," said Kilani. "Ready, Melissa?"

"As I ever will be," she replied.

The two she-wolves headed out into the water. Both shuddered as the water reached their thighs.

"Burr," said Kilani. "This water's chilly."

Melissa just shrugged and dove into the water. Kilani smiled and went in after her. They both disappeared beneath the surface for a few seconds before surfacing, then started swimming hard for the opposite bank. The current was strong and swept them downstream about thirty yards before they swam far enough to stand on the other side.

As they walked out onto the shore, they both turned and waved. Neither wanted to risk calling out just in case their quarry was still close enough to hear them. As soon as they got out of the water, they began surveying the ground for tracks. Kilani went upriver while Melissa went downriver.

"Now we wait," whispered Mika.

"What if we hear fighting?" asked Joe.

"Then I guess we're all gonna get wet," replied Mika with a grin.

Mika sat crouched on his haunches for almost fifteen minutes before he saw Kilani return to the spot directly across the river from them. A couple of minutes later, Melissa joined her. After conferring, Melissa gave them hand signs indicating that neither of them had found anything. Mika motioned for them to stay where they were at.

"Want me to knock down a couple of trees?" asked Joe.

"No," said Mika. "I want you to go over there and join them. We're going to go downriver with three of us on each side. If any of us find signs where they emerged, we'll signal the others."

"And three on each side keeps us strong enough to fight them until the others arrive," said Cassie, smiling.

"Something like that," said Mika, winking at her.

"Watch for tracks and for where they might have beached the log," said Isaac. "I'd have just let it keep floating downriver, but who knows what they might have done."

"Especially since they probably don't think we know what they did," said Cassie.

"Exactly," said Mika. "Go on over there, Joe. I want to get moving. We're not far behind them and they're going to be bedding down soon. The sun will be up in less than an hour."

Joe nodded and headed for the water. Glancing back at Mika he grinned.

"You know my people are desert dwellers, right?" he asked, shaking his head. "I hate the cold."

Mika chuckled softly as Joe waded out into the deeper water, then started swimming for the far side.

"He swims pretty damned good for a desert guy," said Cassie.

"Hey, aren't you from Alaska?" Mika asked Isaac, grinning.

"Sure am," said Isaac, "but I still hate cold water. We don't do much swimming in Alaska. Not by choice, anyway."

"Your sister seemed to do alright," said Cassie, chuckling.

"She's the weird one of the family," said Isaac. "She loves swimming on the like two days a year when the water was warm enough."

Joe stood up and started walking out of the water on the far side of the river. He turned around and gave them a hand gesture.

"Did he give me a thumbs-up or flip me off?" asked Mika.

"I think it was the second one, Chief," said Isaac.

Mika smiled broadly and waved at him. Joe walked up onto the shore and shook like a dog, sending water spraying from his fur. Kilani and Melissa both hit him in the arms for getting them wet again. That drew a round of soft chuckles from Mika, Isaac, and Cassie.

"Alright," said Mika, waving at the others, "let's get moving."

Mika took the lead and started following the shoreline, looking for any impressions in the soft earth at the water's edge. He didn't have to look up to know that Joe was mirroring his movements directly across the river from them. Mika kept his concentration on the ground and trusted Cassie and Isaac to watch their surroundings.

They followed the water's edge for over an hour. The sun was cresting over the horizon and the morning was promising to be a beautiful one. Mika was still tracking when a hand on his shoulder pulled him up short. He glanced back at Cassie to say something, but she had her finger against her lips indicating he needed to be quiet. She just slowly motioned for him to get down. Mika crouched behind a bush, glancing around nervously.

Across the river, the others had vanished into the trees. It had been them that had alerted Cassie in the first place. She was miming that something was going on. Joe had indicated to them that he saw movement and then vanished into the trees.

"Joe saw something up ahead," she whispered.

Mika peered through the bushes. The terrain was sloping upwards along their side of the river. There was a bluff just ahead and where there were rock bluffs, there were usually caves. Especially in Missouri.

Mika lowered himself down onto his stomach and began crawling slowly forward until he could see around the slight bend in the river. Peeking through the brush, he saw that just off the edge of the river, there was an opening in the face of the bluff. It was big enough to drive in a small car without touching the sides or the roof.

"Cave ahead," whispered Mika. "Looks deep. I also see a log pulled up on the bank by the entrance."

"I think we've got the right place," whispered Cassie.

Glancing back, Mika saw that Joe, Kilani, and Melissa had gone back about a hundred yards where they were sure they couldn't be seen from the cave, then swam across to join them. He waited until they were crouching down with them before he crawled back away from the bushes.

"I think this is the place, boys and girls," he whispered. "The log is pulled up on the shore right by the mouth of the cave."

"They were probably planning on using it again tonight," whispered Joe.

"They're lucky it hasn't been raining," said Mika, quietly. "If that river came up suddenly, then that cave would be flooded."

"What's the plan, boss?" asked Isaac.

"We have no idea how deep that cave is," said Mika, "or if there are any other exits."

"That's the problem around here," said Cassie, "there are caves everywhere and they tend to go back pretty far."

"I was afraid of that," said Mika. "We're just going to have to go in after them. Nothing else we can do. If we wait for them to come out, they could slip out another exit and be gone. If we go inside and the cave branches out, we might waste hours trying to find them."

"I wouldn't think they'd go very deep," said Joe. "They'd want to be able to see us coming in after them, but still be able to defend the entrance. Tactically, it makes no sense for them to go any farther inside than they have to."

"What if we lure them out?" asked Kilani.

"What do you have in mind?" asked Mika.

"How about Joe and I go back across the river," she said, smiling.

"Oh, God," said Joe. "More water."

"And we change back to human," said Kilani, watching Joe. "We can take some of the clothes that you have in the bag. We act like a couple of hikers and come out of the woods where they can see us."

"That might work," said Mika. "They've got to be hungry after running from us all night. I know they didn't show any signs of hunting along the trail."

"We'll go over there and make some noise," said Kilani. "Surely they'll come to see who's ringing the dinner bell."

"And when they come out to grab the snack," said Isaac, "we jump them before they know we're there. That might just work."

"It beats the hell out of going in claws and teeth flashing," said Melissa.

"Alright," said Mika. "Make it happen."

Kilani opened the bag and took out clothes for both. Then with a smile, she headed back down the river.

"Great, more water," said Joe, smiling and following her.

They stayed hidden in the bushes until they were sure that both Kilani and Joe had made it safely across the river. They vanished into the trees and Mika crawled back to the spot where he could see the cave. The others stayed hidden behind him.

After a few minutes, Joe and Kilani emerged from the trees and walked down to the edge of the water. Kilani knelt and acted like she was checking the water temperature. Joe stood watching her but subtly kept an eye on the mouth of the cave.

"They're not making enough noise," whispered Mika. "If they're sleeping, then they're not going to notice you."

Joe seemed to anticipate that thought and started throwing rocks into the water while Kilani giggled and talked loudly.

"Good one," she said. "Throw another one."

Joe side-armed a flat rock and it skipped across the river and clacked into the rocks on the far side. Mika smiled and kept an eye on the darkness of the cave.

"Keep it going, guys," he whispered.

After a few minutes, Mika noticed movement in the darkness of the cave. They had caught something's attention. Joe must have noticed too because he stopped throwing rocks and crouched down next to Kilani. She glanced at the cave, then grabbed Joe and started kissing him, pulling him to the ground beside her. Soon, they were making out like a couple of teenagers, paying no attention to the cave entrance.

With their attention focused elsewhere, the creatures stepped out into the light. Cautiously, they checked both directions on the river, looking for any sign of movement. Finding nothing, the three of them crept out into the sunlight. Mika could see that they were holding their hands up to shield their eyes from the sun.

"Wait for it," he whispered.

Kilani and Joe continued to make out while the creatures crept closer to the edge of the water.

"I hope they hurry up," whispered Isaac. "I don't want to watch my sister getting laid."

"Get ready," whispered Mika. "They're about to hit the water."

"We are planning on catching them in the water?" asked Melissa.

"Makes it damned hard to run from us," said Mika, grinning.

No sooner than the creatures started swimming across the river, Mika gave the signal and they all rushed out from behind the bushes and ran down the shore. The creatures saw the trap a few seconds too late to do anything but swim for the opposite bank. When Joe and Kilani stood up and started changing back to wolf-form, the panic set in. The creatures weren't sure what to do.

Mika leaped high into the air and landed almost on top of the creatures, hitting the water with a massive splash. Mika hit the bottom and realized the river was only about five feet deep. Standing up, he grabbed the nearest creature and the fight began. Mika struck swiftly by slamming his fist into the nose of the nearest beast.

Repeating his movements, Isaac and Cassie jumped and landed among the fray. Mellissa sprinted downriver a short distance before entering the water, to cut off any of the creatures that tried to use the current to escape. She had to duck to the side when a massive boulder hit the water just to her left. It had come from the top of the cliff. Glancing up, she barely caught a glimpse of a dark figure ducking back into the trees.

"There's another one on top of the bluff," shouted Melissa, heading out of the water.

When Joe saw how shallow the water was at that point, he leaped almost halfway across and headed for the nearest creature. Kilani was right behind him. They had no intention of missing the fight. Neither of them heard Melissa's alert and didn't react.

Mika dragged a brown colored male out of the water and drove his fist into the beast's face. Slashing violently, the creature tried to break Mika's grip, but he held fast. Before it could attack again, Cassie delivered a vicious blow to the beast's lower back. Grunting in pain, the beast took its eyes from Mika for a critical second. He heard Melissa's voice, but it didn't register what she had said.

Mika took the advantage and slammed his fist into the beast's stomach with enough force to knock the wind out of it in one big rush of air. Wheezing, it tried to catch its breath, but Cassie shoved its head below the surface. When it tried to breathe, all it pulled in was water.

As the beast forced its way to the surface, it tried to lash out at Mika, but Cassie gripped its arms and held them behind its back. Mika, taking advantage, dug his claws into the chest of the beast, and grabbed its heart. With one powerful pull, he ripped the still-beating heart from its chest and held it up in front of the creature. He saw the look of recognition in its eyes as the beast died knowing that it was looking at its own heart.

"Fuck yeah!" snapped Mika.

Glancing to his left, Mika saw Melissa running down the shoreline and start climbing the ridge. She was heading for the top of the bluff as rapidly as she could go.

"Where's she going?" asked Mika.

"I don't know," said Cassie, "but we'd better find out."

Isaac slammed into one of the female wolves and she grabbed his throat with both hands, digging her claws into his neck as she squeezed. Undeterred, Isaac drove his fist into her stomach, loosening her grip slightly. Using the momentum, he shoved his hands up between her arms and knocked her hands away from his throat. Blood flowed down his neck, matting his fur, but at least he could breathe.

Joe dove onto the remaining female but she stepped inside his reach and pushed him over her head. He hit the water and tumbled away in the current. Kilani landed just after him and was immediately grabbed by the she-wolf, who buried her teeth in her throat. Kilani knew that the beast had her clean and tried desperately to break the hold. The grip was too tight.

The she-wolf dug her claws into Kilani's shoulders in preparation to rip her throat out when Joe rose out of the water holding a rock the size of a basketball in each hand. Slamming them together on either side of the she-wolf's head with tremendous force, he felt the bones in her skull give way and crush inward.

The she-wolf released her grip on Kilani and stumbled. Joe brought the rocks together again, completely obliterating the she-wolf's head. The body fell into the water and started to drift away when Kilani grabbed it by the leg.

"We can't let them float away," she said. "We've got to burn them to make sure they don't come back."

As they were dragging the body to shore, they saw the body of another creature with its chest torn open and a heart lying beside it. They could see Mika and Cassie racing towards the trees at the edge of the bluff.

"Where do you think they're going?" asked Joe.

"No idea," said Kilani.

Behind them, they heard a splash and they turned to see Isaac still struggling with the other she-wolf. She was on his back with her legs wrapped around his waist, forcing his head under the water.

"Shit," said Joe, running back into the water.

Kilani raced after him. If they didn't get there quickly, Isaac might very well lose his fight. Joe reached them first and drove a fist into the she-wolf's face. This broke her grip on Isaac's neck and he raised out of the water, gasping for air. Kilani stepped onto Joe's back since he was bent at the waist and leaped high into the air. She came down with thunderous force, driving her fist into the she-wolf's face. The she-wolf came loose from Isaac and fell backward into the water. She was unconscious and started reverting to human form.

"Fuck me," said Isaac. "Thanks for the rescue."

"Let's get her to shore," said Kilani.

"Is she dead?" asked Joe.

"No," said Kilani. "She's just out cold."

"Then what do we do with her?" asked Isaac.

"We ask her where the others went," said Kilani.

"Then we kill her?" asked Isaac.

"Probably," said Joe. "By the way, you were convincing over there."

"Did you enjoy yourself?" she asked, smiling.

"I did," said Joe. "Any chance of trying that again when we're not being hunted by monsters."

"Ask me again when we get back to camp," she replied, grinning.

"I think I'm gonna be sick," said Isaac, shaking his head. "Get a room, you two."

"Maybe later," said Kilani, winking at Joe.

Above them, Melissa rushed out onto the top of the bluff. Glancing down, she could see Joe, Kilani, and Isaac dragging a naked human female to shore, but she didn't see Mika or Cassie.

"They're probably right behind me," she thought.

Going to the spot where she saw the black figure enter the trees, she caught a scent. It wasn't the scent of one of the *Oolonga-Doglalla.* This was something different. Something she'd never smelled of before. It was musky and the smell of a predator. Some primitive part of her brain warned her that it was dangerous.

"Whatever the hell you are," she said softly, "I've got your scent."

Heading into the trees, she pushed through some thick foliage and emerged in a small clearing. Before she could look around, powerful hands grabbed her by the throat and lifted her off the ground. Pulling her around like she didn't weigh anything, she found herself looking into the dark eyes of a monster. It was over ten feet tall and covered in thick black hair. It had the face of a nightmare, more beast than human.

The elongated snout looked like some sort of mandrill and human hybrid. It snarled at her, revealing canine teeth almost four inches long. Her feet were dangling at least two feet above the ground. Kicking frantically into the beast's chest, she tried to get away, but the blow only seemed to anger the beast.

The last thing she was aware of was the sound of her vertebrae cracking as the beast tore her head from her shoulders. Sinking its teeth into her face, it tore the front of the skull off and began crunching it as it chewed. Throwing the body with a powerful burst of strength, it flew back through the bushes and over the edge of the bluff.

Plummeting nearly seventy feet down, the body impacted with the rocks near the mouth of the cave. Kilani screamed and grabbed Joe as she realized what it was that had hit the rocks. Joe pulled her into his arms and held her. The ragged stump of the neck was still pumping blood from the severed arteries.

"What the fuck?!" said Isaac.

When Mika and Cassie emerged at the top of the bluff, they looked down and saw the body. They could tell from the markings on the fur that it was Melissa. She was slowly reverting to human as they watched. Her head was gone and there were no other wounds to the body other than those from the impact with the rocks.

Mika turned and was the first to catch the scent. Cassie moved up next to him and started to head into the trees. Mika put a hand on her chest and stopped her.

"We're not going in there," he said softly. "Get back down to the others."

"But we've got to go after whoever killed her," said Cassie, angrily.

"If we don't get out of here, right now," said Mika, his voice dangerously low, "we're going to join her."

"What could do that to her?" asked Cassie.

"I've seen them before," he replied. "They're called *Gugwe*, and we're not ready to face them. We've got to go, now!"

Reluctantly, Cassie turned and headed back down the bluff. Mika continued to watch the trees until she was heading down, then backed slowly to the path and began following her. He kept a wary eye on the spot where he had caught the scent. In the brush, he could hear a growling snort which was answered by several others.

By the time they had reached the bottom, the others were gathered and waiting for them. Mika was watching the top of the bluff and moving as fast as he could go without running. The look of fear in his eyes spoke volumes.

"What the fuck happened?" asked Isaac.

"We've got to get the fuck out of here," said Mika, still watching the top of the bluff.

"Why?" asked Kilani. "What about the bodies?"

"Throw them in the cave," said Mika. "We'll tell Gideon where to find them later. Right now, we've got to move."

"What's got you so spooked, Mika?" asked Joe.

"Have you ever heard of a *Gugwe*?" asked Mika.

"Yeah," said Joe. "They're nasty bastards. I've never actually seen one."

"Well, you'd better fucking hope we don't today," said Mika. "Those goddamned things move in packs of twenty or more and we don't stand a fucking chance against them. They're bigger than us, stronger than us, and damned near impossible to kill without massive weapons. Silver knives and tomahawks will just piss them off."

Isaac didn't waste any time. He started tossing bodies into the cave. Joe stepped in and helped. In short order, they were all hidden deep inside the cave.

"What do we do with her?" asked Joe, pointing at the unconscious she-wolf.

"We take her with us," said Mika. "She's either gonna give us the information we want or she's gonna wind up like the others."

"What if she wakes up and tries to run?" asked Kilani.

"Then take her out and we keep moving," said Mika. "I want to be far away from here when the sun goes down. If this is *Gugwe* territory, we're in big trouble if we're here after dark."

"Are they that bad?" asked Cassie.

"I hunted with a group a while back," said Mika. "We went after a group of *Gugwe* up in Minnesota. Nine of us went into the woods. Me and one other guy came out again, and I was carrying him. No trace of the others was ever found."

"But that was before you were *Hotamétaneo'o*, right?" asked Kilani.

"Yeah, but we were armed to the teeth," said Mika. "I shot one point-blank in the chest with a 12 gauge slug and the fucker kept coming. It ripped the gun out of my hand and knocked me flying. When I got up, they were ripping the rest of the hunters apart, eating their fucking heads like you'd eat a goddamned apple. I grabbed the only one I could get to and took off. I still don't know if I escaped or if they just let me go."

"It sounds like we need to come back here," said Isaac.

"Yeah," said Mika, "we do. But we're going to need all of the *Hotamétaneo'o* and maybe Gideon's team to get the job done. Until then, we run. Dump everything that's slowing us down and run. If the chick won't run, kill her and keep running. We don't slow down until we're ten miles from here, at least."

"I'll run," said the she-wolf. "And my name is Allison."

"You're one of them," said Cassie. "I don't give a damn what your name is."

"I joined them because the other option was death," said Allison. "Get me out of here and I'll tell you anything you want to know."

"Turn on us and I'll kill you myself," said Mika.

"I understand," she said.

"Alright," said Mika. "Shift back to your wolf-form and let's get moving. You stick to the center of the group. If she tries to fall behind, take her ass out. Isaac, you and Joe bring up the rear. I'll lead the way."

"I won't try to run," said Allison.

"You'd better hope not," said Mika. "Because those goddamned things will do worse than kill you. They'll fucking eat the face right off your skull while you're still screaming."

With that, Mika walked over and picked up the headless body of Melissa, then headed for the trees following the river back upstream. Allison shifted form and headed off with Cassie on her left and Kilani on her right. Isaac and Joe brought up the rear. Mika set a blistering pace, keeping one eye on the trees as he ran. In the distance, he could hear heavy feet keeping pace with them.

The hunters had just become the hunted.

APEX PREDATOR: HUNTER'S MOON

CHAPTER SIXTEEN
SECOND CHANCES

"Those who have one foot in the canoe, and one foot in the boat, are going to fall into the river."
Tuscarora

September 30th
6:00 AM

Grandfather motioned for the others to slow down. They were rapidly approaching a large clearing where a waterfall emptied into a wide pool. The pool fed a stream that ran off through the woods. The tracks were heading for the waterfall. From the look of it, there had to be a cave behind the falls, but there was no sign of them having come out again.

"Watch the falls," whispered Grandfather. "There is a cave behind them."

"They can't get out on the other side," whispered Kayli. "The rocks lead right up to the water."

"So, unless there's another exit," whispered Robert, "they're trapped."

"Precisely," replied Grandfather. "But a cornered animal is all the more dangerous."

"Still," said Kayli, "there's just two of them and four of us."

"It is dangerous to be overconfident," cautioned Grandfather. "Do not celebrate the victory until the battle is won."

"If we're right," said Richard, "then one of them is the Alpha female. She's not going to go down without a big fight."

"Would you?" asked Kayli.

"Fair point," said Robert.

"Watch the entrance," said Grandfather. "I will be right back."

They looked at him quizzically as he slipped into the trees and disappeared.

"Maybe he's gotta take a leak," said Robert.

"Or the other kind," suggested Richard.

"Idiots," whispered Kayli.

Robert and Richard looked at each other and shrugged.

"She's not entirely wrong," whispered Robert.

"Not in your case, anyway," whispered Richard.

After a few minutes, Grandfather emerged from the bushes. He'd reverted to human and gotten dressed. He handed the duffel bag to Robert. He was carrying a wooden flute in his left hand.

"You gonna charm 'em out of the cave?" asked Richard.

"Something like that," replied Grandfather, smiling softly. "I'm going to attempt something. If it fails, be prepared to come into the fight quickly. However, do not come out and attack unless they do so first. Wait for them to make the first move."

"We'll be ready," said Kayli.

Nodding at her, Grandfather stepped out into the clearing and took a seat on a large rock near the edge of the water. Adjusting his legs beneath him, he perched on top of the rock sat serenely near the pool of water, looking like he was preparing to meditate instead of trying to lure out one of the deadliest predators on the planet.

Taking a deep breath, he brought the flute to his lips and began playing softly at first, but it began to grow in power and volume as the song continued. It was a haunting tune that none of them had heard before. It was eerily beautiful and sad, at the same time. It seemed like a simple tune, but the emotions it brought forth were both deep and complex. Feelings of love and loss, happiness and deep sadness, light and darkness, hope, and hopelessness. As magnificent as it was melancholy.

After a few moments, they could see movement approaching the waterfall. The two female creatures emerged into the light, hesitant at first due to the brightness of it. Kayli and the Mohawk twins watched with dread as the creatures closed to within twenty yards of Grandfather.

The smaller of the two crouched like she was about to spring and something unexpected happened. The Alpha female backhanded the smaller creature, knocking her back into the mouth of the cave. Snarling over her shoulder, the Alpha roared her fury at the other female. Cowering, the smaller female approached the Alpha and kept her head down but made no more moves towards Grandfather.

The Alpha female cocked her head from side to side, listening to the music and studying him. She began sniffing the air and continued to have a confused look on her face. Then, her expression softened, and she sat directly in front of him, folding her legs beneath her just like he had.

She sat there for a long time, just listening to the song. Grandfather kept playing and the tune continued to evolve, growing more complex as he played. The visions that came into their minds now was of a father mourning the loss of a daughter. They were separated and forever kept apart. As the song reached its crescendo, the Alpha female wiped tears away from her eyes with the backs of her hands.

Once the song stopped, they all held their breath. Less than six feet separated the Alpha female and Grandfather. With one swipe, she could reach out and take his head off. Instead, she was staring into his eyes and the yellow of her eyes seemed to clear, showing a dark brown beneath.

"You still play beautifully, father," said the Alpha female, her voice thick with emotion.

The Mohawk twins looked wide-eyed at Kayli. No one dared to speak.

"I was hoping that you would remember that song," said Grandfather.

"I had no idea it was you that was hunting us," she said.

"Would it have made a difference?" asked Grandfather.

"Probably not, at least not at that time," she answered, her voice sounding weary. "After all this time, why now? Why try to reach out for me?"

"Honestly, I wasn't sure it was you, *Macha*," said Grandfather. "At least, I wasn't until I caught your scent last night."

"You took a big risk, playing that song," said *Macha*. "I could just as easily have killed you."

"I did not come alone," said Grandfather.

"Ahh," said *Macha*. "That would explain the three wolves hiding in the trees behind you."

'Yes," said Grandfather.

"Have you come to kill me?" asked *Macha*.

"We have to stop you," said Grandfather, flatly. "You must know that."

"It has been more than forty years since I've seen my face," said *Macha*. "Surely, you can't deny me that."

"I have to admit," said Grandfather, "I would certainly like to look into your eyes, one more time, my daughter."

"One *last* time?" asked *Macha*.

"Perhaps," said Grandfather.

"The change is complete," said *Macha*. "The rest of my pack can change at will."

"We know," said Grandfather. "Although very few of them remain, now. Perhaps none of the others were successful."

A thought seemed to occur to *Macha*.

"Where is Will?" she asked, glancing around. "Where is my son?"

"I did not have the heart to tell him," said Grandfather. "He believes that you and his father died in a car crash. It's the story we've told everyone since you were lost to us."

"Is he hunting with you?" she asked, her voice cracking.

"He is," admitted Grandfather.

"Where is he?!" she snarled. "I want to see my son!"

"He is tracking his father," said Grandfather, his voice quivering.

At first, *Macha* stiffened and seemed like she was about to attack, but then seemed to collapse into herself. Then, slowly, she began to revert to her human form. It seemed to take a long time as if her wolf form had forgotten how to change back. After several agonizing moments, a naked Native American woman sat in the dirt in the place where the massive Alpha female had been.

She was beautiful with streaks of grey just beginning to form in her raven-black hair. Her features were smooth and unblemished except for a scar on the right side of her face that had long-since healed. She was White Bear's daughter. When she looked at her father, they could see Will in her eyes.

Grandfather stood up and wrapped a blanket around her, covering her and pulling her head against his shoulder. They could hear her sobbing uncontrollably. The sound of pure anguish was painful for them all, except for one. The other she-wolf crouched to attack, sensing a moment of weakness to claim the Alpha position for herself.

Just as she leaped in for the kill, Robert and Richard exploded from the bushes, slamming into her, and driving her into the deep pool. The three of them vanished beneath the surface of the dark water and it began churning frantically as they battled in the depths.

Macha stiffened as the wolf-spirit tried to take hold of her again, but Grandfather held her and began chanting softly. After a tense moment, she relaxed and returned to sobbing against his shoulder.

"That song will not keep it at bay for much longer," she whispered. "I can't fight it. It's too strong. I should have listened to you and not taken the easy path."

"Shhh," whispered Grandfather. "Do not worry yourself about that, now. For the time we have, let us be father and daughter, once more."

"Promise me, father," said *Macha*.

"Promise you what?" he asked.

"You will not let me turn," she pleaded. "Don't let the wolf take me, again."

"As much as it pains me, my beautiful Aurora," said Grandfather. "I will not let it take you, again."

"Promise me that you won't let Will know," she pleaded, crying softly. "Don't tell him we fell to the darkness."

"He will not know," promised Grandfather. "Not by my lips."

"He's going to kill his father, isn't he?" she asked, crying.

"Yes," said Grandfather.

"He can never know that," she said. "I cannot bear the thought of the pain that would cause him."

"It would be great, but not as great as what he already carries," said Grandfather.

"Tell me," said *Macha*.

The Mohawk twins emerged from the water. They were both bleeding from numerous cuts and bites, but they were alone. There was no sign of the she-wolf.

"Will took two mates in his pack," said Grandfather. "Their names were Sarah *Makawee* and Gabrielle Cameron. They were both murdered by the woman your pack took captive. The first one, the blonde. Her name is Alex. She shot them both."

"I wish we had killed her when we had the chance," said *Macha*. "I knew she could not be trusted. She reeked of deception and lust."

"No one saw it coming," said Grandfather. "Will was devastated."

"He must never know he likely killed his father," said *Macha*.

"He will not," said Grandfather, looking around and meeting the gaze of the Mohawk twins and Kayli.

They all nodded grimly. They would keep this secret for him.

"Thank you, father," said *Macha*. "Our time is running out. I can feel the wolf coming back for me. It is growing stronger as we speak."

"Sing with me, daughter," said Grandfather.

Together, they began singing the Lakota death song. Tears were running down both of their faces as their voices reached a crescendo. The song was rising into the air and both lifted their faces to the sky. Then, *Macha* leaned over and looked into the water, seeing her reflection for the first time since the darkness had taken her.

"I was once beautiful," she said.

"You still are," said Grandfather, his voice cracking.

Macha closed her eyes and began singing the death song again. Grandfather held her tightly and slipped the tip of his knife between her ribs and into her heart as gently as he could. She stiffened in pain but kept singing until the words faded away with her dying breath.

"Rest easy, my beautiful *Macha*," whispered Grandfather, tears streaming down his face and dripping from his chin.

The fading words of the Lakota death song echoed off into the stillness of the morning light. As her voice faded to nothing, Grandfather began singing where she left off. Soon he was joined by the Mohawk twins and Kayli, adding their voices to his own.

All of them wept.

APEX PREDATOR: HUNTER'S MOON

CHAPTER SEVENTEEN
ALPHAS

"Anyone who has ever heard it when the land was covered with a blanket of snow and elusively lighted by shimmering moonlight, will never forget the strange, trembling wolf cry."
Unknown

September 30th
8:00 AM

Will and Cody emerged from the deeper woods to a section that was growing rockier and steadily sloping upwards. Above them, Will could see more than one jagged overhang where the Alpha could have taken shelter to avoid the daylight. The sun was fully up over the horizon, but the air still had a chill to it. That would soon be chased away by the warming sunlight, but that was still a couple of hours away.

The scent was stronger here, so they knew the Alpha had to be close. Will looked around and tried to decide which place he would have chosen. Which one was the most defensible while providing the most shelter and best escape routes, if needed? The choice was easy for him to make. Only one provided a good vantage point from which you could watch every angle of approach.

"Hold here for a minute," Will whispered.

Cody stopped but didn't say anything.

"Let's figure out where he's at before we move any closer," Will said, keeping his voice low. "If not, he'll bolt, and we'll be chasing him all over again."

"He's a coward," said Cody, softly. "The way he let the others do all the fighting, then split off from the females to save his skin. I know he's just a beast, but he has no honor."

"I think he's in that one," whispered Will, pointing at the small cave.

"How can you be sure?" whispered Cody.

"Because that's the one I would have chosen," whispered Will. "Tactically, it makes the most sense."

"Yeah," said Cody. "It has a great field of fire."

"Let's hope he doesn't have a machinegun up there," said Will, smiling. "If he does, we might be in a lot of trouble."

"Copy that, Top," said Cody, chuckling softly.

"We're going to have to be careful how we approach," whispered Will. "He'll see us if we don't approach it just right."

"From the look of it," whispered Cody, "that can't go back more than a few feet. No more than ten, at the most."

"I agree," said Will. "That means there's only one way in or out."

"Then his only way out is through us," said Cody.

"Not if he climbs up over the ridge," said Will.

"Or maybe," rumbled a deep voice behind them, "he's standing behind you."

Will and Cody whirled around to see the Alpha emerge from a thick briar patch. As the Alpha parted the bushes, they could see a hidden grotto with a trickling spring coming from inside. He was a massive wolf with a dark grey coat leading to a lighter grey on his chest and stomach. Standing well over ten feet tall, he rippled with muscle and had numerous scars from past battles.

"So, you think I'm a coward?" rumbled the big Alpha.

"Aren't you?" snarled Cody. "All of the real fighting was done by your Beta and you ran off and left the others when we were getting close."

"Hmm," rumbled the Alpha. "The Beta, as you call him, is my son. His name is *Utsidihi*, and he is old enough to start his own pack. I let him lead to test him in battle. I take it, from your tone, he is dead."

"He is," said Will, tensing for the coming fight.

"That is…" said the Alpha, "unfortunate. It would have been nice to see his real face, his human face, for once."

"You have names?" asked Cody, shocked.

"Of course, we do," snarled the Alpha. "Just because we couldn't shift forms doesn't mean we weren't once like you. I...I was once like you."

"You were *Hotamétaneo'o*?" asked Cody, incredulously.

"Once," said the Alpha. "Long ago."

"What happened?" asked Will, moving slowly to the side to be ready to flank him.

"I chose poorly," said the Alpha, curling its lip into a snarl. "I chose the path of Wolf. I thought I was stronger. No one is stronger than Wolf."

"*Anunkasan*," said Will. "I chose *Anunkasan*."

A deep growl was the only reply from the Alpha.

"Then why did you abandon the females?" asked Cody.

"I intended to draw off pursuit," rumbled the Alpha, "to give them more time to escape. We had no idea how many of you there were, so I gambled you would go after me instead of them. I see it worked."

"Sort of," said Cody. "We came after you. The rest went after them."

The Alpha growled low in his chest, a deep and resonating sound that seemed to vibrate the air around them. Then, he threw back his head and howled. It echoed into the distance, rebounding off the hills and through the valleys around them. Will fought the urge to join him but Cody felt no such urge. Bears don't howl at the moon.

Moments later, there was a reply. Only it wasn't from any wolf. It was a snarling roar that was taken up by several others. When it sounded again, it was closer. Whatever it was, they were coming closer and covering the territory quickly.

"What have you done?" asked Will, glancing in the direction of the roars.

"I had hoped to trap your entire pack," said the Alpha, his voice rumbling with mocking laughter. "You think I'm a coward? I brought you here to die with me so that the others could escape! I might not get your entire pack, but I will take the Alpha with me."

Cody snarled and took a step towards the Alpha.

"You better save your strength, boy!" snarled the Alpha. "Because what's coming for you is more than any of us can handle."

Cody began looking around nervously. Will could feel it, too. Something dangerous was coming and from the sounds that they were now hearing, there were enough of them to cover every possible path of escape.

"What did you do!?" snarled Will.

"I drew you deep into *Gugwe* territory," said the Alpha, laughing. "They're going to kill you both."

"You'll die with us," said Will, looking around the area.

"Oh, I would have died, either way," said the Alpha. "Maybe I could have taken the two of you, but the rest of your pack would have followed me to hell and back. At least, this way, I get the satisfaction of watching the two of you torn apart by the *Gugwe*."

"What do we do, Top?" asked Cody.

"We're surrounded," said Will. "We find a spot that's defensible and we hold as long as we can."

"It's been an honor, Greyeagle," said Cody, nodding grimly.

"What did you just call him?" demanded the Alpha.

"Greyeagle," said Will. "My name is William Greyeagle."

The Alpha staggered back several steps as if it had just been slapped in the face. The look of shock on its face was very human-like.

"You're lying," snarled the Alpha. "Tell me you're lying!"

"I am not," said Will. "I am William Greyeagle, born *Oglala Lakota* and *Aniwaya Cherokee*."

Something struggled for dominance in the eyes of the Alpha. The deep evil of the yellow of the Wolf fought for supremacy with the dark brown of the human. A human part that had been buried by the Wolf until reawakened by the curse of the werewolf. For the first time since the Wolf had claimed the Alpha, his humanity was fighting for control. The unexpected side effect of the werewolf bite was bringing back some measure of humanity to the beasts.

Then there was a change in the Alpha's eyes. The yellow was fought back, and the human portion took control, but they could see that it was taking everything he had to hold on. It was only a matter of time until the Wolf once again reigned supreme.

"I have not heard the name William Greyeagle in many long years," whispered a softer voice now coming from the Alpha.

There was weariness there and deep sadness, as well.

"How do you know my name?" asked Will.

"My name is…" stammered the Alpha, "*was…* William *Enoli.* Black Fox."

It was Will's turn to stagger back like he'd been struck in the face.

"That's impossible," Will said, his voice breaking. "You died!"

"Jay *Matoskah* told you we were dead," said Black Fox. "That was probably for the best. I never wanted you to know that we had lost the battle with the wolf. Your mother and I were both *Hotamétaneo'o*. We chose the wrong path and were consumed by the Wolf spirit."

"How is it you can even speak?" asked Will. "The *Oolonga-Doglalla* we've faced before could barely talk."

"We couldn't," admitted Black Fox. "At least, until we took on the werewolf curse. The blending of the two brought us closer to humanity than we'd been since Wolf took over."

"So, what are you now?" asked Will.

"If the change is complete," said Black Fox, "we are Skinwalkers, at best. I'm not sure if that's better or worse than being *Oolonga-Doglalla*."

"It's much better," said Will. "Now you can choose to fight the wolf! You can be free of the curse!"

"No," said Black Fox. "There is no coming back from this. The Wolf spirit is too strong. Even now, I fight to hold him back. I cannot hold him for long."

"There has to be a way!" said Will. "We can find a way to save you and my mother."

"She is being hunted by the other group," said Black Fox. "Undoubtedly, they will not draw your mother out as you have done with me."

"Grandfather is leading the group chasing her," said Will.

"Even if he discovers who she is," said Black Fox, "there is nothing even he can do for her. Only death can break this curse."

"Hang on," said Cody. "Your son *Utsidihi*. Wouldn't that make him Will's brother?"

Will nodded grimly.

"Yes," admitted Black Fox. "However, he was born in the curse. There was no changing back for him. Even the werewolf curse only allowed him to change into a human. There was little or no humanity in him. He was a wolf, in mind and soul."

Around them, they heard limbs breaking as several large creatures were getting closer.

"The *Gugwe*," said Will, glancing around.

"You have to run," said Black Fox. "They will kill you."

"I won't leave you," said Will.

"My son," said Black Fox, "please let me do this one thing for you. While the Wolf is held back, I can be your father for a moment. As I should have been all along. Let me save you from the *Gugwe*."

"Where do we go?" asked Will. "There's nowhere to run. We've got to fight together if we're going to survive."

Black Fox looked around and sniffed the air.

"Luck is smiling on us," he said. "This is not the entire clan. I smell only eight of their warriors. The rest must be on a hunt."

"Then we fight," said Will.

"Back away from the trees," said Black Fox. "Get into the clearing. In the trees, they have the advantage. Bring them out to us."

"Backs to each other," said Will.

The three of them formed a small circle, far away from the trees. They could hear the heavy breathing of the beasts as they pressed closer. Will could smell the rancid scent of the creatures lingering on the breeze. Although this was the first time he'd ever encountered a *Gugwe*, he knew that if he survived, he would never forget that smell. It was the unmistakable stench of death.

"What are these things?" asked Cody.

"A nasty type of Bigfoot," said Black Fox. "The word *Gugwe* is from the Mi'kmaq tribe. It means face eater."

"Wonderful," said Cody.

When the first creature emerged from the trees, even Cody was shocked. The beast stood nearly eleven feet tall and was rippling with muscle. The face looked like a nightmarish cross between a baboon and a human, with massive canine teeth and muscles along the jaw that made it look like it could chew bone with ease. Gigantic hands ended with clawed fingertips. There was intelligence in those hellish eyes, but it was a feral intelligence. Devoid of concepts like compassion or humanity.

It bellowed a challenge, trying to draw them closer to the trees. When no one moved towards it, the beast snarled again and began slapping those enormous hands against the thick muscle of its chest. Then it began slamming its fists into the ground while snarling at the three of them, jumping up and down and adding force to the blows.

"Don't break the circle," said Black Fox. "If you go after it, the rest will drag you into the trees. It's a trap."

Cody roared back at the beast, letting all the fury that the great bear had within him loose at the snarling monstrosity. The *Gugwe* cocked its head to the side, clearing surprised by the roar.

"I think it was expecting another wolf," said Will. "It's not sure what to make of you."

"Then we're even," said Cody.

"When they attack," said Black Fox, "they'll hit fast to test us, then fall back if we don't fall immediately. Try not to get dragged away from the circle. If you do, there's nothing we can do for you."

"We stand together, or we fall together," said Will. "No one's getting dragged away."

The first creature seemed to look puzzled and sat back on its haunches, seemingly studying them. Just as it seemed to settle in, four of the others exploded from the trees and charged directly at them, snarling and leaping through the air.

"Here they come!" shouted Black Fox.

As the creatures came rushing in, Cody snatched up a rock about the size of a basketball and threw it crashing into one of the creature's face. The force of the impact threw the creature over backward and seemed to crush part of its skull. The beast hit the ground, screeching in pain and flailing its arms and legs.

The other three landed and Will drove his fist into the throat of the nearest one. He felt the soft tissues give way and he knew that he had crushed the trachea. Black Fox leaned to the side and kicked the one closest to him in the stomach. It let out a great whoosh of air but grabbed hold of his leg and tried to drag him away from the circle.

The fourth creature landed and tried to slash at Will, but Cody picked it up in a bone-crushing bear hug. Lifting the creature into the air, they could all hear the bones creaking as Cody continued to crush the beast with incredible force. The beast opened its mouth to try to bite Cody, but he anticipated that move. Ducking his head lower, Cody sank his massive canine teeth into the beast's exposed throat.

Digging his claws into the beast's ribcage, Cody pressed it away from him and threw it back towards the trees. The soft tissue of the beast's throat remained firmly locked in Cody's teeth. It hit the ground with blood spurting into the air, arterial spray diminishing with each pump of the creature's heart.

Black Fox struggled against the creature that was trying to drag him into the trees but was unable to match the beast's raw strength. Snatching up a large rock, Will threw it at the beast and struck it in the shoulder. It hit with enough force to knock the beast onto its back, causing it to release its hold on Black Fox. Instantly, he hopped to his feet and got back into the circle.

"Thank you," he said, nodding to Will.

Will only nodded. He didn't want to distract himself with the conversation, despite the many things he was dying to say to his father. There were three of the creatures either dead or out of the fight. The *Gugwe* had underestimated them. That wasn't going to happen again.

Black Fox doubled over at the waist and snarled, holding on to the sides of his head. It was clear that he was in agony, fighting against something that none of them could see. Then it occurred to Will, he was likely fighting the spirit of the Wolf that he'd managed to push back. Will knew that once the beast had control, regaining it would be virtually impossible. At least, not for any length of time. Will had felt the same struggle when he'd been trying to resist Old Wolf. He had understood from the beginning that once the wolf won, there would be no coming back.

Sensing a moment of weakness, the remainder of the *Gugwe* rushed in to attack. Will was able to dodge the first assault, but the second creature slammed into him and bore him to the ground. Two of the beasts leaped on Cody and Will could hear his enraged roars as he tried to resist the sheer power of the two massive *Gugwe*.

Just as the last creature was diving onto Black Fox, Will saw him look up at him. The evil yellow had returned to the eyes and there was a malevolence that wasn't there before. Black Fox was gone, and the Wolf was back in control.

As they hit the ground, Will rolled to the side to keep the beast from pinning him to the ground. He was able to force the beast off balance and rolled it away from him, getting quickly to his knees. Before the beast could regain its footing, Will dove on its back and wrapped his legs around the beast's waist and his arms around its throat. Applying an LVNR, Will began to exert all the pressure he could apply to choke the beast out.

Ducking beneath the creature's attack, the wolf that had been Black Fox slipped inside its grasp and sank teeth and claws into the fiend. The teeth locked into the beast's face as the claws sank deeply into the soft flesh of the throat. Not to be taken without a fight, the *Gugwe* tore deep into the flesh of the wolf's back, digging into both muscle and bone.

Blood flowed freely from the ragged wounds on the wolf's back, but it seemed to not feel it at all. With a savage twist and a push, the wolf ripped the throat and most of the face from the *Gugwe*. As the creature fell back, it was clear that the wounds were mortal. Most of the beast's face was gone and you could see the open sinus cavity and the frontal lobe of the brain, which was severely damaged.

Spitting out the flesh, the wolf looked around for its next target. Will wasn't sure if it was going to attack the *Gugwe* or them. There was only rage and hate in the wolf's eyes. It showed no sign of recognition when it looked at Will. If the *Gugwe* that Will had dodged hadn't attacked him, Will was certain that the wolf had been coming for him next.

The creature began going limp in Will's arms, slipping into unconsciousness. Not merely being content to knock it out, Will twisted and snapped the beast's neck. Dropping it to his side, Will started to get to his feet when the other wolf started towards him, snarling.

"I know you're in there, father," said Will, staring the wolf in the eyes.

The beast took another step towards Will, clearly intent on attacking him. Cody seized the moment to throw one of the two creatures that he'd been struggling with directly at the wolf. The other *Gugwe*, seeing how the fight was going, broke away and ran for the trees. As it ran, it began howling and shrieking loudly. They all knew it was calling for reinforcements.

Will got slowly to his feet, bleeding from numerous cuts and slashes. Cody helped him up but wasn't in any better shape. He had several deep wounds to his chest, shoulders, arms, and back that were bleeding profusely. Some of them were undoubtedly going to leave scars.

"Are you ok?" Will asked, glancing at Cody.

"Do I have a choice?" asked Cody. "That thing is going to be back with more of them. We can't hold off another attack. We were damned lucky to hold off this one. If they'd all come at us at once, we wouldn't have."

The beast that was fighting the wolf broke free and sprinted into the woods after the other one. The wolf got to his feet, still staring after the retreating *Gugwe*. It turned slowly to face Will and Cody. For a long moment, they all just stared at each other, each unsure what the other was going to do.

Then, in the distance, they heard more of the *Gugwe* coming. From the sound of it, there had to be a dozen or more. They were still quite some distance away, but they would cover it quickly. They knew that they only had a few minutes before they were going to be overwhelmed.

Cody took a staggering step and fell to his knees. Will grabbed him and kept him from falling on his face. It was clear that Cody was struggling to keep from passing out. Now that he was lower to the ground, Will could see that the damage he'd taken was more significant than he had originally thought. There were several bites taken out of his shoulders. They would heal, but not quickly enough to get him back into the fight before the *Gugwe* arrived.

"Are you ok?" asked Will, kneeling beside him.

"You gotta get out of here, Top," said Cody. "Run while you can. Those things will kill us all. We can't hold them all off."

"I won't leave you," said Will, resolutely.

"Then we'll all die together," said Cody. "Someone's got to bring the others here to finish off this clan. You go and I'll hold them as long as I can."

"No," said Black Fox. "I'll hold them. Get your friend out of here."

Will turned to see that Black Fox had regained control. The pain that was etched on his face made it clear that it was taking everything he had to do it.

"I won't leave you, father," said Will. "We can find a way to help you."

"There is no way," said Black Fox. "We both know it. I can't hold the wolf for much longer. At least let my death have some meaning. I do not wish to go on living as that monster. Let me die as I should have died. As a *Hotamétaneo'o*. As your father."

"We can't come back for your body," said Will.

"There will be nothing left to come back for," said Black Fox. "The *Gugwe* will devour it all."

They could hear the creatures were much closer. They would be on them in a matter of minutes. At the rate they were covering the distance, they all knew that the first of them would arrive very soon.

"I don't want to lose you, again," said Will, his voice cracking.

"My son," said Black Fox, "I'm grateful that I was allowed the chance to see you, again. Take your friend and run back the way you came. They will not follow you past the river. Go!"

Will hesitated and was going to argue when Cody pitched forward and passed out. He began reverting to human form, which allowed most of the wounds to close but not fully heal. He was going to need rest and time to recover. If they stayed, he would never regain consciousness.

"Go, my son," said Black Fox. "I will buy you the time you need to escape."

They locked eyes for a long moment before Will had to look away. He knew that if Cody was to survive, he had to get him out of there. He also knew that Black Fox was only barely keeping the wolf at bay. The only way he stood a chance was to release the wolf as soon as the *Gugwe* arrived. Buying them time to escape would be the last good thing he could do or could ever hope for. The wolf would not be overpowered again. It was a testament to Black Fox's strength that he was able to do it twice.

"Go!" snarled Black Fox.

His eyes were beginning to tinge yellow. Will knew that his hold was slipping. To make matters worse, he could hear trees breaking not fifty yards away. The *Gugwe* were almost on top of them.

Grabbing up Cody, Will tossed him over his shoulder and nodded grimly at his father, for the last time. Will could see tears in his father's eyes as he turned to face the first of the *Gugwe* as they emerged from the trees. With a snarl of challenge, Black Fox raced towards them with frightening speed.

The last glimpse Will got of him was as he dove into four of the *Gugwe*, taking them all down with the sheer ferocity of the attack. Will turned and sprinted off through the trees with Cody over his shoulder. He would have to run, non-stop, for hours. He knew that Black Fox's sacrifice would only buy him a few minutes and then the *Gugwe* would be hot on his trail.

Calling on both the Old Wolf and the Dire Wolf, Will asked for their strength to get them through this. He felt instantly stronger but knew it was not going to last. He had to make every second count.

Behind him, he heard the shrieks of victory as the *Gugwe* celebrated their kill. He knew that meant Black Fox was dead. He wanted to turn around and try to avenge his father's death, but he knew it would be in vain. He would only join him in death and consign Cody to it, as well.

Pushing the pain away, Will ran. He ran with every ounce of strength in his body. To slow down or stumble meant certain death. In the distance, he could hear branches breaking and the snarls of his pursuers.

The *Gugwe* were coming and they were gaining ground.

APEX PREDATOR: HUNTER'S MOON

CHAPTER EIGHTEEN
TRAIL'S END

"All who have died are equal."
Comanche

September 30th
6:45 PM

The sun was nearly set when Will staggered into the campground. He was exhausted and stumbling under the weight of Cody, who was still unconscious. Jason was the first to see him and called for the others to come help as soon as he saw him.

Mika reached him first and Will collapsed into his arms. He was already reverting to human form before he fell. His endurance had reached its end. All in all, he'd run over twenty miles to get away from the *Gugwe*. They hadn't stopped at the river. They had only stopped just a few miles back, heading back into the deep woods and their territory.

"I've got you, brother," said Mika, easing Will onto his back. There were bloody wounds all over his legs, arms, and torso. Some were lingering wounds from battle, the others from jagged rocks and trees that he crashed through staying ahead of the *Gugwe*.

"*Gugwe*," he wheezed, coughing.

"Yeah," said Mika. "We know. We ran from them, too."

Will was gasping for air, taking deep breaths and trying to slow his heart rate.

"Calm down, brother," said Mika. "We've got you. You're safe. We're all here, now. Did you get the Alpha?"

"He's dead," wheezed Will. "He sacrificed…himself…for us."

"What?" asked Mika. "How'd that happen?"

"The Alpha was…" gasped Will, "my… father."

"What?!" asked Mika.

"I'll explain later," said Grandfather, kneeling beside Will.

Cody was lifted by the Mohawk twins and taken towards one of the trailers. Jason went with them to begin tending to his wounds. Grandfather began checking over Will. Rain Wind-singer grabbed her kit and followed Jason. She was a veterinarian, but her skills were still especially useful. Humans were still animals, after all.

"Did you know?" asked Will.

"I did not," said Grandfather, "until yesterday. If I had known the Alpha was your father, I never would have let you go after him."

"Then the Alpha female," said Will, softly.

"Was my daughter and your mother," said Grandfather, his voice thick with emotion. "*Macha Ehawee.*"

"Is she…?" asked Will.

"Yes," said Grandfather. "But she did not suffer."

"When I am stronger," said Will. "I want to know everything."

"I promise," said Grandfather. "Rest now."

Will tried to say something else but fell into unconsciousness. His wounds were severe, and he'd lost a great deal of blood, but he'd made it back to them. There were pieces of wood and rock sticking out of his skin in several places and on his back were four massive claw marks with two claws still protruding from the wounds.

"I don't get it," said Mika.

"What do you not get?" asked Grandfather.

"I thought that his parents died in a car wreck," said Mika.

"That was the story we told everyone," said Grandfather. "It was far easier than explaining what happened."

"Why didn't you tell Will?" asked Mika.

"Because if he thought that his parents were out there," said Grandfather, "he never would have been able to stop looking. I knew that once they fell to the darkness, we could not bring them back."

"If he'd thought that they were one of the *Oolonga-Doglalla*," said Kayli, "he never would have been able to fight them without being afraid he was fighting them. He wouldn't have been effective."

"She's right," said Grandfather. "He might never have become one of the *Hotamétaneo'o*."

"I don't know," said Mika. "I kinda feel like lying to him was the wrong thing to do. He's not going to be happy about it."

Grandfather nodded but said nothing.

"Let's get him inside," said Mika. "We need to clean him up and get him to bed."

They carried Will into the trailer and began cleaning his wounds. Cody was already laying on the big fold-out couch. His wounds had been cleaned and bandaged. He was burning up with fever, but Jason and Rain were already working on him.

Grandfather and Mika cleaned up Will's wounds, carefully removing all the things stuck in his wounds. Then they wrapped them in clean bandages. Once that was done, Grandfather began to sing the healing songs while Mika covered him over. After he finished, Mika headed out of the room. The look of anger on his face was evident as he glanced back at Grandfather. Cassie caught up with him and looped her arm through his.

"Want to tell me what that was about?" asked Cassie.

"I'm just pissed off," said Mika.

"About what?" she asked.

"Let's grab a couple of beers, first," said Mika. "I want to go outside to talk. I need some air."

They went to the fridge and Mika took out two of the Boulevard Wheat beers that Will liked so much. Popping the tops off, he handed one to Cassie and headed for the door. Once they took a seat by the fire, Mika drained about half of his beer in one long pull.

"Wow," said Cassie. "You are pissed. Want to talk about it?"

"Apparently," said Mika, "Will's parents have been alive all this time and they've been lying to him about it."

"How's that possible?" asked Cassie.

"They were the Alpha male and female of this pack," said Mika. "They didn't die in a car crash. They became *Oolonga-Doglalla*. They used to be *Hotamétaneo'o*."

"Well," said Cassie, "that's not exactly something they could explain to a child. From what I was told, Will lost his parents when he was still small. Jay was only protecting him."

"Then why didn't he tell him once he was an adult?" asked Mika.

"I don't know," said Cassie. "But I'm sure he had his reasons. Will's only been a *Hotamétaneo'o* for what, a few months? Maybe he was working up to telling him. Or, maybe he didn't know they were still alive and didn't bring it up to avoid hurting Will for nothing."

Mika finished his beer in one more drink and set the empty on the ground.

"I don't know," said Mika. "I get it, but I don't. Does that make sense? I understand why they didn't tell him, but it still bothers me. Especially since Will went out to kill his father and didn't even know it."

"You might want to go easy on Grandfather," said Robert, kneeling beside Mika and handing him another beer.

"Why's that?" asked Mika.

"I was there when he found out," said Robert. "I promised not to say anything, but the cat's out of the bag now. He had to put his only daughter down. It was one of the most painful things I've ever had to watch, and she wasn't even my daughter."

"He killed his daughter?" asked Mika.

"He had to," said Robert. "She couldn't hold the wolf back any longer. She asked him to."

"Goddamn," said Mika. "That sucks. Fuck, I guess I hadn't thought about how that went down. Shit, I feel like an asshole, now."

"I'm sure he understands," said Cassie.

"Well, we know one thing, now," said Mika.

"What's that?" asked Cassie.

"When we were running from the *Gugwe*," said Mika. "When they stopped chasing us, I thought we'd just made it out of their territory. Turns out, they were going after Will."

"I hope we never run into those things again," said Cassie. "Those things were terrifying."

"I'd say that in this line of work," said Mika, "we'll run into them eventually. Besides, there's worse out there."

"There is?" asked Cassie, glancing around at the darkness.

"There always is," said Mika.

Grandfather emerged from the camper and headed for where Mika and the others sat.

"I'm sorry," said Mika, before he could say anything.

"You have nothing to apologize for," said Grandfather. "This entire situation was never something I imagined could happen. I was told that hunters from the Crow Reservation had wiped out the pack that I believed they were part of. I thought they had been killed shortly after they had turned. It was just far easier to let Will think they died in the accident instead of them falling into darkness."

"So, what do we do about the *Gugwe*?" asked Mika.

"I contacted Gideon," said Grandfather. "He told me that Team Uller and Team Odin were going to deal with them. He asked us to stay out of the area, so we aren't accidentally caught in the line of fire."

"Probably for the best," said Mika. "I don't think those soldiers would ask too many questions if a gigantic wolf showed up. Honestly, I'm surprised he didn't want us to handle it ourselves."

"Gideon said our team has been through enough, for now," said Grandfather. "Half of the team is hurt, and we lost three of our own fighting this pack."

"He's got a good point," said Mika. "We need to heal and rest."

"I'm going to bury my daughter with the other *Hotamétaneo'o*," said Grandfather, "if you don't have any objections."

"Not at all," said Mika. "She was *Hotamétaneo'o* before any of us were."

"Thank you," said Grandfather. "Now, if you all will excuse me, I'm going to get some rest. It's been a very long day and I'm not as young as I once was."

"When are you going to tell me the story of Wovoka?" asked Mika. "I want to hear about Greasy Grass, too."

"I will," said Grandfather, "but not tonight. I think we've all had enough excitement for one day. I need to rest."

"Get some sleep," said Mika.

It was just after sunrise when Will emerged from the camper. His wounds were healed, but he still had a haunted look in his eyes. Grandfather was sitting by the fire, brewing coffee. Jason was already preparing breakfast. Most of the others were already taking their seats, except for Cody, Mika, and Cassie.

"Good morning," said Will, sliding into a camp chair.

"How are you?" asked Jason.

"To be honest, I still feel like crap," said Will.

"You should have stayed in bed, Greyeagle," said Kayli. "You need your rest."

"I need food," said Will, trying to smile. "I think my stomach thinks I'm mad at it."

That drew a few chuckles.

"Besides," said Will, "I have too much work to do to lay in bed all day."

"What work do you need to do?" asked

"I heard we lost Melissa," said Will, frowning.

"Yeah," said Joe. "The *Gugwe* got her. They kept her head, but we got the rest of her back here."

"We have a funeral to prepare for," said Will.

"Your mother will be laid to rest with the others," said Grandfather.

Will glanced at him but said nothing.

"I brought her back with us," said Grandfather. "She's in the back of the big camper with Melissa."

"What about your father?" asked Jason, nodding at Will.

"He's gone," said Will. "The *Gugwe* took him. There's nothing left to bury."

"I would expect nothing less from the *Gugwe*," said Grandfather. "They are terrible adversaries."

"Did I hear that Mika had taken one of the she-wolves prisoner?" asked Will.

"Yes, he did," said Grandfather. "We turned her over to Gideon's team shortly after Mika made it back with her."

"Good," said Will. "I didn't want her anywhere near this camp. What happened to that Beale, guy?"

"Gideon didn't say," replied Grandfather. "I was given to understand that it wasn't very pleasant."

Will didn't say anything. Glancing over his shoulder at the sound of the camper door opening, Will noticed Cassie and Mika emerging and heading for the fire.

"Cody's fever finally broke," said Cassie, leaning over and hugging Will. "I'm glad you're up and around."

"Thank you," said Will, returning the hug. "I had to get up. Mika snores too loud."

Everyone chuckled and Mika only smiled.

"You think you have it bad," said Cassie, "he's right next to me."

Even Will smiled at that one. Mika slid into the chair beside Will and Cassie headed over to help Jason with breakfast. The Mohawk twins jumped up and went to help and soon they were all gathering around the big table to start filling their plates. Just as they were sitting down, Cody emerged from the camper. He looked pale and still had a thin sheen of sweat on his face, but he was better than anyone expected him to be.

"Mind if I join you?" asked Cody.

They made room at the table and several people made their way over to pat him on the back or hug him. Once they were all seated again, the food was served, and everyone began digging into the breakfast feast that Jason had prepared. Cody was awake and his appetite was back. Despite their losses, they all were happy to be together and enjoying the meal.

Once they had finished, everyone pitched in to help clear dishes, clean up the area, and put away supplies. Once that was completed, they all took their seats and leaned back to digest.

"We're going to be heading back to Grandfather's house," said Will. "We'll be breaking camp, shortly. We have to honor our fallen and prepare for what is to come."

"Like what?" asked Mika, glancing at Will.

"When I'm healed," said Will, "I'm going after Alex and Julia."

"We're all going after them," said Mika.

"No," said Will. "I have to do this alone."

"You do not," said Grandfather. "Sarah and Gabrielle were part of our family, as well."

"I'll track them alone," said Will. "Once I've located them, I'll call for help in taking them down."

"I don't like the thought of you going alone," said Cassie.

"He won't be," said Cody. "I'm going with him."

Will glanced at Cody.

"It's not up for debate, Top," said Cody. "You go, I go. That's how it works."

"I'll go, too," said Mika.

"No," said Will, shaking his head. "You're their leader. You've got to stay here."

Mika frowned but didn't argue.

"Just come back to us," said Cassie.

"I can't promise that," said Will. "All I know for sure right now is, I have to find Alex and Julia. After that, we'll see. I'm not sure I can be here for a while. Everything reminds me of Sarah and Gabrielle."

"I understand," said Mika. "But remember, we're all your family, too. We all want you to come back to us."

"Thank you," said Will.

"Let's get this camp broken down," said Mika. "We have to honor our fallen."

They all busied themselves breaking camp and getting all their gear put away. Will and Cody both pitched in as much as they could, but they were a long way from back to full strength. Everyone was glad to have them back, but they all felt that this might be the last they saw of Will and Cody for quite some time. The loss of Sarah and Gabrielle had changed Will. Just how much, they weren't sure. Honestly, neither was he.

APEX PREDATOR: HUNTER'S MOON

CHAPTER NINETEEN
FROSTBITE

"There is such a thing as anesthesia of pain, engendered by pain too exquisite to be borne."
Jack London

December 15th
6:00 PM
Flathead County, Montana
Approximately 1 mile south of the US/Canadian Border

The large black Ford F-450 XLT 4 wheel-drive with the cab-over camper pulled into the mostly empty parking lot of Lachland's Roadhouse and stopped just outside the front door. Lachland's had a sign out front that read "the Last Great American Burger before Canada." The building itself was a wooden structure that had faded to a grey color since most of the original paint was gone. There was a hand-painted sign above the door that read, "No guns, no tats, no service."

"You sure this is the place, Top?" asked Cody.

"Yeah," said Will, putting the truck in park. "My sources say they set up shop here and slip across the Canadian border to hunt. That way, it's not supposed to flag any law enforcement agencies in the US."

"Pretty smart," said Cody, "but they didn't consider that Gideon has contacts in Canada."

"So do I," said Will with a shrug. "I have a few cousins that live on the far side of the border but are still registered with the tribe."

"How do we play this?" asked Cody.

"We'll go inside and check the place out," said Will. "If everyone inside is a wolf, then we'll clear it out. If not, then we'll have to be a little more careful."

"Do you think that Alex and Julia will be here?" asked Cody.

"They were," said Will. "That was verified just a couple of days ago."

"Still," said Cody, "we almost had them in Memphis last month, but they managed to slip away."

"We killed six of their new pack there," said Will, "so, it's not a total loss."

Unzipping his coat, Will took out a pair of the Glock .50 GI pistols from Guncrafter Industries. Gideon had them customized for him to be fitted with suppressors. Extended magazines put the capacity out to ten rounds per pistol and holographic sights finished the modifications. Will had drilled with the pistols and could shoot the center out of the Ace of Spades at twenty yards while moving.

Cody, being far larger than Will, opted for something a bit bigger. He was carrying a pair of modified H&K UMP-45's that had been customized to shoot the .50 GI round. They were also fitted with suppressors and holographic sights. The main difference was Cody's could go fully automatic.

"Ready Top?" asked Cody.

"Yeah," said Will. "Keep the guns hidden until we verify what we're up against."

"And if they're all wolves?" Cody asked, cocking his head to the side.

"Try to keep at least one alive to question," said Will, "just in case Alex and Julia aren't there."

"I'll try," said Cody, smiling.

Zipping up their coats, they climbed out of the truck and stepped into almost two feet of snow. Will's moccasin boots were insulated and treated with mink oil to keep them dry, so he wasn't concerned. His jeans were tucked into the boots, anyway. Cody was wearing army jump boots with jeans over the tops of them. His pants were going to get wet, but he didn't care. The cold didn't bother either of them.

Opening the door to the Roadhouse, Will walked in first and scanned the room. There were eight people in the room. Will could tell from a single sniff of the air that they were all wolves. Four were acting like customers, one was a bartender with another one being the waitress. There was a cook at the grill and a guy that had to be the "bouncer" sitting at the end of the bar. He was nearly as big as Cody.

Will felt all their eyes on him and Cody as they walked inside and headed for the bar. Taking seats where they could keep an eye on the entire room at once, Will nodded at the bartender.

"Can we get a couple of beers?" asked Will, smiling and trying to act like a normal customer.

Will didn't recognize anyone in the room so he knew that they couldn't know who he was. However, it was likely that Alex and Julia had warned them about Native American people coming looking for them. The fact that they were close to several reservations made it impossible for them to know if the two newcomers were trouble or not. From the looks they were getting, Will had the distinct feeling that they were now on the menu.

"Sorry," said the bartender. "We're all out."

"Out of beer?" asked Will, shaking his head. "Some roadhouse. How about a couple of burgers, then?"

"Fresh out," said the bartender, frowning.

Will noticed one of the male customers got up from his table and headed for the door. Instead of leaving the roadhouse, he stopped and locked the door.

"I think you picked the wrong place to stop for a beer, *Tonto*," said the bartender.

"No, I'm pretty sure that I'm where I'm supposed to be," said Will, smiling. "Maybe you can help me with something."

"I think you don't understand the situation you're in," replied the bartender.

"I think I've got a pretty good idea," replied Will. "But, if you tell me where Alex and Julia are, I might be inclined to let some of you live."

They all started laughing as they started to shift into their wolf-forms. Their laughter abruptly stopped when Will and Cody both came to their feet, guns in hand. Before their transformations were complete, they opened fire. Will kneecapped the bartender with one well-placed bullet to each knee. Cody opened with automatic fire, taking three of the creatures apart in the first salvo. Their chests were blasted apart with the massive hollow point rounds.

While the bartender was still screaming, Will dropped to one knee and shot the wolf that was standing by the door. He put two rounds into the beast's forehead, killing it instantly. The cook came running out of the kitchen, snarling and leaping over the bar. Cody stitched him from the crotch to throat with a short burst from his left-hand weapon. He was dead before his body hit the ground.

The remaining two ran for the windows, looking to dive through to safety. Cody put an extended burst into the back of the waitress-wolf as she tried to get to the nearest window. The remaining one, the bouncer-wolf, leaped into the air as Will turned, putting a single hollow point through the beast's right ear, and blasting out the left. The beast's momentum carried it into the wall, narrowly missing the window.

As the mayhem came to an end, the only sound that could be heard was the groaning of the bartender. Will and Cody scanned the room slowly, turning in a full circle before stopping.

"Clear," said Will.

"Clear," echoed Cody.

"Go check the back," said Will. "I'll get us those beers."

"On it, Top," said Cody, heading for the back of the roadhouse.

Will strolled around the bar, putting the pistol in his left hand back into its holster. The pistol in his right hand remained trained on the bartender, who was still holding both knees but had not yet turned back into a human. He was glaring at Will with hatred in his eyes but said nothing.

Using just his left hand, Will picked up an empty mug and put it beneath the tap. Pulling the tap, he began filling the large glass mug with Amber Bock. Once the mug was full, he sat it on the bar and filled another one. All the while, the pistol in his right hand never wavered from its target.

"Look at that," said Will, grinning. "I found some beer. I guess you weren't out, after all."

The wolf said nothing but continued to glare darkly at Will. Cody emerged from the back and shook his head. He met Will's gaze and nodded briefly, indicating something had been accomplished.

"All clear, Top," he said. "Nothing back there but a cooler with some questionable beef hanging from the hooks and a storage room with chips and beer."

"Questionable beef?" asked Will.

"The kind with hands instead of hooves," said Cody, shrugging.

"Ahh," said Will. "Long pig."

"Thanks for the beer," said Cody, taking a seat at the bar and picking up a mug. "I don't think I'd trust the food here, though. I'm giving the food a bad review on Yelp."

"You're probably right," said Will.

Turning to face the bartender-wolf, Will picked up the beer and took a long pull from it.

"You know," said Will, "I'm not a fan of most American beers, but this isn't bad. I'll have to remember the name of it."

"I've had worse," said Cody, nodding and lifting his mug towards Will. "It's better on tap, though. It's not quite the same from a bottle."

"You might as well go ahead and change back to human," said Will, nodding at the bartender. "If you make any sudden moves, you're going to die."

"I'm not telling you anything," snarled the bartender-wolf.

"Of course you will," said Will, smiling. "You see, you can either tell me or I turn you over to a military organization I know, and they WILL get it out of you."

"You fucking ruined my legs," snapped the bartender-wolf.

"Better than your head, right?" asked Cody. "Legs will heal, eventually."

"They're not here!" snarled the bartender-wolf. "They went into Canada with the hunting party."

"See," said Will, patting the bartender on the cheek, "that's a complete lie. It's a good try, but a lie none-the-less."

"How would you know?" demanded the bartender-wolf.

"Because I was in contact with some friends about an hour ago," said Will. "They intercepted your hunting pack just before they reached the border. Six of them, to be exact. They took them all out, quick and clean. No survivors."

That caught the bartender-wolf off guard and Will could see it in his eyes. He wasn't prepared for that eventuality or he would have come back with a story about there being more than six. That would also be a lie and Will already knew that.

"Look," said Will, "we've been aware of this place for a few days. The only thing we don't know is where Alex and Julia are. Give me that and we're gone."

"You'll let me live?" asked the bartender-wolf.

"Well, no," said Will. "But we'll finish it fast. If we turn you over to the Hunt, they'll make it last weeks or months. They'll bleed you for every detail you ever even suspected. They'll know who sat next to you in preschool."

"You do that," snarled the bartender-wolf, "then they'll be long gone. I'll fight them as long as I can."

"Which won't be long, I promise you," said Will. "The public doesn't even know your kind exists. Trust me, there won't be a bit of public outcry for the shit they do to you. It'll make Gitmo look like goddamned Club Med."

Will could see the indecision in the beast's eyes.

"Look, turn back into a human so we can talk normally," said Will. "I'll give you something to cover up with so you're not naked. Then we'll talk."

Reluctantly, the bartender-wolf began slowly reverting to human. The wounds in his knees closed but Will knew they were a long way from being healed. It would be a long time before he could walk again, much less try to run from them.

Tossing him an apron that he found under the bar, Will waited until the transformation was complete before lowering the pistol. It was clear to the bartender that Will could shoot him in the face before he could transform again.

Cody reached over the bar and refilled his mug. Once it was full, he took a long pull from the mug and then turned to watch the door. Will turned back to the bartender and smiled.

"Now, where were we?" asked Will. "You were about to tell me what I want to know, right?"

"Look, man," said the bartender. "You let me go and I'll tell you whatever you want to know."

Will put the pistol away and drew a long knife from his belt. It was beautifully crafted with an elk antler as a handle. The blade itself was inlaid with silver and etched with the image of an eagle in flight. The blade had been forged with white ash in the process and blessed by four different shamans of different tribes. It had been custom-built for Will by the Mohawk twins. Will was pleasantly surprised to find out they were expert bladesmiths.

"Take a good look at this knife," said Will, turning it so that the glistening edge caught the light. "It was specifically forged to kill creatures like you. I know it works. At least two of your pack-mates from Memphis could attest to that if they were still alive to tell the story."

The bartender swallowed hard. Will wasn't particularly surprised that none of the males Alex had turned had been particularly tough men. The last thing she wanted was for someone to challenge her for the Alpha position. She likely found this guy in some coffee shop and lured him in by promising he'd be stronger than ever before. Little did he know that she only promised him that to make herself stronger. He was cannon fodder. Alex never did anything that didn't benefit her.

"My people understand the value of a good knife," explained Will. "They have so many uses. The functionality of a blade is amazing."

The bartender looked nervous, his eyes never leaving the gleaming blade.

"For example," said Will, "did you know that if you're good enough at it, you can skin an animal without killing it? It's agonizing, I'm sure, but completely possible. Agonizing for the animal, that is. I happen to find it fascinating and always wanted to try it. Of course, I'd never do it to an animal. You, on the other hand…"

"I… I…" stammered the bartender. "I don't know where they went."

"Oh, I think you do," said Will. "Or, more to the point, you should hope you do. With the storm coming in, it's highly unlikely anyone is going to come through that door and stop me from skinning you alive. To be honest, if anyone does come in, they're likely on that military team I was telling you about. You see, they have this entire place surrounded, as we speak."

"I don't know!" whined the bartender.

"You can do better than that," said Will, smiling and slapping him on the leg with the flat of the blade. "You know something. Think harder."

The bartender winced and cried out as the silver in the blade caused an instant burning sensation on the skin of his thigh. The contact was only for a split second, but the pain had been intense. There was an outline of the blade on his leg and you could even see the outline of the eagle etched into the blade.

"You might want to do what he says," said Cody. "He's got more reason than most to want you dead. Now, what he wants are Alex and Julia. You, you're just collateral damage."

"I'll tell you everything I know," vowed the bartender. "You have to promise me you'll let me live."

Will considered it for a moment before speaking.

"Okay," he said, slowly nodding. "If the info is good. If you give me some vague bullshit, I'll string you up from the ceiling fan and start removing strips of flesh."

"They left this morning," whined the bartender. "They knew you had to be getting close. They keep moving all the time, never in once place for more than a week or two."

"Where are they going next?" asked Will.

"That's the weird part," said the bartender.

"What's weird?" asked Will.

"Do they have kangaroos in America?" asked the bartender.

"Only in zoos," said Will. "At least, as far as I know. Why?"

"I only overheard part of what they were planning," said the bartender. "They didn't know I was in the storeroom."

"What did they say?" asked Will.

"They said they were going to take a long route to make sure they weren't followed," explained the bartender. "They said they were going to go down the west coast, then cut back through Texas to Louisiana. They're supposed to meet a guy named Lafontaine somewhere in Louisiana on the 15th of January. They said they were going after what sounded like a kangaroo. It seemed like they were excited about it."

"Are there kangaroos in Louisiana?" asked Cody, glancing over his shoulder at them.

"They're not looking for kangaroos," said Will. "They're hunting a Rougarou."

"What's that?" asked Cody.

"It's kind of like a werewolf," said Will, "but some believe that it's stronger because of voodoo magic. Almost impossible to kill."

"That's not good," said Cody, frowning.

"No, it's not," said Will.

Turning back to the bartender, Will crouched down on his heels and put the blade in his face.

"Where in Louisiana?" asked Will.

"I don't know," said the bartender, whimpering.

"What about this Lafontaine guy?" asked Will. "Did he have a first name?"

"I only heard one other name," said the bartender, "but it wasn't mentioned at the same time. I heard the name, Pierre."

"Pierre Lafontaine," said Will, frowning.

"Yeah," said the bartender. "I mean, I guess. I never heard the names put together. They said something about going to Pierre to do his part."

Will put the edge of the blade right beneath the bartender's right eye and cut into the skin just enough to bleed. It began to sizzle when it met the blade and steam rose into the air.

"That's all I know," said the bartender. "I swear!"

Will stared into the man's eyes for a long moment before standing up and taking a step back.

"I believe you," said Will.

Standing up, Will headed for the door. Cody got up to follow him.

"That's it?" asked the bartender. "You're letting me live."

"That's the agreement we made," said Will.

"Oh, thank God," whined the bartender.

"Gideon," said Will as he opened the door. "He's all yours."

Gideon stepped out from the back of the roadhouse wearing arctic fatigues and the full Team Odin combat load. Behind him were two others wearing similar gear with their faces covered.

"We'll take good care of him," said Gideon, nodding at the other two.

"Wait!" screamed the bartender.

"I said I'd let you live," said Will, over his shoulder. "Never said I'd let you go."

Will and Cody climbed back into the truck and fired up the engine. While they were letting the big engine warm-up, a Humvee with an enclosed back pulled into the parking lot, then backed up to the door. Will gave them a nod as he backed up and headed out of the parking lot.

"Where to now, Top?" asked Cody.

"We have a rough destination and a date," said Will. "We have to figure out who this Lafontaine character is and where they are in Louisiana."

"I've got enough signal on my phone I think I can start looking up things on the internet," said Cody.

"You do that," said Will. "I'll get the nav system on the road to Louisiana."

"We're gonna get 'em this time, Top," said Cody, smiling.

"Yes, we are," said Will. "For the first time since this hunt started, we're one step ahead of them and time is on our side."

APEX PREDATOR: HUNTER'S MOON

CHAPTER TWENTY
VOODOO BAYOU

"Hope you got your things together
Hope you are quite prepared to die
Looks like we're in for nasty weather
One eye is taken for an eye"
Bad Moon Rising – Credence Clearwater Revival

January 15th
9:30 PM
Pierre Part Parish
Louisiana

Two small boats, locally called "pirogues" (pronounced pee-row), slipped silently through the black waters of the dark swamp. One man rode in each boat, guided only by a lantern held on a pole attached to one of the boats. As they glided soundlessly through the filthy water, the only signs of life they could see was the light reflected in the dozens of luminous eyes and the occasional bat swooping through the air to catch one of the millions of bugs that seemed to be everywhere.

There was a symphony of insects singing in the darkness and the croaking of frogs but moved in the deep swamp at night. It was as if the swamp itself grew malevolent and unwelcoming in the darkness. Cajuns all along the bayous and swamps throughout Louisiana warned their children to stay out of the swamps at night. Tales of creatures like the Rougarou, demon alligators, *Père Malfait*[1] , and many others, each more horrifying than the last.

The two small pirogues were both propelled along by a single paddle with an extended handle so it could be used both as a paddle and as a type of push pole. Motioning for them to come to a stop, the older man in the pirogue with the lantern pushed his boat right up next to the other one.

"Dis 'ere is de' closest I go," said the older man.

---

[1] *Père Malfait* – the Cajun Boogey Man. Supposedly lives in the swamp and covered in Spanish Moss and other rotting plant life. Small children are told if they don't behave, *Père Malfait* will get them.

His name was Henri "Papa" Hebert, pronounced Ay-bear. He was in his late sixties and wore a pair of bibbed overalls over a blue t-shirt with no shoes on.

"Thank you, sir," whispered Will, from the other boat.

"Call me Papa," said Papa. "Ev'ryone do. You sure you gwon down t' Voodoo Bayou? Dat dere a bad place. Bad *gris-gris*. People gwon down dere don come back an' dey never gonna did."

"That's where I'm heading," said Will. "Is it much farther?"

"Bout haf mile dere bouts," said Papa Hebert, "you gonna see wat's lef o' de ol' Lafontaine plantation house. Ain't much lef deese days, jus' some pieces o' walls and de chim'ney. Take de' right-side o' de bayou dere. Maybe haf mile down, you see de ol' church. Dat's Voodoo Bayou. If you see de black iron fence, you gwon too far."

"I think I can take it from here," said Will, shaking the older man's hand. "Thank you."

"You take dis," said Papa Hebert. "Dis a *gris-gris* bag. Keep de' bad *JUJU* away. Its powerful *mojo*."

Will accepted the bag and nodded his thanks.

"Maybe I see you come mornin'," said Papa Hebert. "Maybe not see you no more."

Papa turned his pirogue around and headed back the way they came. Will watched him go until he was completely out of sight. Listening to the sounds of the swamp around him, Will noted that the insects were still going strong. That meant no big predators were in the area. Well, besides the alligators. Papa Hebert told him they would be in their dens when it was this cold, but Will felt like there had to be alligators everywhere, just waiting for him to fall in the water.

Resuming his paddling, he moved along the water, careful to make as little noise as possible. He moved as silently as a shadow, sticking close to the side of the bank to avoid being seen in silhouette on the open water. It suddenly occurred to him just how alone he was out here in the deep swamp.

"I hope Cody's having better luck than I am," thought Will.

Cody was circling in from another direction, using an overland route to avoid being seen. His guide was an old swamper who used to run illegal alligator traps in the swamp and knew how to avoid being seen. He hoped that their plan worked because reinforcements would be a long way away.

The air was cool but not like it would have been back in Missouri, especially in January. It was in the lower fifties and there were still a lot of bugs in the air. Papa Hebert had told him that there wouldn't be many bugs in the swamp at this time of year. If that was the case, Will decided he didn't want to see summertime in the bayou. The place had to have mosquitos the size of pterodactyls.

Ahead, the ruins of what once had to be a large manor house appeared in the darkness. Will let the pirogue drift along silently, not making a sound. He scanned the ruins for any signs of movement but there was nothing there. Will half expected for there to be a sentry, watching for anyone trying to slip into Voodoo Bayou, but there was nothing. They expected all the locals to stay away from the area at night.

Taking the right fork in the bayou, Will began slowly pushing the pole to propel him silently on through the night. Once he made the turn, it seemed like the darkness grew deeper. Not even starlight pierced into Voodoo Bayou. He knew it had to be because the trees completely covered over the water, but it still felt evil and oppressive. The air seemed thicker beneath the canopy.

Rounding a bend in the bayou, Will caught a glimpse of light up ahead. It was flickering and had to be either a fire or a lantern. There wasn't any electricity out here in the swamp. There was no noise from a generator, either. He could see shadows moving in the light. There was someone there tending the fire.

As he got closer, he saw the ruins of an old church. Only a part of two walls and the steeple remained standing. He could see inside where the old pulpit still stood, overgrown with vines and vegetation. There was a large fire burning right in the middle of what had once been the main room. Around it, at least a dozen figures stood hunched, keeping their voices low enough that all he could her was unintelligible murmuring.

The breeze was blowing in his direction as he slipped the pirogue right up to the bank, twenty yards from the walls of the old church.

Crouching low in the darkness, he saw Alex and Julia. They were holding court over the group that was assembled. It was mostly women with the few men looking more scared to be there than the women. Hiding there in the darkness, Will heard Alex whispering to them.

"If you join me," she said softly, "I can promise you strength as you've never known before. You won't get old. You won't be hurt by almost any weapon. You'll be nearly invincible."

"What's de' catch?" asked one dark-haired Cajun woman, wearing a white skirt and puffy-sleeved white blouse.

"You swear your allegiance to me," said Alex. "I'm your Alpha. Julia is my mate, so you'll show her the same respect you show me."

Will expected that they all were recruits with only Alex and Julia being able to shift forms. He was shocked when all but two of them began shifting forms. The dark-haired woman and another blonde woman were the only two that didn't shift.

"Chose now," snarled Alex. "You can swear it and be reborn or refuse and be devoured."

Both women knelt before Alex, who bit each of them in turn on the arm. Will expected it to take a while before the two women could turn but was astounded to see them begin to shift almost immediately after being bitten.

"Shit," he thought. "That's not good."

In the distance, an owl sounded. The creatures looked up and waited for a moment before resuming their murmuring amongst themselves. Will waited until they were focused on the new members before sneaking through the shadows towards the entrance of the church.

Once he was crouching near the broken front steps, he glanced around the railing. Inside, the creatures were all snarling and growling, welcoming their new pack-mates. Glancing down at his watch, Will noted the time by the faintly glowing luminous display. It was just after ten.

"Well, here goes nothing," he thought, with a shrug.

Standing up, he walked through the old door frame and into the entryway of the old church. Instantly, all movement and noise stopped. All eyes were on him now and he could see the looks of shock on the faces of Alex and Julia.

"I'm just here for them," said Will, pointing at the Alphas. "The rest of you can go to hell for all I'm concerned. I want them."

Alex almost panicked but recovered quickly. Checking the air, she glanced around for a moment before looking directly at Will and smiling.

"The rest of your pack isn't here to protect you," said Alex. "You're outnumbered and don't stand a chance against all of us."

"Oh, I wouldn't be so certain of that," said Will, flexing his knuckles.

"You're strong, Greyeagle," said Julia, "but you can't take us all."

"Maybe," said Will, "but how many of you are willing to die to stop me? I promise you; I won't go out alone."

"Rip his head off," snarled Alex.

The pack hesitated, unsure of what to do next. This human was dangerous enough to make their Alpha's nervous. They could smell the fear coming from her. What was special about this one lone human?

"I said kill him!" roared Alex.

"Hang on," said Will.

Everyone froze, staring at the audacity of this lone man in the face of an entire pack of wolves.

"I've learned a few things since we last met," said Will, smiling.

"Like what?" demanded Alex.

"I learned a magic spell that will kill you all with the snap of my fingers," said Will, holding his hand up and glancing at the uncertainty in their eyes. Even Alex and Julia looked worried.

"You're bluffing!" snarled Alex.

"Am I?" asked Will, preparing to snap his fingers.

"Get him!" roared Alex.

Will snapped his fingers just as the creatures were about to launch themselves at him. The sound of dozens of suppressed rifles filled the night and came from every direction at once. In the span of two heartbeats, the entire pack fell dead and began reverting to their human forms. All except for Alex and Julia. They were left completely untouched.

"You were saying?" said Will, mockingly.

"What the hell was that?" whined Julia.

"That is what happens when you bring a highly trained Special Forces team," said Will. "They're still out there, in the darkness. So, if you try to run, they'll cut you down."

"What do you want?!" demanded Alex.

"What do I want?" he replied, looking at her like she was a complete idiot. "You killed my mates and you dare to ask me what I want. I want your blood. Both of you. I swore a blood oath to kill you both and I intend to do just that. So, you can die facing me or die with a bullet in your head when you try to run."

"If we kill you, we walk free," said Alex.

"Oh, hell no," said Will, laughing mockingly. "You die here, tonight. End of story. You can either die on your feet or die like the cowards that we all know you are. Even if you kill me, you won't outlive me by more than a heartbeat or two, at the most. Team Odin will put so many holes in you both, they'll be able to see moonlight through you."

Will could see the looks of absolute panic setting in on their faces. They both knew that there was no chance of getting away, this time. Will was going to be as good as his word and either kill them himself or watch them die.

"I didn't shoot anyone!" whined Julia, moving towards Will. "It was her. She shot them. She told me that if I didn't join her, she'd kill me too."

"And I'm sure that she would have," said Will. "But you made your choice. You stood there and did nothing while Sarah and Gabrielle died. I don't care if you didn't pull the trigger. You're just as guilty as she is, as far as I'm concerned."

"Well, if we're going to die either way," said Alex, "then we might as well take you with us. Get up, Julia. I'll deal with you later."

"There won't be a later," snarled Julia, turning to run.

She took two steps before the massive form of Cody in bear-form emerged from the darkness and backhanded her across the church and into the pulpit.

"She's yours," said Will, beginning to shift. "Alex is mine."

As Will began to advance on Alex, she scooped up something and threw it into the fire. Before he could react, a howl erupted from the deep swamp.

"You think you can kill me?" snarled Alex. "I just finished the spell to summon the Rougarou. You can't beat it. It's like nothing you've ever faced before. It's from voodoo magic older than recorded history. It will destroy you!"

"Maybe," said Will, "but you won't be alive to see it happen."

Fully changed, Will still towered over Alex. Even powered by the *Oolonga-Doglalla* she stood just over nine feet tall. Will was close to eleven feet with Cody towering over twelve feet. Will covered the distance between them in two massive strides.

To her credit, Alex didn't try to run. Instead, she leaped at Will and tried to go for his throat. Will caught her and slammed her into the ruins of the steeple, bringing it down on top of her. Before she could dig herself out, he dragged her out by the leg and drove a fist into her face. He saw her eyes roll back into her head.

"It can't be over this easily," thought Will, leaning closer.

Alex appeared to be blacking out when suddenly she lunged forward and dug her claws and teeth into the side of Will's head, slashing deep furrows into the flesh along the right side of his face. When he forced her away, he knew that the skull on that side of his face was exposed.

"I can taste the blood of the firstborn," she roared. "When I eat your heart, I'll be invincible."

Roaring in fury, Will caught her by the throat and picked her up off the ground without effort. She kicked him several times in the stomach, but it did nothing. Will continued to lift her until they were eye to eye. Grabbing his wrist, Alex desperately tried to break his grip.

"I should have done this the first time I met you," roared Will.

Alex started to say something, but it was cut short when Will forced her down onto her knees and moved over behind her.

"Now we're talking," she wheezed, expecting him to take her as his new Alpha.

Instead, he dug his claws into her spine at the base of her neck and pulled. At first, there was resistance, but with a roar of fury and a wet tearing sound, Will ripped her entire spine from her back with the head still attached to it. As the light faded from her eyes, he turned the head so he could look into them as they went dark.

"This is for Sarah and Gabrielle," he said through clenched teeth.

As the light vanished from her eyes, Will heard another roar of the approaching Rougarou followed by the sound of numerous suppressed weapons. There was a snarl followed by screaming as at least two members of the team were ripped apart. Their weapons did not affect the Rougarou.

Cody tossed Julia's head next to Alex's body and stood beside Will, looking out into the darkness.

"I never liked her anyway," said Cody, nodding at the head.

Then, the massive form of a wolf-like creature exploded through the back wall of the church, landing on the far side of the fire. It was as big as Will and rippling with muscle. There were scars all over its body from healed wounds and they could both see the bullets that it had just been hit with being forced from rapidly healing wounds. The beast locked eyes on Will and Cody, then roared its challenge. It had been summoned to kill them and that's exactly what it intended to do.

"What do we do, Top?" asked Cody. "Bullets didn't hurt it, at all."

"We hit it with everything we have," said Will.

Roaring a challenge, Will crouched in anticipation of the coming attack. Cody bellowed his challenge and took a few steps to his right, creating a gap between him and Will. Diving through the flames, the beast dove right on top of Will, taking them both to the ground. Will felt the beast overpowering him and tearing a chunk out of his shoulder.

Before the beast could press the advantage, Cody slammed into it and knocked it rolling off Will. The beast was up in an instant and dove onto Cody. Trying to catch it, Cody expected to be stronger but was shocked when the beast forced him over backward and slammed him to the ground. Snapping its jaws open and shut, it was trying to take out Cody's throat. It was only through complete desperation that Cody was able to hold the beast back, but it was slowly getting closer.

Just as he could feel the long teeth brushing the fur on his neck, Will drove what was left of the old wrought iron cross into the beast's side, piercing deep inside the beast and into the lungs and chest cavity. Will kept pushing and shoved the beast into the fire.

Staggering back, Will reached out to help Cody to his feet. Will's left arm hung uselessly from where the beast had torn a chunk from his shoulder. The right side of Will's face hung by strands of flesh with the bloody skull visible in the moonlight.

Will saw too late the look of shock in Cody's eyes as he helped him up. The beast drove a massive fist into Will's already damaged left shoulder, knocking him rolling away from the fight to lay in a heap beside Alex's body.

Cody drove his shoulder into the monster's stomach like a linebacker going for a tackle. The beast caught Cody and hooked his arms beneath Cody's, then lifted him without effort. With a twist and a turning throw, the beast sent Cody flying out into the darkness, to land with a splash in the bayou.

Turning to Will, the beast gently pulled the wrought iron cross out of its side and tossed it into the fire. Will watched as the wound began to slowly close. There were bubbles in the blood of the ragged wound, but it would not be open for much longer.

As Will tried to force himself to his feet, his hand fell on something familiar. Glancing down, he found the *gris-gris* bag that Papa Hebert had given him. Remembering his words, Will picked up the bag and held it in his fist.

"What do I have to lose?" thought Will.

As the beast stepped towards him, Will summoned the last of his strength and drove his bad shoulder into the beast's stomach. The beast was not knocked off its feet and it began slamming fist after fist into Will's back, trying to drive him to the ground.

In desperation, Will shoved his entire fist into the open wound and deep into the monster's chest cavity. Howling in pain and rage, the beast tried to force him back, but Will held on as if his life depended on it. Deep down, he knew that it did.

Feeling around inside the beast, Will felt the beating of its heart. Shoving the *gris-gris* bag into the heart, he yanked his hand out of the monster's side and fell back. The beast kicked him in the chest and sent Will sprawling into the dirt, exhausted and with nothing left. He was done and he knew it.

The beast took two steps towards Will, then began having spasms as something took hold of the monster. Will could see the skin begin bubbling as magic fought magic, each battling for supremacy. The beast's features began to shift as the power of the Rougarou was shook by the power of the *gris-gris* bag.

The look of confusion on the beast's face would have been comical had the situation not been so dire. Will saw the look of the beast begin to shift back towards the human. Before the transformation could be completed, one of the Wild Hunt snipers put a large caliber round right through the beast's head. It exploded apart and the beast stumbled backward.

Before it could fall, Cody bellowed his fury and slammed into the animal. Picking it up above his head, he brought it down on his knee with the force of a freight train and the beast's back snapped like thunder. Cody kept forcing the beast farther and farther over his knee until he bent it double. Standing up, he tossed the creature into the bonfire and the flames greedily accepted this new offering.

Out of the darkness emerged figures clad all in camouflaged uniforms, wearing body armor and carrying suppressed weapons. Two-headed for Will. Will rolled his head in their direction but could only see out of one eye. Kneeling next to him, Gideon put his hand on Will's uninjured shoulder.

"It's done," said Gideon. "They're all dead."

"Let's get these men to the doc," said the other man.

His nametag read Clark and he wore the rank of Captain. Will tried to thank them but felt himself slipping into unconsciousness. His last thoughts before darkness took him were of Sarah and Gabrielle. He hoped they could rest in peace, now.

APEX PREDATOR: HUNTER'S MOON

CHAPTER TWENTY-ONE
AFTERMATH

"A journey of a thousand miles begins with a single step."
Lao Tzu

January 16th
0630 hours
Team Odin Headquarters
Fort Leonard Wood, Missouri

Will awoke in what could only be an army barracks. They all looked alike. The real giveaway was the wall-lockers. On the other side of the room, Cody lay in a bunk identical to the one Will was in. Glancing around, Will saw a woman with dark hair and a Mediterranean complexion standing near the end of his bed. Her name tag read Olivetti and she wore the rank of Captain on her uniform.

"You're awake," she said, smiling. "How do you feel?"

"Better than I expected," said Will, trying to sit up.

"You're likely still a bit weak," said Captain Olivetti. "Take it easy."

"Yes, ma'am," said Will, leaning back.

"Now that's unusual," said Olivetti. "Most of the team tend to ignore my advice. Some more than others."

Will touched his face gingerly. He felt fresh scar tissue covering part of the right side of his face, but at least his eye still worked.

"You're the doctor," said Will, "and I want to heal quickly. Where am I?"

"I'd better let the Major explain that," she said. "I'll be right back."

Heading out of the room, Will waited for a few moments before four men arrived. He recognized Gideon and the Captain he'd seen before he passed out named Clark. The others he didn't know, so he checked the nametags and ranks. One was a Major named Saunders and the other was a Command Sergeant Major named Hammond.

"Good," said Saunders. "I'm glad you're awake."

"Where am I?" Will asked, again.

"Team Odin's facility on Fort Leonard Wood," said Saunders. "Ordinarily, we would have taken you to the base hospital, but explaining your unnatural healing abilities might have been difficult. We brought you here to rest and heal, instead."

"Thank you," said Will.

"We could use people like you," said Saunders. "This team encounters all different kinds of threats. Your military background and unique abilities could make you a very valuable member of the team."

"In what capacity?" asked Will.

"Well, you'd be reinstated in the Army," said Saunders. "Back at your old rank, First Sergeant."

"What about me?" asked Cody. "If he goes, I go."

"I was hoping you'd say that," said Saunders. "I like a package deal. Same thing. Reinstated at E-6. Both of you would be assigned to Captain Clark's team."

Will glanced over at Cody.

"I wasn't planning on going back to the others anyway," said Will. "I just hadn't told them yet."

"I'm with you, Top," said Cody.

"Alright," said Will. "We're in. On one condition."

"What's that?" asked Clark.

"We don't have to cut our hair," said Will. "I've gotten too close to my people and our sacred religion to cut my hair again."

"I'll make it happen," said Saunders. "They make exceptions on beards for the guys who are Norse Pagans, now. I don't see why we can't accommodate that."

"Outstanding, sir," said Will.

"Excellent," said Saunders. "I'll set the ball in motion and expedite all the paperwork. Gentlemen, welcome to Team Odin."

"Hooah," said Cody, smiling at Will.

"Hooah," repeated Will.

Author's Bio: D.A. Roberts

D.A. Roberts is an author of fiction, primarily in the horror/dystopian and science fiction genres. Born in Lebanon, Missouri, he now lives in Springfield, Missouri with his wife and sons. When not writing, D.A. serves his community in Law Enforcement.

Best known for his "Ragnarok Rising Saga," he blends the zombie genre with elements of Norse Mythology. The series has been called "a thinking man's apocalyptic world." This is a unique approach that creates a new sub-genre in Apocalyptic Fiction.

He is also known in science fiction for "The Infinite Black Series." This series is based on the hit video game from Spellbook Studio. Download and play the game for free at www.Spellbook.com.

In November of 2018, D.A. took on the challenging role of C.E.O. of J. Ellington Ashton Press.

In March of 2020, D.A. was elected as the president of the Horror Author's Guild.

Find more about his work at

    www.daroberts.net
    www.jellingtonashton.com
    www.amazon.com/author/daroberts
    https://www.facebook.com/DARobertsAuthor/
    https://www.haguild.com/

D.A. ROBERTS

Printed in Great Britain
by Amazon